THE GOOD TURN

SHARNA JACKSON

PUFFIN

PUFFIN BOOKS

UK | USA | Canada | Ireland | Australia
India | New Zealand | South Africa

Puffin Books is part of the Penguin Random House group of companies
whose addresses can be found at global.penguinrandomhouse.com.

www.penguin.co.uk
www.puffin.co.uk
www.ladybird.co.uk

First published 2022
001

Text copyright © Sharna Jackson, 2022
Cover artwork and chapter headers © Paul Kellam, 2022
Map illustration © Luke Ashforth, 2022
Interior images © Shutterstock

Set in 13/17.5 pt Baskerville MT Std
Typeset by Jouve (UK), Milton Keynes
Printed and bound in Great Britain by Clays Ltd, Elcograf S.p.A.

The authorized representative in the EEA is Penguin Random House Ireland,
Morrison Chambers, 32 Nassau Street, Dublin D02 YH68

A CIP catalogue record for this book is available from the British Library

ISBN: 978-0-241-52359-9

All correspondence to:
Puffin Books
Penguin Random House Children's
One Embassy Gardens, 8 Viaduct Gardens, London SW11 7BW

PUFFIN BOOKS

THE GOOD TURN

About the author

Sharna Jackson is a writer of books, scripts and games that are mostly about art, mystery and murder. She grew up in Luton, where she spent most of her younger years under a blanket, reading stories. When she grew up, she moved to Brighton, London, Kent and Sheffield and had lots of different jobs, mostly in museums or making apps. Sharna now writes full-time, and her books include the award-winning, bestselling *High Rise Mystery* and *Black Artists Shaping the World*. She lives on a ship in Rotterdam, which she pretends to sail when no one is looking.

To those of us who came before.

Contents

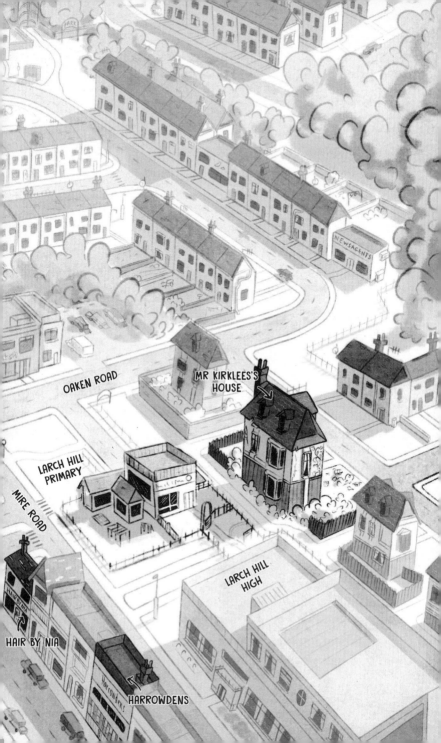

The Copsey Code

I swear I will do my best to love others (and myself, naturally), to ask
'What would the Josephines do?'
when things get way too much, to do good things, and to **always** keep to the Copsey Code.

Signed:

....

Co-signed by:
Josephine Williams
Wesley Evans
Margot Anderson

THINKING

Consider, ponder, wonder!

Do you know what I dislike most in the whole world?

The wasting of time. Mine specifically.

I figured this out today – as soon as I realized Mr King was making us draw dens for the rest of the afternoon. *Dens and shelters?* Sir, please. It wasn't that it was a *bad* activity. It was fun, educational and practical – everything I enjoy. It just wasn't a two-hour thing. It's a five-minute filler, at best.

Listen, I like Mr King – really, I do. I pride myself on seeing the very best in everyone. But, I have to admit, this made me wonder about him. He's been here at Larch Hill Primary forever – even in the dark days, before the internet. He taught my mum too, and, well, she's getting kind of old.

I reckon Mr King's over his job. He must be. Wouldn't you be? Imagine sitting at the same coffee-stained desk, staring at the same dusty screen, setting the same simple tasks for most of your samey life? Sad. It could never – will never – be me. I'm going to get out there, get things done and make change – that much I promise.

Mr King tapped noisily at his keys, squinting through the thumb-smudged lenses in his thick tortoiseshell glasses. Occasionally, he'd stop typing and rub his balding head, polishing it, perhaps hoping a genie would pop out and grant him three wishes. If one did appear – and anything is possible; I don't dismiss the supernatural because who *really* knows – I'd step right up to that spirit and request relevant, challenging schoolwork, and then world peace. Mr King could keep the last wish. That's only fair.

I leaned back in my chair to look at the clock. This one in our classroom is weird. It doesn't tick and I don't like that. The steel second hand just spins silently, yet time never moves fast enough.

It just drags.

I decided I'd change that clock. Yes. I'd fundraise and swap it for something more suitable. Maybe a sponsored silence? I think our class would love that because it's easy, and they can be lazy sometimes. If they didn't want to raise funds, well, I'd just bring in the clock from my kitchen.

That clock would hopefully speed everything up, making the time spent here at school more efficient. Imagine if Year Six could be done and dusted in three months, instead of taking a whole school year? How brilliant would that be?

I'd have time for better, more important things – my other projects and plans – *and* I'd get to university way ahead of schedule. Just last week, I ranked my top ten choices and ordered their prospectuses – that's their booklets, basically. Four have arrived in the post already. I could've been looking through them on this wasted Wednesday afternoon – considering subjects to study, ranking all the famous, important people who attended, making up my mind – but no, instead I was here, drawing dens and shelters.

Mr King – really?

It was three fifteen now, according to the annoying clock, so a full five minutes to go. The afternoon was over and absolutely nothing remarkable had been achieved.

I picked up my pencil and looked over my work, thinking of quick ways I could improve it, but, honestly, I couldn't. It was finished and had been for an hour.

My friends and neighbours, at school and at home – we sit together and live close by – were still going. Wesley, my oldest friend, had pushed his bottle-green sleeves up over his brown elbows. They poked left and right as he slid and shifted his piece of paper over the desk to colour his design, making sure the shading and shadows were just right. This task was very Wesley. He's great at art and designing things – talents he gets from his mum, Ella. Ella's always creating and making interesting things for people in our close to look at and play with. She's been having a bit of a break recently, though, because she hasn't been feeling too well. Plus, it's November now, so it's getting too cold to be outside all the time. I stared at Wesley, who was concentrating very hard. I could tell because he was squinting and his tongue was sticking out a bit, and I've known him forever. Well, since we were five.

Margot, my newest friend, was focused, too. She sat with her back ruler-straight in her seat. Her head was tilted towards her left shoulder, and her dark-brown plaited pigtail grazed it. She wasn't drawing – that wasn't Margot's strongest skill. Honestly, she wouldn't mind me saying that – she agrees with me

4

on lots of things; it's why we get on well. Margot was writing – adding so many notes to the page that her tiny sketch was surrounded and swamped by her words. Since Margot and her dad, Michael, moved to Luton from London at the start of September, Wesley and I have noticed she's always noting things down – so much so that Wesley doesn't trust her and thinks she's a spy. I'm pretty sure she's not. She just wants to be a writer – she doesn't know which kind yet. In any case, it's good she's practising now, because she'll only get better, surely.

I sighed and leaned over my work. Margot and Wesley were calm and content, and I just wasn't. I rarely am. 'This is unacceptable,' I muttered. I spun my sheet round to share my work. I jabbed at my drawing. '*This* is something the Year Ones do on a rainy, wet-play day.'

Wesley glanced over at my work. 'Nah, it's not – and it looks good, Josie. You've got a solid structure there, and nice work on your fabric cover. I'd stay in that den, no problem. Relax. It's decent.'

'I don't need to relax, I'm not tense, and that wasn't my *actual* point,' I replied. 'It *should* be decent. This is Year Six. Six! Not One. At this point, in the middle of the autumn term, we should be way past this. Why are we sketching? I want to be stretched!'

'Stretched?' asked Margot, putting down her pencil. 'What, like in yoga?' She raised both of her arms above her head to demonstrate. 'We had to do that at my old school. In assembly every morning and –'

'Nah, she doesn't mean yoga,' said Wesley, cutting in. 'Josie wants more work. She simps for school, big time.'

'No, I don't! I just think this task could have more value.' I nibbled the end of my pencil, then drummed it against my lip. 'I'm going to talk to Mr King.'

I dropped my pencil, pushed my chair away from the table and stood up.

'Oh no, don't! Don't!' pleaded Wesley, pulling at the sleeve of my cardigan with both of his hands. 'Not again! The bell's about to go any second – don't ruin the day for everyone. Nobody wants homework!'

'I'm not asking for any and I'm not ruining anything. I'm helping,' I said, pushing his palms away. 'You'll appreciate this one day, wait and see.'

'I totally won't,' said Wesley, leaning back in his chair. 'Never will. Some of us have lives – things to do outside of school, you know?'

'*Exactly!*' I said, throwing my arms in the air. 'That's exactly why the time we spend here should be worth it.'

Margot's head spun between Wesley and me.

'I-I think you're right, actually,' said Margot, standing up. 'Come on, Jo. I'll go with you!'

'Tragic,' said Wesley, narrowing his eyes. 'You're both such disrespectful suck-ups, I swear. Mr King will make you regret this.'

CHALLENGING

Question everything and everyone!

Margot and I weaved our way to the front of the class through tables of pupils perched on purple plastic seats. When we reached Mr King's desk he didn't look up, but he knew we were there.

He expected me.

'Miss Williams,' he said, his eyes fixed on his screen. 'And Miss Anderson, of course. How can I help?'

Margot nudged me forward – encouragement I didn't need. Mr King and I have been here before, many, many times.

'How are you today, Mr King?' I said brightly. 'Well, I hope!'

'Hmmm,' he replied. 'All good . . . so far.' He clicked his mouse with ink-stained fingers.

'I just have two tiny things today, sir. One, it's November now, so with your permission I'd like to start organizing the class Christmas party, please?'

'Ooh – I'll help, too,' Margot added eagerly. 'Might as well.'

'Fine. Your second thing?'

I took a deep breath. 'Mr King, sir, I know you have lesson plans that you must stick to –'

'Or Mrs Herbert will fire you,' Margot cut in. She looked at me. 'Right? That's how it works here?'

'But I feel we could be doing more than colouring in, sir,' I said. 'It's almost the end of the day and I haven't really *done* anything yet.'

'You've done plenty, Miss Williams, believe me.' Mr King raised his eyebrows. 'Too much, maybe.' He took his hands away from the keyboard and pulled his glasses towards the end of his nose, squinting through their lenses. 'This is not just *colouring*, Josephine,' he said. 'It's *design*! Design and technology! There's a lot to consider here. You need to think about your den's structure, your choice of material, the ground it will sit on – whether it's wet, dry or sandy. It needs a lot of thought, and good, deep thinking needs patience.'

'But, sir, I *am* patient –'

Mr King snorted and raised his eyebrows. 'Your mother was patient. You . . . not so much.' He removed his glasses, folded their arms and placed them on his desk. 'Do you *really* want to be challenged, Miss Williams?' He crossed his arms and leaned forward.

'Yes, sir! Please!'

'If you're sure now?' he said quietly.

I nodded eagerly. 'That's exactly what I want!'

I looked over at Margot. She smiled and shrugged. 'Yeah, go on then. Why not?'

Mr King raised his eyebrows then quickly clapped his hands close to my face. Margot jumped, shocked and confused. She grabbed my arm to steady herself, but I knew what was coming.

I'd pushed Mr King too far. 'Six K!' he said loudly. He stood up next to the whiteboard with Margot and me by his side. 'I understand this afternoon's work was too easy, and you need something more difficult?'

Margot's guilty eyes hit the floor as the reality of our situation dawned on her. I looked up at Mr King instead, my lips pursed. I could take it. I *was* right about this, after all. He smiled encouragingly back at me with the most energy I'd seen him have all day.

Sighs and shouts rippled through the sea of green jumpers. My classmates were livelier than ever now too.

At the back of the class, Wesley covered his mouth to contain a laugh.

'No, no! Sir? Sir?' shouted a desperate Bobby Patel. He thrust his hand in the air and bounced in his seat, his black hair flopping on his forehead. 'Mr King! Josie's my mate, yeah, but don't listen to her this time.' Bobby turned to look at me. 'This was hard, Jo, very hard. We don't need anything else, I promise, sir!' The class agreed loudly with Bobby.

Let me tell you a bit about Bobby. Bobby loves telling everyone we're friends, but we're not really. His big brother, Sundeep, works with my dad. They're estate agents at the branch of Harrowdens not too far away from school – or home – on Mire Road. My dad focuses on selling houses and Sundeep on businesses, but sometimes they help each other. Or, in reality, Dad helps Sundeep – judging by what I hear him tell Mum. Sundeep and Bobby have been to my house twice – the first time for five minutes. But Bobby *is* all right, really – just a bit naughty and nosy. Either way, I read that you can only be a real, good friend to two people at once, so I had no capacity for him at the moment.

'So, you *don't* want extra homework then? That's not what I've heard,' said Mr King, turning to me.

The class erupted into screams. Bobby slumped forward, placing his face on the table. He screamed out a muffled 'No!'

A balled-up piece of paper flew across the room, missing my head by millimetres.

'Jo, why can't you ever just, like . . . leave it?' said Kelly Marshall, a tiny girl with a huge voice. She sat at the front of the class – directly in front of Mr King – and as she spoke she twisted her long, ginger curls round her frustrated fingers. 'We know you're extra – that's you, yeah, that's your business – but keep us out of it!' Kelly's friends on her table agreed with her.

'Yeah! Wes – tell her to calm down!' said Jenny Lui, spinning in her chair to stare towards the back of the room.

'Oi, nah! It's nothing to do with me!' Wesley protested. He was shaking his head vigorously. He mouthed 'Told you!' at me, then set his laughter free.

'Ready, Six K?' asked Mr King.

Six K weren't ready. Some of them stood up in protest. Others slapped their foreheads and the tables in front of them. A few stomped their feet. It was such an overreaction. Six K didn't know how lucky they were. They didn't understand that learning is a privilege. It was pitiful, really.

'Open your exercise books, and write this down –' Mr King shouted over the commotion.

Before he could finish his sentence and improve everyone else's evening, Mr King was interrupted by the bell, which rang loudly through the room. The entire class – me excluded, but even Margot – cheered. As she ran gleefully back to our table and packed her pens away, I questioned her motives and loyalty.

Mr King raised his voice over the roaring end-of-school-day noise. 'Erm, excuse me, Six K, the bell is –'

'A sign for me, not for you!' shouted the class in unison – me included – finishing his sentence. Mr King loved saying that. Wesley gleefully grabbed his chair and slammed it on the table in front of him. 'We know, sir, but it's home time! We've got places to be, people to see!'

The class ran towards their pegs. They pushed against each other as they collected their coats and sprinted towards the corridor, towards 'freedom'. Wesley and Margot waited by the door, wearing their bags.

I looked at Mr King. 'That's not what I meant by "be challenged", sir.'

Mr King smiled. 'Just a little lesson in the importance of considering consequences, Josephine,' he said. He fumbled behind him for his chair and sighed as he sat down. 'You won't believe this, but I was once like you.'

'I doubt that, sir,' I said.

'Me too,' said Wesley.

Mr King laughed. 'Listen, Miss Williams. I believe in you. You're a very capable, promising young lady –'

Wesley stifled a laugh. 'Very capable of getting on our nerves.'

'– and we are all incredibly proud of you here at Larch Hill Primary – you're going to go far –'

'Far away from this dead town!' said Margot with a grin. She raised her right hand to high-five Wesley, but his arm remained stiffly by his side.

'– but, as I told you and Miss Anderson,' Mr King continued, 'you *must* have patience. Think of others. Think of the impact of your actions!'

He was right, and I knew it.

'You know I'm right, don't you?' Mr King said gently.

I stayed silent. He laughed.

'I see you agree.' He put his hand on my shoulder. 'Channel all this energy responsibly and respectfully. Encourage your neighbours to be part of the process, too.' Mr King glanced at Margot, who nodded enthusiastically, then at Wesley, who sighed and shook his head. 'I know Mr Evans would love that,' he said.

'I wouldn't. I've asked Mum to move, actually,' said Wesley. 'Neighbours no more.' He glared at Margot through narrowed eyes. 'The close is waaay too crowded these days.'

Margot smiled. 'Yes, *your* house is crowded, Wesley. If you ever need space away from the rest of your . . . litter of siblings, then you'd be very welcome. Come over any time!'

'No, thanks,' said Wesley, folding his arms. 'I'm good.'

Mr King coughed awkwardly and turned to me. 'You'll change the world one day, Josephine. Just be considerate and measured. That's my challenge to you.'

'Erm, sir?' said Wesley, panic rising in his voice. He looked over his shoulder, through the window that looked into the now-very-crowded corridor. 'Talking about challenges, you're gonna need to get involved out there.'

GATHERING

Bring everyone together!

'Stop! Stop it!' a muffled voice screamed. It sounded like Kelly. A flat white cheek pressed itself against the glass between the many multicoloured puffa jackets pushing against the window. It was quickly followed by a slapping pair of pale palms and a swish of red hair. It was definitely Kelly.

Mr King shook his head, muttered under his breath and strode over to jerk the classroom door open. He leaned out, held on to the door frame and poked his head above the crush developing in the corridor. This was a regular occurrence here at Larch Hill Primary. I knew why. Every year, class sizes get bigger, so the space for everyone – and the money to make that space better – gets smaller. When my mum was here, there were just four classes with twenty-two children in each of them. Now, there are eight classes, each with at least thirty students. Thirty of us! That's too many. Mum said there were even playing fields here once, but 'temporary' classrooms have sat on them for at least ten years instead – almost my whole life.

'You lot! Keep moving! Go home!' Mr King bellowed.

'Can't, sir!' Kelly squealed. 'We can't move! Something's happening down on Oaken Road.'

Mr King sighed. 'What now?'

'Dunno, sir,' she replied. 'I'm not there, am I? I'm here! It's standard, though.'

'Right,' said Mr King. 'Some of you in here now, until this clears.'

'Nah,' said Kelly. 'I'll risk it out here – it's safer than doing more work in there.'

'Innit!' Bobby shouted. 'That's a trap! How's this for an idea: let me set off the fire alarm real quick – that will get everyone scattering, sir. Then you can go home to the other Mr King quickly. What d'ya think?'

'I think not, Bobby. In. Now,' he said.

The crowd groaned, and some of them slumped and sighed their way back into the room. Our classmates stood around their tables in small groups, talking. To make space, Wesley, Margot and I moved to the back of the room.

'Wanna bet something's on fire again?' said Wesley. 'Something's always going on down there by that exit.'

I nodded. 'Always,' I said. 'And I don't like it.'

'Really?' asked Margot. She reached into her bag for her pen and notebook. After pulling them out, she looked back in. 'Wait, wait!' She tucked her notebook under her arm and fished out a handful of individually wrapped, round red chocolates from her satchel. 'These are for you, Josie – I forgot to give them to you at break,' she said. 'I know you like these truffle ones, so I picked them out of the box for you.'

'Thanks!' I said, unwrapping one quickly, and popping it in my mouth.

'Erm, what about me?' said Wesley. 'Where's mine?' I handed him one, but he gave it straight back to Margot.

Margot shrugged. 'See, I *knew* that's how you'd react. I thought you'd accuse me of poisoning them or something else ridiculous.'

Wesley laughed. 'Yeah, exactly. I was just about to.' He looked at me. 'You see how she's buying your friendship though, Josie? It's tragic.'

I tried to reply, but my mouth was full. I shook my head instead.

'I'm not trying to buy friends.' Margot snorted. 'We just had some at home, and I thought I'd share. It's so not a big deal.' She opened her notebook. 'Anyway, you were saying something's always going on – what kinds of things?'

'Well,' said Wesley, eyeing Margot with suspicion, 'anything that could be set on fire, is set on fire. It's that lot at the high school, one hundred per cent. They're seriously trouble. Once, yeah, they torched a car. It was kind of sick – but terrible, well terrible. And scary.' He exhaled loudly. 'I don't wanna go there next year. I'm scared, can't lie. That school is huge and spooky – especially in winter and, honestly, teenagers are terrifying. Well threatening. The boys there are feral.' He shuddered. 'I don't wanna be part of it. Might ask Mr King if I can stay here forever.'

'Why?' I asked, swallowing my chocolate. 'How will you grow and develop if you do that?'

Wesley shrugged. 'I won't.'

I shook my head. 'That's the worst thing I've ever heard you say, Wesley.'

'I knew that would get you good.' He laughed.

'It *is* pretty sad, actually,' said Margot, looking down and scribbling notes as we spoke.

'You don't know me like that, so what do you know?' asked Wesley, pursing his lips. He peeked into Margot's book. 'What you writing, anyway? It better not be about me.'

She snapped it shut. 'No. Don't look at my notes. They're not for you.'

'Who they for, then?' said Wesley. He leaned forward. 'Who you working with?' he whispered.

Margot sighed. 'I'm not a spy, Wes.'

Wesley shrugged. 'Well, that's *exactly* what a spy would say. And it's *Wesley* to you, yeah? Like I said, you don't know me like that.'

'Not yet,' she said.

'Not ever.'

'Suit yourself,' Margot replied. She put her notebook away, then turned to me. 'I'm not staying at this school forever, Josie. I'm with you.'

'Course you are,' Wesley muttered under his breath.

'Exactly, Margot,' I said. 'No chance, no way, no how. We –' I pointed to the three of us – 'obviously won't get involved in any bad behaviour or funny business when we get to high school, will we? We'll go, get it done and get out.'

Margot nodded. 'Yep, then I'll go back to London, probably. You'll love it, Josie.'

'I'm still thinking about universities in London. I need to get those other brochures first, though. Six to go.'

'I ain't moving to London,' said Wesley. 'Definitely not with you, anyway.'

'I didn't invite you, so . . .' she said. As her voice trailed off, shouts rose from the corridor. She leaned in. 'Really, if this disruption happens all the time, what's being done about it? Surely there's some kind of committee to sort it out? Or the police, possibly?'

'There used to be a youth club attached to their school,' I said. 'So their students had somewhere to go if home wasn't really an option.'

'That sounds really positive. What happened to it?' asked Margot.

'The manager took all the money and disappeared.'

'No way,' she gasped.

Wesley nodded. 'Oh yeah. That was a big deal. Huge. Front page of the *Herald and Post* and everything. Mum did an awesome mural there, and she never got paid either.' He kissed his teeth. 'Rude.'

'Yes, that *is* bad,' said Margot, nodding along.

'We – I don't mean us; I mean a whole-town "we" – aren't doing enough.' I bit my lip and thought for a moment. 'Mr King did just say I would change the world – you heard him – so maybe I should start right here, on Oaken Road.

'No, don't start nothing,' said Wesley. 'He was only saying that to calm you two down. I knew he'd get you for that stunt. You deserved it.'

'I didn't, I –'

Before I could offer reasons why I was right, the class door swung open, slamming loudly against the wall.

The class gasped their surprise, but quickly fell silent – a rare occurrence. It could only mean one thing. One *person*.

Mrs Herbert.

Our head teacher was here. She walked in, scanning the room with her cold grey eyes.

'Sorry, children,' she said, panting slightly. 'Didn't mean to scare you there.' She laughed and smoothed down her black suit jacket. 'Mr King, a moment?'

She put both her palms on his desk and leaned over.

Mr King looked up at her. 'Larch Hill High boys?'

Mrs Herbert nodded. 'Fireworks and graffiti this time,' she said in a low voice.

Mr King tutted. 'Again?' He shook his head. 'This town . . . this town has really changed,' he whispered. 'You don't regret accepting this job?'

Mrs Herbert tutted. 'Absolutely not,' she said. 'It's been seven years. I'm used to it.'

'See, called it,' said Wesley. He shuddered. 'Told you – it's those teenagers every time. Now we're gonna have to walk the long way home to avoid them.'

WALKING

Talk it out while you walk it out!

After the crush cleared and our classroom emptied, we started our walk home, taking a quick look at Oaken Road first. By that point, though, there wasn't much to see. Through two narrow windows on the bolted and locked exit next to the stationery cupboard and Jim the caretaker's weird little office, full of supplies and industrial cleaning solutions, we could only see Jim. He muttered furiously to himself, face twisted with frustration and rage as he scooped up the remnants of smoke bombs and Catherine wheels with his gloved hands.

'Playing with fireworks is *so* dangerous,' whispered Margot.

'Innit. See what I mean now?' said Wesley.

She nodded.

Jim threw the fireworks with force into the big, smouldering bin. He was lit only by the floodlights above, which had just turned on. Poor Jim. He had a thankless job, and he deserved better.

The three of us then took the long way home: through the playground to Lindley Road, Copsey Avenue and Copsey Close, our cul-de-sac. I've lived there my whole life; I was even born in my house, but not intentionally. I was just eager, I suppose, so nothing's changed there.

I love that we live together on the close. My house – number ten – is in the middle; from mine, Margot's on the left in number seven, and Wesley's to the right in number twelve. It's nice, and convenient, having friends nearby – even if they didn't get on well with each other yet. They would; they just needed time and opportunities away from school. It's a shame Margot wasn't around this summer – she and her dad would have loved the barbecues, parties and fun we had here almost every weekend (weather permitting). If only they'd arrived before it got dark so early, before my mum was too pregnant to pay attention, and before term started, Wesley would've got to know Margot much better too. He would've seen that she's all right, really – not a spy – and that she means well.

So, our trio was a work in progress. I called us the Copsey Three in my mind, even though it made us sound like old-time outlaws from the Wild West. I knew not to say any potential group names out loud. Wesley would accuse me of being 'up to something', but Margot would like it, or at least pretend to – which would get him tutting and cussing. On Lindley Road, I made a firm decision to keep hold of it though, until I really needed it. The Copsey Three was way too strong to simply discard. It just needed its moment.

On Copsey Avenue, the road leading to ours, I looked up at the houses, like I always did. Although the streets have similar names, they are very different – it's a real tale of two towns. The houses on the avenue were built around 1900, so no one remembers that happening. Our houses on the close were developed in 2000. Dad said the builders had called it 'a new community for the new millennium' and everyone was excited. Luton was, according to the papers, looking up. The houses on the avenue were huge, and while ours weren't tiny they were much smaller.

The biggest house on Copsey Avenue directly faced Copsey Close. If I ever looked out of Mum and Dad's bedroom window, I could see it. The house didn't have a number, just a name: Beechwood. That's how you know a house is fancy – no digits on its door.

Beechwood was a Victorian house. I know, because I did a project on those types of houses in Year Four for fun. I could tell Beechwood used to be extremely elegant, but now, honestly, it needed work. The door was peeling; the window frames were flaking; ivy was growing around the glass; and the front garden was littered with limp leaves and crisp packets. I decided to gently tell Mr Kirklees about his lack of upkeep and offer some help when I saw him next. He's always lived there, but we never saw him much. We all knew of him, though. He gives Larch Hill Primary money sometimes, for summer fetes, discos and Christmas parties. Yes, I'd ask Mr Kirklees to sponsor ours when I helped him. Mr King would be proud of me for that.

'What's that in the doughnut?' said Margot, squinting, breaking my concentration on the fundraising plans. This doughnut, you can't eat it – it's what we call the circular part of the road that our houses on Copsey Close face. Cars that miss the junction for the motorway turn round there all the time, and the extra pollution is no good for anyone.

'It's a mattress!' said Wesley gleefully. He dropped his faded, battered old backpack on the ground by my feet. 'Early Christmas present!' He ran straight down the middle of the road. 'Budget bouncy castle!' he shouted at the sky, his arms in the air.

Copsey Close isn't the idyllic street my dad thinks it is, or wants it to be. Because he's an estate agent, he *thinks* he's an expert. I did my own research though, and it turns out that many people get run over in doughnuts like ours across the world because cars reverse out of their driveways without checking properly first. It's a terrible fact, and one that needs attention.

Margot gingerly kicked at the faded light-blue mattress with the tip of her shiny shoe as we watched Wesley enjoying himself, jumping between shadows and street lights. 'Mum never lets me do this on my bed!' he said.

'With good reason, Wesley! If I was your mum, I wouldn't let you either,' I said, picking up his bag. 'There could be springs poking out –'

'And you don't know where it's been,' said Margot, grimacing. She clutched her brand-new leather satchel by her side. 'I bet it's covered in disgusting stains from God knows where . . . and who.' She stuck out the tip of her tongue, narrowed her eyes and scanned the houses on the close. 'I bet it's those students in number three,' she said, pulling at her pigtail, unravelling the plait. 'That's something they'd do – dump stuff in the middle of the street. Or your mum, Wesley. I could see her doing that.' Margot bit her lip and stifled a laugh.

Wesley immediately stopped jumping and stepped off the mattress.

He stared at Margot. 'Don't you *ever* talk about my mum, Margot. She's not like that. She would never.'

Margot grinned. 'I know, silly. I was trying to be funny.'

'Well, you failed. It wasn't.' Wesley snatched his backpack from my hand. 'I'm going in. See you tomorrow.'

He stomped towards his house and knocked on his front door. Kayla, his little sister, opened it wearing her oversized uniform. She smiled and let him in.

'That was mean, Margot,' I said quietly once Wesley's door had closed. 'Wesley's family is everything to him.'

'I didn't mean it,' she replied. 'Truly. I thought I was being funny, and it would make you laugh.'

'Hmmm,' I said. 'If you're interested in writing comedy, consider developing your humour? Start by researching what makes a good joke.'

'That's a good tip, thanks,' said Margot. She turned towards her house. 'Right, I'm off too – Dad *says* he's coming home early, but we'll see. He's bringing sushi and I haven't had it for ages!' She rubbed her stomach. 'Can't wait.'

Raw fish would never be my first choice, but I shouted 'Enjoy!' as I let myself into my house. Margot waved back at me from her doorway and closed her door.

NAMING

What's in a name? Everything!

I stepped into the house and switched on the hallway light. I peered into our living room, looked past our dining table and out of the patio doors to our garden. No movement. Silence. My parents weren't home yet. I put my bag down in the hall, took off my shoes and headed to the kitchen. Inside the fridge, I reached for a carton of milk. I considered heating leftover rice and peas to eat first, but quickly thought against it – Dad said he'd bring an Indian takeaway home tonight, and I didn't want to spoil my saag aloo by being stuffed. No, it wouldn't be so special then. Instead, I drank directly from the carton and wiped away my milk moustache when I was done.

When I closed the fridge, I noticed a note attached to its dark-silver door. I lifted the Caribbean-map fridge magnet that held it in place and lifted it close to my face.

'THOUGHTS, PATRICK?' was its title. Below it, on the pale-yellow paper, was a list of boys' names.

Daniel was at the top, followed by many others, including:

Reuben

Samuel

and Benjamin.

At the bottom 'It must have meaning!' was underlined twice, followed by two kisses. I groaned, screwed the note into a tight ball, pushed it in my cardigan pocket and stomped up the stairs.

In my room, I flopped on to my desk chair and threw my laptop open. He wasn't even here yet, but I already didn't like my brother. He was taking over. Everything was about him now and I was in second place. That meant I was losing, and I don't like to lose. I wanted to win, and to be loved. *What about me?* I whined internally. *Why are my mum and dad like this?* I sighed and pulled the note out of my pocket. My name better have meaning too. I needed to know, so I followed my regular research routine.

New tab. Google. Type.

My name was French, but I knew that already. What was less clear was why my parents chose it for me. There were no French people in our family – none that I knew of anyway.

Josephine is also the female version of Joseph, of course, obviously.

I didn't know that Josephine apparently means 'God adds', but I was glad to find that out. It works for me because I do add a lot to any situation, that's true. The trouble with God was we didn't know Him that well. We didn't really go to church except for christenings and weddings, so Mum and Dad weren't giving Him the chance to contribute much to my continued development. Maybe I needed to find Jesus, and go to Sunday school. There would probably be a few Josephines there, living up to their names.

Which led me to wonder how popular my name was.

New tab. Google. Type.

According to the most recent data I could find, only 187 girls were named Josephine in England in 2013, and it was apparently due for a comeback. I hoped it wasn't, as it was mildly unique – I'm the only one around here with that name and I like that.

If Josephine was an old-fashioned name, as this website suggested, I was curious to know if any famous or significant Black women had my name in the past.

Another new tab. Hello again, my great friend Google. Type.

First result: Josephine Baker. She was a famous Black entertainer and activist who lived between 1906 and 1975. She was very accomplished and cool – she famously wore a skirt made of bananas, which became iconic, but she was so much more than that outfit. Staring at her image, I wondered whether I wanted a banana skirt, but quickly decided I didn't. It wasn't me; I didn't think I could pull it off. Josephine Baker *did* have a day named after her, though – now that I would like.

I kept searching and scrolling. Then I found her.

Josephine Amanda Groves Holloway.

I sat forward in my chair, elbows on my desk, in awe as I read about this Josephine and her achievements.

In the 1920s, after Josephine went to university in Tennessee, she began working in her community with women and girls who needed help. At this time, she became interested in the Girl Scouts and started her own, unofficial troop for Black girls – 300 girls joined within a few years. In 1933, Josephine decided to make her group official, and she took a petition to the Girl Scout Council in Nashville. The council said no – officially because of lack of money, but actually because of racism and segregation.

Josephine kept going, though. It took lots of work and nine long years – almost my whole life – but in 1944 her troop was recognized and made official Girl Scouts. She never stopped thinking about them, even when she retired, and when Josephine died in 1988 she left lots of land to her group in her will so a camp named after her, Camp Holloway, could grow.

I peered at a black-and-white image of her staring proudly into the camera, saluting the photographer in her crisp uniform with a girl mirroring her movement at her side. For a moment, I wondered if reincarnation was real.

Maybe she was me in a past life.

I had to look away as the similarities between us – the strong eyebrows, high forehead and steely, determined gaze – were too much, too great to comprehend. I narrowed my eyes and rubbed my temples. I thought about the things Josephine Holloway did – going to university and making real change. I thought about what I wanted and needed to do, and they were exactly the same.

I thought about the Copsey Three.

I thought back to what Mr King said.

Everything was falling into place. It felt . . . right. I knew exactly what to do next.

This. This was it.

I reached for my phone and sent a message to Wesley and Margot in our group chat.

Be here. One hour? I've got a good idea!

Margot instantly sent a heart in return. I knew Wesley had read my message – the two ticks had turned blue. He waited to reply, though, because that's what he does. Three minutes later, he sent the rolling-eyes emoji to me separately. That meant he was coming, but didn't really want to.

Downstairs, my front door opened. 'All right, Jo?' Mum shouted up the staircase.

'Never better!' I hollered truthfully in return.

Putting my phone down, I turned back to my laptop. I opened PowerPoint, the best computer programme to exist – bar none – and got to work.

PRESENTING

Knowing your audience is glorious!

'The Copseys is all about community action. A unique opportunity to make, go and do. To create. To initiate.' I clicked forward to the next slide in my presentation. A screen grab of the world filled the screen. 'The Copseys is the three of us – to start – but we will, eventually, become a global movement of young people creating change, and doing good in and for their communities. We'd need a strategy for that first.' I clicked again to a photograph of pin badges. 'To show what we've done and to chart our progress, we'll earn a range of badges – some early ideas include cleaning, giving, designing and writing.' I moved forward. 'To make sure we are all committed, we'll wear uniforms, create a pledge that we say at every meeting, and a Copsey Code of Behaviour that we all follow and –'

'*Pfft!*' Wesley spluttered. 'Uniforms? *Codes?* Nah, Josie. Please. Stay off the internet. It's no good. Not for you – not for us.' He stood up. 'This was you, I bet.' He brought his shoulders to his ears, squinted and pursed his lips. He wriggled his fingers at chest height. ' "Hmmm, yes, typey, typey type-type. Wow – look! Inspirational, fun ideas for our future!" ' He stopped talking and his shoulders slumped. 'Now we're Scouts, Margot. We're some kind of Girl Guide.' He shook his head.

It wasn't the most flattering impression, but I saw myself. I'm comfortable admitting that. It's good to know your weaknesses, isn't it? It's impossible to turn them into strengths otherwise.

'It *is* typical Josephine,' said Margot. She lay back flat on my bed, her loose dark curls around her shoulders, her left arm dangling off the edge. She ran her fingers through my shaggy white rug and stared up at the glow-in-the-dark stars on the ceiling. Margot's very comfortable at my house. Possibly too comfortable sometimes.

This – the Copseys – was A Good Idea. No, it was A Brilliant Idea. I'm not going to undersell it. I'm not shy.

Wesley and Margot would get on board.

They'd have to.

'Ahem.' I cleared my throat to regain control of both our conversation and my presentation – it's a good technique to use in business meetings, I've heard. 'No, no – this is not typical *at all*,' I said. 'Also, for the record, I claim no ownership over either of you: you're free to do what you like. Controlling you would be very much against the code – you see, that's a concrete example of how it could work.'

'Thanks for your permission to live freely,' said Wesley, laughing, but only a bit. 'Very kind of you.'

He crouched to sit back on the bed. He landed squarely, on-purposely on Margot's stomach. He was clearly still upset with her over her comments about his mum and that mattress.

'Wesley!' she shouted, pulling at his jogging bottoms, then pushing him on the rug. 'Now, now – no pets on the bed, remember? Williams house rules.'

Margot laughed, but Wesley didn't.

'Ahem. Look.' I sat on the floor next to Wesley. Margot lay on her side, leaning over my work. 'Think how good this will look on our CVs when we're older –'

'On our what? Our TVs?' said Wesley. He rubbed his undercut. 'Nah, I don't want to be on telly, thanks. That's a mug's game, that is. A scam.'

'No, not *TV*. CV! It stands for curric . . . curricula . . .' said Margot. 'You know what, I don't actually know what it means, but it's just like a list of jobs, subject scores and hobbies or whatever that you use to get into uni.'

'Exactly that,' I said. 'That's why we have to think ahead. Strategize now to win later. To get into the good universities – like we promised – the work to stand out starts now. It's like how you practise your creative writing, Margot – it's great for your future.'

Margot nodded proudly. 'Thanks. I try.'

Wesley scowled at Margot. 'Yeah, but university is like . . . seven years away,' he said, quickly counting on his fingers. 'We've got loads of time.'

'Not if we don't create our own opportunities we haven't.'

'Why are you so old inside, Josie?' Wesley rolled his eyes. 'You act just like my nan, and she's like sixty-five.'

'Rude,' I said. 'And I don't know why you're being like that – I'm being proactive. Changing the world like Mr King said I would. Wasn't it you, Wesley, who said Copsey Close is, I quote, "dead"?'

I would never say that. Not out loud, anyway.

Margot liked that quote. 'Ha, right? Totally dead!' She cackled and clapped. 'I'm with you on that.' She stiffened her body. '*Corpsey* Close – that's what I said to Dad when –'

'When you first turned up. Yeah, we know,' said Wesley. 'You've been telling us every week for, what, a year now?'

'Since the first of September,' she replied. She tilted her head and smiled at him. 'It's only been two and a bit months.'

'Feels much longer. But let me remind you, Margot. You ain't from here, so any opinions on the close or our town don't count, OK? You can pipe right down – only we –' Wesley swung his finger between his face and mine – 'can cuss. You can run down West London – Spannerjones, or wherever it is you're from.'

Margot sat up. 'It's Hammersmith *actually*, but I like that, can I have it?' She reached for her notebook. Wesley raised his hands, sighed and looked out of the window. Margot turned to me. 'Local pride aside, Josie – and beautiful presentation, by the way, excellent font choice – I get the point, and I'm mostly on board. My big question is will you *actually* do this? You seem to say things, but not always finish them.'

'Facts,' said Wesley from the window. 'That's harsh but true.'

'I mean, last week, you wanted to campaign to make ten-pin bowling an Olympic sport –'

'I still do. That can be part of –'

'– and now this. I like it, but tell me your process,' Margot said. She stroked her chin. She looked at me through narrowed eyes. 'What happens in there?' she said, tapping my forehead, then opening her notebook. 'Where did this come from? Why are you like . . . like this?'

'She's always been like this,' said Wesley. 'This is what Josie does. She's extra. Kelly nailed it when she said that in class earlier.'

It wasn't a compliment then, it wasn't a compliment now, but I decided to take it as one. I might as well.

'Well, I was curious about the origin of my name, so I was researching that –'

'On the internet?' said Wesley under his breath. 'Shocking.'

'Then I discovered Josephine Holloway, my hero. That was it. I just knew. The concept came to me, instantly.'

'Wait, I thought your hero was Michelle Obama?' said Wesley. 'Who's Josephine Holloway when she's at home?'

'Just Jo or Josie to her family, probably,' Margot mused. 'Or Mum, maybe?'

'To be clear, you can have more than one hero, Wesley. I still love Michelle O. And Margot – I'm sure Josephine Holloway was all of those things. She was also a visionary, you guys. In a nutshell, she created the first Black Girl Scout troop in America, like eighty years ago. Imagine how stressful that was and the courage it took – especially in those days.'

'Yeah,' said Wesley, nodding his head. 'OK, that's well brave – I'll give you that.'

Margot murmured her agreement. 'Inspirational,' she said. 'I have cousins in America – in Harlem, actually. I'll ask them about her.'

'You ain't got no Yankee cousins,' said Wesley. 'You only said that to make yourself sound more interesting, and cooler.'

'No, Wesley,' said Margot. 'I do, I –'

'Ahem!' I coughed. 'So I thought, *that* Josephine put herself out there, fought racists and made lives better. What's *this* Josephine going to do to change the world? We have the same name, we're both Black and we're committed to making things better. I can't not act on this information.'

'I mean, you could,' said Wesley. 'You could just be like, "Great work, That Josephine," close your laptop and focus on something else, like your mum and the new baby –'

'No,' I said firmly, cutting him off. 'Impossible. It's too late. I'm inspired. Think about how great it could be – pledges, badges, our code.' I clicked the last slide on my presentation. 'The Copseys,' I said, with an element of drama to my voice to really persuade them now – another useful business tip. 'A brand-new concept for youth community action. The three of us, together. Changing minds, changing lives.' I held my hand out and maintained eye contact with Wesley for a little longer than normal. He snorted down a laugh, but when I looked at Margot she was grinning.

LIGHTING

Go towards the light - there, you will be all right!

Margot clapped her hands together. 'OK, sold. Love it. I'm in. I'm totally in,' she squealed. 'Can I write the handbook?'

I nodded. 'Definitely – that job's got your name on it. Wesley, you're on badge and uniform design.'

'Am not,' said Wesley, pursing his lips. He looked at Margot. 'So that's it? That's all it took? You're a proper pushover, Margot. You're so . . . new. Josephine, nah. I've known you too long to give you a quick answer. That's way too easy. I know your tricks – your PowerPoints don't work on me, pal. You can wait.'

'Take your time,' I said, knowing it wouldn't be too long.

He sighed. 'Can't you just join the Guides and let me rest?'

'This is different! Something we're doing ourselves and –' I started.

'Where's the excitement in that, though, Wesley?' interrupted Margot. 'This is way more fun, right?'

Exactly, Margot.

'That's what I –'

Before I had a chance to reply in full and list all my reasons, a little voice shouted loudly outside my bedroom window. 'Wes! Wes!'

'Ignore her,' said Wesley. 'They're all annoying me today. So yeah, I'll think about –'

'Wesley? Where are you? We're well hungry – can you come do us some chips?' the voice pleaded.

Margot snorted. 'Your sister sounds like a Victorian urchin. It's very Dickens down there.'

'Oh, shut up, you,' said Wesley, his face tight. He opened my bedroom window and leaned out.

Margot and I peered out beside him. A rain-rusted tricycle lay on its side and had done so for months now. Kayla, Wesley's little sister, stood beside it, her long school jumper covering her knees.

'What, Kay? Where's Mum? We're busy,' he shouted into his concreted yard two houses away. 'Homework.'

'Yeah, right!' shouted Kayla in return. 'Come on, come home! Mum's feeling rough and Jayden's losing it. He just smashed the TV controller into Jordan's face and Jordan's eye is, like, bubbling. It's grim. Please. Chips with chilli sauce on the side will fix this. Come on, Wes, please! You know I'm not allowed to turn the oven on!'

Wesley sighed loudly, cursed under his breath and slammed my window shut. He put on his black jacket. 'Doughnut tomorrow, usual time?'

Margot and I nodded.

'Yep. I'm looking forward to your decision then,' I said with a smile.

'Yeah, right!' Wesley scowled and ran down the stairs. 'Bye, Mrs Williams!' he said sweetly in the direction of the living room. He shut my front door gently.

We knew Wesley was home when we heard his front door slam shut. Yellow light from his kitchen shone into his yard, over their tricycle. The chips were coming.

'Imagine having so many people in one small space,' said Margot with a shudder. She stared into Wesley's yard. 'All those little bodies breathing the same air in that tiny house. Gross. I don't know how he does it, honestly.'

'Don't be like that,' I said. 'Ella's a great mum, and she's doing her best – she just hasn't been doing too well lately. But she works hard, and she's fun. You'll like her. This summer, just before you came, their family completely covered the pavements in the close with brilliant colourful chalk art. It was great. Remember, not everyone has spare money, spare space and sushi, Margot.'

'Yeah, I suppose,' she said.

'And, if you want to be friends with him, you have to be kinder.'

'Do I want to be friends with him, though?' She shrugged. 'I like you better – *we* should be best friends.'

'We could *all* be best friends,' I said. 'Start by being nice to Wesley and his family.'

'All right,' she said. 'I was just saying that –' she gestured down to Wesley's yard – 'couldn't be me. I'm lonely sometimes – and a bit bored – but I'm glad I'm an only child.'

'Hmmm,' I said. 'I thought that once, but things can change quickly, when you least expect it.'

'Oh, yeah, sorry,' said Margot. She paused for a moment. 'Actually, no, wait, I'm not sorry – that was the wrong word. I take that back. Your parents are lovely. It's going to be great when the baby comes. Joyous!'

'Great for who? My parents, yes. For me?' I paused. 'Doubt it.' I stared out of the window, looking beyond my garden and into The Outback – the overgrown, jungle-like bushland behind our close. Mum said I'm banned from going in there as it's too dangerous. These days, though, she probably wouldn't notice if I moved out and lived there. If she did realize, well, she'd probably just be happy she had extra room for all the new baby toys. I rolled my eyes and looked up to Chicane Cars, a five-floored abandoned factory that stood just behind The Outback. Chicane Cars, once the shining jewel in the town's crown, was now an ugly thorn in its side. A sad reminder of our glory days. Years ago, most of the adults in town worked there – or knew someone who did. People moved here just to work there. When cars stopped being made here, and production moved to Germany, many people lost their jobs. *That's* when problems in the town began. Some people left, then the building was sold to a random company in the Cayman Islands. The company haven't done a thing with the building. Nothing! They haven't repaired it, and they're in no hurry to replace it with something better. Chicane Cars had been closed and derelict forever.

Or so I thought.

Then why could I see bright light in there?

I'd never seen *anything* in there before, not in the eleven years I'd had this room. No lights. No movement. Nothing.

Maybe I was seeing things. I had to be. The earlier Josephine Holloway-reincarnation inspiration must've been playing tricks with my mind.

I rubbed my eyes then leaned closer to the window.

Yes, there *was* a light in the dark. In the first row of windows at the top left of the factory.

'Come on, get a grip,' said Margot, pulling my arm. I'd forgotten she was still here.

'What?' I quickly glanced at Margot, then back to Chicane.

The light had gone off. My eyes darted around the building to find it, but there was nothing. Nothing but darkness.

Margot nudged me in the ribs. 'Don't be such a stereotype.'

I looked back at her. 'What are you on about?'

'I see what's going on here. It's textbook "older child feeling threatened by the new baby". You know, if you were like five and small I'd have sympathy, but, well, you're not. You're eleven and quite tall!'

'Oh, right. No, no, I'm not upset about the new baby. It's fine,' I semi-lied.

'I don't believe you. Come on now, what would Josephine Holloway think of this sad face?' Margot reached out and lifted my cheeks.

'I'm not sad, I swear. I just thought I saw something in Chicane and –'

Margot wasn't listening. 'You're a Copsey, aren't you? That's what we're called, right?'

I nodded. I knew she'd like that name.

'Then pull it together, co-Copsey.' Margot slipped on her shoes and reached for her pink satin bomber jacket. 'See you in the morning. If I have any big ideas in the night, I'll text them over.'

CODING

*Commit to your code - it will
save you down the road!*

'Jo?'

I held my hair above my head with one hand and looked at myself in the long mirror on the back of the bathroom door. Today – this typical Thursday, just like every other weekday since I was four – I wore black tights, a grey pleated knee-length skirt, a crisp white shirt, a green-and-grey striped tie and a bottle-green cardigan. I turned from left to right. Acceptable. I loved my school uniform. It really simplified this getting-ready-in-the-morning business and freed up time to think about other, important things – specifically the Copseys now. I couldn't wait to catch up with Margot and Wesley to get thinking, planning and plotting.

'Josie?'

Wait, Mum. A minute, please.

I leaned over the sink and reached for a black hairband. I pulled my tight curls into a puff on the top of my head. I wet my hands and lightly coiled any curls that had frizzed with my fingers. I wondered how Josephine Holloway did her hair in the mornings and assumed she appreciated uniforms, just like I did. I could tell by that proud smile in her picture. Feeling her spirit in the bathroom, I saluted my reflection.

'Josephine?!'

I knew what Mum wanted. It was Thursday morning.

'Yes, Mum?' I shouted back. I mimed along with what I knew she was going to say next.

'Remember to put the bin in the doughnut when you go, yeah?'

I've never forgotten. It *was* Thursday morning, after all. 'Yes, Mum.' I sighed.

Sitting on the bottom step, lacing my shoes, I heard Mum wincing and whining in the living room. I peeked round the door frame. She was fully stretched on the long leather sofa, head propped on a pillow, her eyes tightly closed. She was dressed head-to-toe in black and her long, straightened black hair hung perfectly curtain-like over the arm of the sofa. Mum didn't have her shoes on yet, and I could see why. Her feet and ankles had swollen to twice their size – they looked like they belonged to the Incredible Hulk.

I had sympathy, of course I did. She's my mum and I do love her. But those ankles were the consequences of her and Dad's . . . actions.

Mum breathed deeply and her mini-mountain stomach rose and fell.

'You all right?' I said through the spindles on the staircase.

Mum opened one eye and looked across at me. She smiled. 'Yeah, yeah, I'm all right – your brother's just draining me this morning.' She pointed at the baby's cave. 'Vampire, this one.'

'That's a nice name,' I said. 'I like that one the best.'

Mum narrowed her eyes. 'Is that so?' She struggled to sit up and burped. 'Sorry, sorry, that takeaway last night has given me nothing but heartburn. She sighed. 'That's a lie. It's made me tired, too. Ah, with you it was so *easy*. I should've appreciated it at the time.' Mum shook her head.

'Well, you are *much* older now,' I said.

She laughed. 'Excuse you, Miss Williams. I've still got it. I'm young!'

'If thirty-one is young, then sure – you've got it.'

Mum looked in my eyes with her lips pursed, then moved her gaze up to my head. 'Hair's looking great today. Your curls are popping. You want to come to the salon after school? I'll wash it for you, if you want? I've got some new products in.'

'I can do my own hair, Mum.'

'I know, I know – you're a grown girl. But it would be nice, no? Pamper yourself a little?'

'Resting would be better for you, I think.'

Mum lay back down. 'Yeah, good point. Oh, Jo? Remember the –'

'Bin. Yep, haven't forgotten. Bye, Mum. Try to relax.'

'See ya, Jo Jo. Be nice to Mr King, OK?'

'Why would you say that? I always am.'

Mum laughed as I shut the front door.

I dragged our blue bin on to the road. It was recycling week, and our bin was overflowing with Amazon boxes of various sizes – once filled with stuff for the baby, but not a single thing for me. I opened the lid and punched the boxes down. There are rules around refuse here. If the lid doesn't close, they won't take it, which means wet cardboard on the close for a fortnight. The bin men are ruthless and for that, they have my respect.

'All right?'

That's Wesley's way of saying good morning. He leaned on his closed bin, waiting for me. There was no sign of Margot yet.

I nodded. 'Morning, Wes.'

He stood straight and pulled his bin into the road. 'So, listen, I thought about your Girl Scout thing overnight.'

'You did?' I hid a smile by biting my bottom lip.

'Yeah, I did – and I see you laughing. Don't be smug. Look – I'm in. For a little while, anyway.' He looked back at his house and lowered his voice. 'I need some space. It's too much in there. Something's up with Mum; she was in bed all evening with her door closed. She never closes her bedroom door unless something's going on.' Wesley sighed. 'I sound well selfish, but I do a lot of "dad" stuff around the house – I have to – but I can't be both parents. I can't. I don't want it.'

We stood in silence. We don't know where Wesley's dad is, so we don't talk about him any more. No one does – not to Wesley's face anyway.

'You know you can come over whenever you want, Wes.'

He nodded.

'And I'm sorry,' I said quietly.

'Sorry about what?' said Margot, jumping into our conversation, seemingly from nowhere. She put her arms round Wesley and me. Wesley immediately squirmed away. 'What have I missed already? I'm only two minutes late.'

I looked at Wesley, who stared at his scuffed school shoes. 'Ah, not much,' I said. 'Just the amazing news that Wesley's now officially part of the Copseys!'

'Really? That's cool,' said Margot. She smiled widely at Wesley and reached into her bag. She pulled out a piece of paper inside a plastic sleeve. 'I did a little work last night. Dad didn't come home after all, so I had time. It's the first draft of our rules – I've called it the Copsey Code, which has a ring to it, right? I've kept it to six points and tried to get all our voices in there. Thoughts?' She handed it to me.

By following the Copsey Code, you promise to be:

1. Truthful and trustful
Don't tell lies – it's bad energy.

★

2. Proactive – and never procrastinate
Don't waste time – not ours or yours. See an issue?

Solve the issue!

★

3. Resilient
'If at first you don't succeed, dust yourself off, try,

try again.' It's an oldie but a goodie – live by that!

★

4. A true ally
Be a friend and support everyone.

★

5. Thoughtful
Think laterally to help someone today!

★

6. Caring
Respect yourself, others and the whole world.

'This is *perfect*, Margot. And your writing is so good – it has so much impact! Two birds, one code. I love it! Wesley, what do you think?'

Wesley peered at the paper. 'It's good, yeah. I don't think we need official rules, though. We're not stupid.'

'But it is good to have them written down now,' I said. 'It makes everything clear and consistent – and we can share them when we start recruiting others.'

'Already?' said Wesley. 'You need to calm down.'

'Well, not yet – we need an expansion strategy first. If this goes global, we need a plan.'

'But first things first, right?' said Wesley. 'Start small and slow, Jo.'

'Absolutely,' said Margot. 'But, if you fail to plan, plan to fail.'

'Oh, that's good!' I replied. 'Write that one down.'

'Way ahead of you!' said Margot, beaming.

Wesley shook his head. 'What have I let myself in for?'

'Challenges and change,' I said. 'And companionship. All the Cs. It's going to be great; I promise it's what you need.' I patted Wesley on the back.

'Next step – maybe uniforms?' said Margot. She looked at Wesley smugly, but with a tinge of hope.

He sighed. 'If I have time, I'll sketch something, but I'm telling you two now, I ain't wearing no uniform. Not gonna happen. See the Copsey Code, point one.'

NEIGHBOURING

Love your neighbour, love yourself!

I looked up at Beechwood as we ran towards Copsey Avenue. Today, it seemed different and I quickly realized why. Mr Kirklees stared out of the round window at the very top of his house, where the roof turned to a triangle. He sipped what I assumed was tea from a large blue-and-white striped mug. His paper-thin, translucent hands trembled as he brought the mug to his lips. His dog had its paws on the windowsill.

'Look, it's Kirklees,' said Wesley. He lowered his voice. 'Long time, no see, Kirky.'

'So *that's* Mr Kirklees? Hmmm,' said Margot. 'What do you reckon is in his cup? And what's he looking at?' She wrinkled her nose.

'Tea, and, what, an old man can't look out of his own window in the morning?' replied Wesley. 'Leave him be.'

Mr Kirklees must have heard us, because he looked down and grinned widely, flashing his white teeth while waving enthusiastically. In the process, he almost dropped his mug, and some of his tea splashed over the rim. His red cheeks rose to his eyes, which narrowed in response. He mouthed a cheerful hello, and the dog wagged its tail.

Wesley and I waved back, but Margot's arm stayed firmly by her side. She peered up at the window. 'How old did you say he was?' she asked. I shrugged. 'His teeth are far too clean and straight for a man who's over sixty.' She wore a fake smile in case Mr Kirklees could lip-read. 'It's unnatural. What's his deal? Where's his family?' She looked down from the window to the front garden. 'It's tired and tatty, but that's a whole lot of house for one person.'

'He's always lived alone, I think – as long as I can remember, anyway,' I said.

Wesley nodded. 'Yeah, I heard his wife died in the seventies, and his kids left town years ago – well before we were born.' He rubbed his chin. 'You know what? We should do something nice for him as part of your Copsey thing.'

'Great minds, thinking alike,' I said. 'I had the exact same thought yesterday on the way home. Maybe we can start by painting his windows and door?'

'They are looking a bit rough, yeah,' said Wesley. 'I'm sure he knows that, but *we* can't be getting on ladders and doing it properly. We've gotta be realistic. Start small and slow, like I said.' He pointed into Mr Kirklees's garden and shook his head. 'Look at all that rubbish – we could easily sort that in five minutes. We could just do it today after school.'

'That's a great idea,' I said. 'A quick way of us getting a badge –'

'Badges, yeah, but also making an impact,' said Wesley. 'That *is* the point of this, isn't it?'

'Of course! What are you trying to say?'

'Nothing. Just checking,' he said, smiling at me sideways.

'Well, let's do it then!' I said.

'I can't.' Margot sighed. 'I have clarinet tonight.'

'No activism for you, then.' Wesley laughed. 'I bet you think litter-picking is beneath you anyway.'

'Hmmm, not *really*, but maybe a little bit,' said Margot. 'But you'd better not do it without me.' She stared up at Beechwood, back at Mr Kirklees. 'Seriously, what is he looking at?'

'Does it matter?' said Wesley. 'It's another beautiful Luton morning. Maybe he's just watching the morning sun rise over the Area of Outstanding Natural Beauty we call The Outback?'

'Ooh!' I shouted. 'Or Chicane! Wesley, I forgot to tell you. Guess what? I saw lights in there last night!'

Wesley immediately stopped walking. 'You what? No way! You sure?'

I nodded. 'I'm pretty certain.'

'Nah. You must be mistaken. It's dark in there. Too dark – even teenagers don't go in there.' He shuddered. 'I hate Chicane. My dad's dad used to work there, you know? Yeah, Grandad Alan was there for years and apparently never said anything good about it – he hated that we moved near it. Might be the reason we don't see that side of the family – the Welsh lot – that much any more.' Wesley sighed. 'The council should step in and get rid of it, tear it down. Give us a shopping centre or something.'

'Eww, no, not a shopping centre,' said Margot. 'Who goes to actual shops these days? And all that pollution? Yuck.' She stuck her tongue out.

'Everyone goes to shops!' Wesley shouted incredulously. 'Josie's mum and dad both work in shops on Mire Road, don't they?!'

'Ah, but those aren't shops, not really. They're spaces where people do things for others. It's totally different.'

'You've lost me, Margot. Lost *it*.'

Margot sighed. 'It doesn't matter. Forget it. Either way, I'm not getting why lights in a factory is such a big deal. Who cares? Maybe someone bought it?'

'Cross your fingers,' said Wesley. 'Think of all the "spaces where people do things for others" we could have right on our doorstep, eh, Margot?'

She giggled and nudged Wesley with her shoulder.

'You don't have to touch me about it – you can just laugh,' he said.

'I did think about someone buying it,' I said. 'But, if that was the case, why wouldn't they just look in the day? Surely it's too dangerous in the dark? It's falling apart. It has to be.'

'It was ghosts then,' said Wesley. 'Definitely ghosts. Grandad Alan, maybe.'

'Maybe,' I said.

'Maybe?' said Margot. 'Come on, Josephine. I thought you were better than that. I love a tall tale – no one appreciates a scary story more than me – but ghosts aren't real. Ghosts aren't technically possible.'

'"Ghosts aren't technically possible"? That's well wrong – they are!' said a voice behind us with a snort.

Margot shook her head and rolled her eyes.

We didn't need to turn round to know Bobby was behind us. He ran to catch up, and together we walked through the school gates.

'Ghosts are totally real!' said Bobby, his eyes wide. 'I've seen one! The one I saw tried to bite me, I swear. Then it moved in with us and lived in my wardrobe for a bit. I couldn't sleep for weeks . . . It was a dark time. A very dark time.' Bobby leaned past Wesley to look at me. 'Get your dad to ask Sunny, innit – he'll back me up on that.'

'See!' said Wesley. 'Knew it. Don't say anything else though, Bobs. I don't need the heebie-jeebies before nine.'

The bell rang just before Margot could call us idiots. I know she really wanted to.

PICKING

Pick and choose, but never lose!

At morning break, Margot sat next to me, while Wesley kicked a ball between two black jackets with Bobby and others from our class. She shuffled close and grabbed my arm.

'So, about later,' she said.

'What about later?' I asked, turning to her.

'You're not going to tidy Mr Kirklees's garden without me, are you? I really can't get out of clarinet. I'm going for Grade Three soon, so I've got to be great. Dad's promised me a present if I pass.'

'Well,' I began. 'We'll only be five minutes and –'

'So?' Margot sat up straight and she raised her voice. 'Josie! I *have* to be there. I want to earn my badge – our first badge – too, and be part of the official start of the Copseys.'

I looked up at Wesley, who was celebrating scoring a goal. He ran with his arms in the air and his jumper over his face. Margot pulled my arm and stared at me. 'Don't do this without me. Promise.'

'OK, Margot. Don't worry, I promise we won't.'

When the bell rang at three twenty, Margot went to her clarinet lesson, making sure I would include her in our plans before leaving. She did this by raising her brows and nodding a lot before skipping away. Wesley and I walked home. When I say we walked, I did, but Wesley slumped. With his backpack heavy on his back, he leaned over at the waist. He reminded me of Atlas, you know – that myth about the old man holding up the sky with his back. When I told him this, he looked at me like he'd smelled something rotten. It's famous and very easy to google, so his overreaction was unnecessary.

'So, we drop our bags, you grab some black sacks and we get going to Kirky's?' he said, dragging his feet in the direction of home. 'Sounds like a solid plan to me.'

'It does,' I said. 'But we have to wait for Margot.'

'Why?' Wesley shouted. 'It's a quick thing! We can do it before she gets back!'

'We could. I did think that, but that's not fair or right, is it? We have to start strong and start together.'

Wesley sighed. 'I've gotta say something.'

I looked at him. 'Go on . . .'

'I'm not into Margot,' he said, shaking his head. 'I've been thinking about her code all day. *She's* the one who really needs to follow it, don't you think?'

'We all should, that's why –'

'She looks down on me and my family. She doesn't even know us! That thing she said about the mattress in the doughnut? I'm still heated. I reckon she thinks she's better because she's minted and from London. Who cares about London, anyway? She's not there now, is she?'

'No, she's not, she's –'

'Well rude, I know! I only put up with her because you like her, but she's mean and mouthy. If she was a boy, I'd knock –'

'Wow, no, Wesley! Copseys don't condone violence in any form. Come on now!'

He kicked at the pavement, scuffing his shoes. 'Yeah, I know. You know I wouldn't really – she's just annoying. She's a snob and she thinks I'm budget.'

'I know she doesn't, but I get why you'd think that. I told her to work on her sense of humour.'

'She needs to because she's definitely not funny.'

'I'll talk to her again, I promise. But give her a break – she *is* new. You said that yourself.' I opened my front door. 'Meet you back here in an hour?' Wesley kissed his teeth and disappeared inside his house.

'Should we knock or just do it?' asked Margot. She held a bin bag in her hand and looked up at Beechwood. The lights were off and it was dark inside. 'I don't want him to come outside either way, but isn't this, like, trespassing?'

'Probably,' said Wesley. 'But it's trespassing for good, innit?' He covered his hand with the sleeve of his jacket before picking up a crisp packet and putting it in his sack. 'I'm just doing it, going for it.'

I bent down and put a wet newspaper in my bag. 'You're right. If we knock, he might stop us, and then no badge for us.'

'Or no good feelings because we did something nice,' said Wesley. He hopped over a hedge on to the lawn. 'This is a right state.' He sighed. 'Poor Kirky.'

'I don't know about *poor*,' said Margot. 'I mean, look at his house – it's huge. This is not a poor person's place.'

'Money isn't everything though, is it?' Wesley snapped.

'Never said it was,' she replied. She picked up a can. 'Family and friends are just as important – more important, if you ask me.'

'I didn't ask you, and I don't believe you believe that.'

'I do,' said Margot quietly. 'I really do.'

Wesley looked at her for a moment, quizzically and slightly sympathetically, then continued cleaning. He coughed. 'I'm done over here – how are you two getting on?'

'I think we're finished,' I said, closing my bag. I stepped backwards to survey the scene. Mr Kirklees's garden was clean, or at least it looked like it in the fading light. 'This is great, Copseys! We're done!'

Three hours later, Wesley and Margot were definitely done. Their attention and enthusiasm had waned.

'So, to recap, we've earned *and* designed our first badge, plus the map for our handbook – thanks, Wesley, they look great. We've nailed our pledge – nice work, Margot. Excellent progress, don't you think?' I said. 'Now, I've got a longlist for the rest of the badges – shall we sort them into categories?'

'Honestly, Josephine,' said Margot, 'I'm tired.' She stretched on my bed. 'Clarinet, cleaning and being this creative has drained me.'

'I'm done, too,' said Wesley, 'and I better check in at home.' He peered at his phone. 'Yeah, it's nearly eight – gotta bounce. This was good, though. More tomorrow, after school?'

He stood up, looked out of my window and over into his yard. 'No moves or noise coming from mine. That means they're up to – Oh! Oh no!'

Wesley's hand flew to his mouth.

Margot looked at me with a combination of confusion and concern.

'What?' I asked cautiously.

He didn't reply.

He opened the window instead.

'Wesley!' said Margot, her voice trembling. 'You're scaring me!'

'The teens,' he whispered. 'Or the ghosts. They're back there. In Chicane! Grandad Alan, you wouldn't haunt it, would you?'

Margot and I scrambled to our feet and joined Wesley at the window, pushing him out of the way.

I wasn't convinced this was paranormal activity. I thought ghosts loved the dark, so why would they turn on a light? In any case, the lights were certainly on. In the top-left row of windows, just like last night. I turned to face my friends. 'See! I *told* you!'

'You *were* right, Jo!' said Margot. 'Finally, some real excitement in the LU4 postcode!'

'We have to get to the bottom of this,' I said. 'Right? How about we make this the second official task for the Copseys? Push uniforms into third place for now? We'll definitely earn a few badges along the way.'

Margot punched the air. 'Whoo, yes! I'm in.'

Wesley turned away from the window. 'I'm not in. I don't like this. Remember what Bobby said?'

Margot snorted. 'Wesley, please – don't be idiotic.'

'I'm not an idiot,' he said flatly. 'I just want to live.'

I reached for my laptop and scanned through our badges. 'OK, how's this for a plan? To know more, we must get closer. How about we earn our camping badges tomorrow night and sleep in The Outback –'

'Sleeping outside in *November*?' said Wesley. 'By *ourselves*?' He shook his head. 'I dunno, Jo.'

'I've got two super-cosy sleeping bags,' said Margot. 'And we'll be together. It will be fine. More than fine – fun!'

'Hmmm,' said Wesley, scrunching his face tightly. 'I really dunno – just the thought of this is making me feel sick.'

'Look,' I said. 'We'll find out what's going on in Chicane. Then, once we know, we can forget about it, Wesley. Lay the ghosts to rest –'

'RIP!' added Margot for emphasis.

'So, what do you think?' I asked, staring at Wesley.

'I think I love it,' Margot squealed. 'It's all so Scoutsy! It's a yes from me. Wesley?'

'I dunno.' He sighed. 'I really, really don't like it.'

MAKING

Make it happen!

I barely slept last night. I lay on my back, staring at the glowing stars on the ceiling and listening to rain hit my window and the paving slabs in the garden. I was happy about earning our first badge and wondered if Mr Kirklees had noticed our work yet. I was also excited to achieve our second badge, but I was honestly nervous. Not about the logistics of camping, or the lights in Chicane – I'm not like Wesley. Those were easy things to figure out. They were achievable and solvable. I couldn't concentrate at school either. My mind wandered all day. The truth was, I was worried about my parents. I spent most of the day trying to figure out how I was going to get round Mum and Dad – Mum especially. She's already banned me from The Outback, and she *hates* camping. Really hates it. Mum thinks camping is dangerous and unnecessary. When Ella, Wesley's mum, offered to take me with them to the coast last summer, Mum kissed her teeth and swatted her away, saying, 'Ella, that's madness! Why sleep outdoors when you're blessed with an indoors? You have a house, and hotels exist! Make it make sense!'

The best course of action – the one I kept returning to, the one very much against the Copsey Code – was to lie.

'You're doing the right thing. A small story will save the day,' said Margot as she lay on my bed after school.

'I don't feel good about doing it,' I replied, looking out of my open window. The ground was still wet and I could smell the damp. Mum would *never* say yes, especially now it was damp. I could hear her now. '*So, you want to catch a cold and die, then get kidnapped and die again?*' I looked back at Margot. 'Don't worry. I'll figure it out. First, update me on the equipment.'

'It's all done,' said Margot. She rolled off the bed and joined me at the window. 'It's at Wesley's. Pop-up tent, quilted ground sheets, sleeping bags –'

'Where did you get all this?' I asked.

Margot shrugged. 'The shed. We used to go camping down in Surrey, like, all the time. "Family-bonding time" Dad called it. I say *family* – but that's a lie. It was just me and Dad. Her Mothership never came, just gave me money I couldn't spend – not in a forest, anyway.' Margot rolled her eyes. 'She stayed at home, bonding with a bottle of wine.' Margot mimed someone – her mum, I assumed – gulping from a glass.

We were quiet for a moment, then I looked sideways at her. 'What's your dad going to say when he sees your stuff is missing?'

Margot laughed. 'As if. He wouldn't notice me missing, let alone the equipment, Jo. He's back in London, back to the law. Mr Michael Anderson, QC, is a very busy man, you know? And no sitter for me tonight – not that I need one. I'm twelve next year!' She blinked. 'Anyway! It's all good! I've packed a hamper full of food – you're going to love it. All you need to do is get your little bag and we can –' She paused, putting her hands on her hips. 'Look at that idiot!'

I knew who 'the idiot' was. I looked over into Wesley's yard. He was roughly pushing a big rolled-up green bag through a too-small gap in his wire fence – our exit to The Outback. Margot banged on my window.

Wesley jumped, swore, let go of the bag and scowled up at us. 'What you banging for?' he shouted. 'I'm doing what you said, aren't I?'

Margot leaned out and looked into Wesley's yard. 'Just be careful – and quiet, for God's sake. Give us ten minutes.'

Bag over my shoulder, I slumped down the stairs behind Margot, who gleefully jumped down each step. In the living room, Mum lay on the sofa, hands crossed over her stomach. Dad sat on the floor in front of her, staring at the TV with a game controller in hand and a mug of tea by his side.

'Wow, Nia!' said Margot. 'You look incredible. How are you feeling?'

Dad looked up at Mum and stifled a laugh. Mum turned her head to look at us. 'I'm feeling over it,' she said. 'This kid's got more kicks than the Premier League. But, on the bright side, I'm finished up in the salon as of today. I'm embracing lying-down life now.'

Margot laughed. 'As you should – I would have quit work ages ago if I were you.'

'If you were me, though, you'd have bills to pay,' said Mum with a smile. She looked at the bag on my shoulder and tried to sit up. 'Where you going?'

I looked at Margot, who nodded. I took a deep breath. 'Is it all right if I stay at Margot's tonight?'

'Yeah, fine with me, Jo,' said Dad. He took a sip of his tea. 'No schemes, no scams, just sleep.' He looked up at me and winked. I smiled back, but I felt terrible.

'Thanks, Dad.'

Mum looked at me through narrowed eyes. 'What's wrong with your own bed?'

I laughed and it sounded so fake. 'Nothing. It's very comfortable. I just want to hang out with Margot.' I held my breath.

'Nah, you're scheming,' Dad said through laughter. 'Is it the Olympic-ten-pin-bowling thing? I like that idea, you know – I might actually have a shot at a medal if you make that happen. You're always doing something, but put *that* one into action.'

'Right?' said Margot, completely comfortable in the lie. 'It's great, isn't it? We'll do some light planning, think about who we can contact, fundraising, that kind of stuff.'

Mum looked at Margot, then at me. She sat back down. 'Yeah, fine, fine – just no walking the streets in the dark, OK?'

I bit my lip and held my breath, staying silent. Where we were going, there were no roads, but I knew what she meant. It was a technicality, but one I could use to my advantage, maybe.

I exhaled. 'OK, Mum. I won't be on the streets. I promise.'

QUILTING
Duvet? No, DO IT!

Of course we went straight to Wesley's. I pressed myself against his porch in case my parents were watching from our front window. I knocked gently on his door, then put my ear to it. Judging by the commotion inside – commentary and cussing – I knew no one would hear us. Wesley's doorbell was broken, and its exposed wire ends were wrapped in electrical tape. So I crouched down and opened his letter box. Through it, I could see his legs in his kitchen. He was by the sink, washing up.

'Wesley!' I hissed. Wesley jumped and swore. A light-green plate he must have been holding fell to the floor and smashed.

'Seriously, will you two stop scaring me today?' he said, his legs moving closer to the letter box. He pulled his front door open. 'I'm already on edge as it is – scared of the dumb, dangerous things you want us to do – so give me a break, will you?'

'Calm it down, Wesley,' said Margot, pushing past him and stepping into his house.

Wesley stared at me. He closed his eyes, and his hands balled up into little light-brown fists. I put my hand on his shoulder. 'Breathe,' I whispered. 'This will be worth it.'

'Will it, though? It better be,' he said, holding the front door open for me.

The broken plate added to the general untidiness of Wesley's house. It couldn't not, what with Ella being under the weather and his siblings being so messy. In the living room Jordan and Jayden, Wesley's younger twin brothers, were sitting on the floor, still in school uniform playing a football game on their Xbox: I didn't know which one. A new one seems to come out every year, but they all look the same to me. Kayla was holding her phone in the air, attempting to copy the dancing she saw on-screen. Every time she stepped in front of the television, the boys would shout 'Kayla!' in unison. Margot watched them with wonder while Wesley shuffled in the hallway, stuffing his belongings into his backpack.

'I don't like this. I don't like this idea at all,' he huffed. 'It's stupid and dangerous.'

'You really don't have to come,' I said with a slight shrug. 'I'll understand.'

'No cap, I have to. I can't leave you fools out there alone, can I? You're smart, but you've got zero common sense. None.' Wesley shook a tattered bag. 'Also, it's all right for you two – that camping stuff Margot's got is *elite*. It will be plush for you. My sleeping bag is well old.'

'It does the job though, doesn't it?' I said. 'At least you have one – I don't have any of this stuff at home.'

'And you never will, knowing your mum. Where did you tell her you were going? Cos I know it wasn't the truth,' said Wesley.

'Margot's,' I said quietly.

Wesley chuckled. 'You'd better hope she doesn't find out.'

'She won't!' shouted Margot from the living room. 'It was a beautiful little lie.' She poked her head round the door frame. 'Nearly ready?'

'Yeah, almost,' said Wesley. 'Let me just chat to this lot.' He stepped past Margot and into the living room.

'Guys?' he said. None of his siblings looked up. 'Guys!' he demanded. 'Please?'

Kayla sighed at her phone.

'What, Wes?' she replied. 'We're busy.'

'Listen, Kay – I'm leaving you in charge until Mum comes down. I'm going out for a bit.'

'Oh yeah? Where?' said Kayla, looking up, scanning me and Margot. 'Out with your *girlfriends*?'

Jayden laughed. 'Nah, he's doing his *homework*, right?' Kayla nudged Jayden in the back with her pink-socked foot. He looked up at her and together they laughed. Kayla flopped on to the sofa and returned to swiping through her screen.

Wesley shook his head. 'You lot are rude and messy.'

'I agree,' said Jordan, not looking up from his game and keeping his eye on the ball. 'Don't worry, Wes. We've got it. I'll check on Mum in a bit.'

'Thanks, Jords,' replied Wesley. 'All right.' He turned to me and Margot. 'I'm not ready, but we can go.' He looked around the hallway and up the stairs. 'Ah, nearly forgot this.' Wesley reached through the bannisters and pulled down a tatty patchwork blanket from the stairs. The fabric was separating at its seams.

'Is that raggedy thing your groundsheet?' asked Margot.

'No,' said Wesley, stuffing it into his bag. 'It's my . . . quilt.'

'Your *quilt*? Like a blankie?' Margot laughed. 'Do you need it to get to sleep? That's really sweet, actually.'

'No,' said Wesley. 'It's not and I don't. Not that it's your business, but I just like it. It's got my name stitched on it and everything. See?' He pushed it close to my face. It did. 'It was Grandad Alan's, then my dad's and now it's mine, and I want it with me.'

'Wait – the grandad you think is haunting Chicane?' I asked.

'Hang on. Using your knowledge, which makes no sense, if you're so afraid of ghosts, is it a good idea to bring your blanket?' said Margot, wrinkling her nose. 'What if it summons your grandad, and he wants it back?'

Wesley shrugged. 'It will either bring us luck, or very much the opposite. If it's the opposite, well, it's your's and Jo's fault for making me do this.'

ORIENTEERING

Follow your own path!

Margot kicked at the rusted tricycle in Wesley's backyard. It scraped loudly against the concrete.

'Don't!' I hissed, jabbing my finger in the direction of my house. 'My mum and dad are *just* there. Let's not get caught before we start, please!'

Margot raised her hands. 'Sorry, sorry,' she whispered.

'Right, so I've screen-grabbed an aerial-view map of The Outback. I *think* I've found the perfect spot for us.' I paused. 'And I have the torch and compass on my phone.' I took a breath. 'Copseys, are we ready to earn our second badge?'

Margot nodded enthusiastically, but Wesley said, 'Nope.'

'Let's go!' I said, ignoring him.

'Ooh, wait! Shall we say our pledge?' Margot put her hand on her heart and began without confirmation. 'I swear, I will do my best, to love –'

'Nope, no. Stop,' said Wesley. 'Too cringe. If I'm going, I'm going now.' He took a hopefully-not-last look at his house, then twisted his body round the wire fence and disappeared into the dark-green wilderness.

It was happening.

Margot stopped reciting and followed him through what I've now named Wesley's Gap. When I reached the other side, I grinned at my friends and picked up the heavy green bag we saw Wesley rolling earlier. Margot grabbed a flat, circular bag. I nodded at them and they nodded in return.

We were on our way.

The Copseys were really real now. I inhaled deeply, breathing in the scent of the bushes and a sense of achievement. I exhaled, breathing out a little fear and a few concerns.

We were out at night, on our own in The Outback. We call it that for obvious reasons – because it backs on to our houses. It's not connected to Australia, but now we stood amidst it in the dark, it might as well have been. I had a thought: we could start our first international group in Australia and have a twin-town arrangement. I made a mental note to talk to the others about this later and add it to our strategy.

Before Copsey Close was developed, a small, majestic group of trees apparently stood here and that's what our close was named after. The houses on the avenue had a great view of them, apparently. If that was more than legend, and it really existed, those special trees were long gone – replaced by unremarkable weeds, thick nettles and copious amounts of rubbish. Faded plastic bags from long-closed corner shops curled around our jeans. We kicked our way through cans and swatted midges, moths and branches away as we stomped through the undergrowth together, one behind the other.

'How far away are we?' said Wesley, looking over his shoulder at Margot and me. 'It better not be much longer, Jo.'

I looked at my phone. 'Hmmm, a minute more, I think. Chicane needs to look a bit bigger. We're heading east, towards the Lea, by the way.'

'The River Lea? There's a river in Luton?' said Margot. 'Didn't know that.'

Wesley snorted. 'Not only is there a river here, Margot, this is where it starts! Then it flows all the way to the Thames. Maybe you can float back to London on it?'

'That's not a bad idea,' said Margot. 'Maybe you can wash your blankie in it, too?'

Wesley stopped suddenly, causing Margot to bump into him and me into her. He laughed. 'Sorry about that – thought I heard something in front of us.'

'You're not funny,' said Margot, pushing Wesley's backpack and causing him to stumble forward.

'Oi!'

'Please, Copseys, can we concentrate? We're nearly there,' I said. I looked down at my phone, then up at our surroundings. 'Wesley, you should see the river, now – can you?'

He squinted. 'Yep – we're here.'

'We are?' said Margot. 'I'm not sure why I was expecting more, but I'm a bit disappointed. Is this it?'

I ignored Margot. This was a good spot. I'd scoped it out on Google Earth before we came and now I looked at it in real life it was a fine location. We were next to the river (I say river; it's more of a stream), and Chicane Cars was directly on the other side of it. The factory loomed over us in the dark and its lights were off – for now. Between our feet were old wrappers, and newer beer cans and bottles. I knew it would be like this. That is why I'd packed bin bags for more litter-picking in the morning. When I looked back at the close, wondering if Mr

Kirklees had seen our work yet for the hundredth time today, I noticed my bedroom light was on.

The pang of guilt I felt when I thought about my parents mostly faded when I remembered the extreme and unnecessary attention they were giving to my brother. Yes, they probably wouldn't miss me or care, really. Not that much, anyway. Still, I felt a little bit bad. Bending the truth can be beneficial, sure, but breaking the rules so blatantly wasn't my favourite feeling. Lying wasn't good for me.

'Yes, this is it,' I said, swallowing hard. I took Margot's heavy bag from my shoulder and set it down. I smiled up at my friends and stomped my feet. 'The ground seems flat enough – let's set up!'

'Great!' said Margot. She kneeled on the grass and unzipped the circular bag. 'Step back and prepare to be amazed!' She pulled the material out of her bag, undid three orange clips and flicked it. A tent appeared, from seemingly nowhere. 'Voila!' she said. 'Home sweet home – for tonight anyway.'

'Sick!' said Wesley. 'That was well speedy! If we were using mine, we'd still be here in an hour, threatening to kill each other with rusty tent poles.'

'It's cool, isn't it?' said Margot proudly. Wesley looked around the tent. He poked his head inside and stroked the top.

'It is,' I said. 'Is that all we have to do?'

'Well, there are some pegs and other bits, but we don't need to bother with those.'

'Are you sure?' I said.

Margot shrugged. 'Maybe?'

'Well, you know best,' I said. 'Let's unpack.' I stepped back and smiled. 'Look at us! Look how far we've come!'

CAMPING

Close to nature, close to home.

We sat cross-legged in our coats on our sleeping bags. The lit torch between us filled the tent with warm, yellow light. It was actually quite beautiful. I looked over at Wesley. He smiled back.

'You've cheered up,' I said.

'Yeah, well, it's nice, innit? Quiet. Peaceful.' He lay down. 'I might live here forever, you know?'

'Maybe I will, too,' said Margot. 'It's nice having company.'

'It is?' said Wesley. 'Can't relate, really. I have nothing but company all the time. Sometimes, I don't want it.'

'Grass is always greener, isn't it?' said Margot.

'Yeah.' He sighed.

'Well,' I said. 'I'm glad you're both happy – and I don't mean to burst your blissful bubbles here – but don't get too comfortable. We're on a mission. If we see the lights or hear anything, we're investigating – right?'

Margot nodded but Wesley's face fell. 'Wait, can't we just stay here and earn the camping badge?' He reached for his quilt and covered his knees.

'Your blankie won't save you from ghosts,' said Margot. 'You do know that, don't you?'

Wesley waved his gloved hands at Margot. 'No! Don't do that. Don't say the g-word, not here. Don't encourage them.'

'All right, all right,' said Margot, smiling. 'I won't.' She reached for her cool bag. 'Here, eat something. I've got plenty of things: sandwiches, buns, cheese and crackers. I've even got three patties in here. One each.'

'Yes!' said Wesley, diving into the bag. He grabbed a tinfoil parcel and ripped it open before stuffing the contents into his mouth. 'Beef?' he asked through cheeks full of food. His eyes crossed in delight. 'Beef.' He sighed happily.

'This is great, Margot. Thank you.' I rubbed my chin. 'It's silly maybe, but I had thoughts of us cooking tonight,' I said. 'Catching a fish from the stream, frying it on a fire. You know – real camping.'

Margot and Wesley looked at each other and burst out laughing.

'Absolutely not,' said Margot.

'Yeah, no way,' said Wesley. 'It's a nice dream, Josie, but no chance. Last summer when we camped on the coast, I went to a river with my net. I had the same idea as you, the same dream – one that quickly turned into a nightmare. All I saw down there was a rat eating a dead baby bird.'

'Eww,' said Margot.

'Innit,' said Wesley. 'I saw Mother Nature that day and she wasn't pretty, I can tell you.'

I thought for a moment. 'Ooh, how about an ecosystems badge! What do you think?'

'I think –'

Before Wesley could even roll his eyes in reply, there was a sound. Music.

Music outside the tent. Stunned silence inside.

Our bodies froze, but our eyes danced. They asked fearful questions and sought comforting answers.

'What's that? What's that? What's that?' Wesley hissed repeatedly.

'Just music,' said Margot. Her chest rose and fell rapidly. 'It's just music. Nothing to be afraid of.' She had her hands on her head. 'It's just teenagers, or, you know, one of those urban explorers – those people who go round abandoned buildings filming stuff for YouTube or wherever, right? Right?'

I leaned forward and unzipped the tent.

'No, no, no!' said Wesley, gripping my shoulder. 'Don't let them in! I don't want teens or spirits inside this tent!'

I poked my head out and looked up at Chicane.

It was time.

'The lights are on!' I said, turning round. 'In the exact same place as the last two nights.'

'Zip the tent back up then!' Wesley pleaded. 'Are you mad?'

Margot breathed deeply next to him. 'Think of the story you could write! Think of your story, Margot!' she whispered to herself. With her eyes squeezed shut, she reached for Wesley's hand. He gripped it tightly in return.

I slowly crawled out.

'That's it, she's dead,' said an exasperated Wesley. 'RIP to you!' He pulled desperately at my leg with his free hand, and I kicked him in the chin in return. It was an accident – kind of.

'Oww, Jo!'

'Sorry, Wesley, but I have to see! I need to know.'

Kneeling outside, I turned to the factory and listened closely to the music.

Cent, five cent, ten cent, dollar!

Cent, five cent, ten cent, dollar!

'I know this song!' I said. 'I don't think teenagers would listen to this one. It's my grandad's favourite. I danced to this with him at my auntie's wedding. It's a soca classic.'

'Cool story, Josephine,' Margot shouted. 'Lovely memory, but get inside!'

I didn't go back inside. I got to my feet instead. I took a step towards the stream and was considering how to cross it when the music stopped.

The light switched off.

'Oh no!'

'No, it's not "oh no". It's good!' said Wesley, his quilt over his head. 'It's great!'

I returned to the tent with a delighted sigh. 'That was *amazing*!' I panted. 'I was so *close* to figuring this out. First, we saw lights. Now, we've heard music. I don't think it's teens, or a new buyer for the factory. I wonder what's next?' I shrugged. 'I guess we just wait and see. Pass me a patty, please, Margot?'

Wesley stared at me.

'What?' I said, biting into the flaky yellow pastry. 'Mmmm, this is *good*!'

'No, this isn't good!' he said, slapping the patty out of my palm.

'Wes! I was enjoying that!'

'Well, you're not now. Let's go. We've camped. It's over. I award you your badge. Margot, what do you think?'

Margot gulped. 'Well . . . you make some good, strong statements.' She flicked patty flakes from her sleeping bag on to the floor of her tent. She sighed. 'But if Josephine wants to stay then, well, maybe we should.'

'For God's sake, Margot – stop kissing her butt for once!' shouted Wesley. 'Be your own person! I'm not gonna die out here for you two, I told –'

'Wait, what's that?' I whispered.

Outside, the sound of slow footsteps crushing cans and crisp packets surrounded the tent and grew louder.

They, whoever they were, were coming closer. Coming for us.

'It's back!' whispered Wesley, his face contorted in terror. 'If you make it, tell my family I actually do love them.'

From outside, a low voice said with a chuckle, 'Rhatid! A likkle campsite?'

We jumped in unison. My heart found itself in my mouth and it didn't taste as good as the patty.

'Abandon tent! Abandon tent!' I shouted. We scrambled to our feet, grabbing what we could, and burst out on to the grass. I reached back into the tent for my bag and phone. 'Go, go, go – don't look back!'

Wesley ran ahead while Margot grabbed my hand and pulled me forward. I immediately broke my own rule and glanced behind me.

I saw the outline of a man. A tall, thin man, slightly hunched over, was ambling towards the tent. He looked solid, not transparent like a ghost looks – not in my mind, anyway. He must have seen me looking because he suddenly stopped and turned away.

We disappeared into the dark of The Outback and ran. Trip hazards were no longer our concern – getting home was. When our houses on the close came closer into view, waves of relief ran over me. Wesley dived through his gap and Margot followed, pulling me through behind her.

We were back. We were safe.

Wesley stood in his yard, panting, bent over at the waist with his hands on his knees. 'I left my quilt,' he said between breaths. 'I need my quilt.'

Margot and I leaned against the wall. Margot looked at me, her eyes bright and wide. 'That was scary – and amazing! Scamazing!'

'I hope it was worth it,' shouted a flat voice from two doors down. 'Get home.'

Wesley and Margot looked at the ground, but I stared up at my bedroom window. Mum leaned out of it.

'Mum, wait, I can explain. I –'

'Get home. Now.'

She slammed the window shut.

DEBRIEFING

Evaluate your efforts, always!

'Well, that's that then,' said Wesley between deep breaths. 'The Copseys are finished, and so are you, Jo. Your mum's going to end you for lying, and I've lost my blanket for nothing.'

I looked up at my bedroom window, then quickly back to my friends. 'Wesley, you *cannot* be serious. How can we give up now? It's just started!' I whispered. I grabbed his arms. 'Look at what we've achieved already!'

'*Achieved?* We've achieved nothing but stress and loss!'

'Not true, Wesley,' I said. 'We helped Mr Kirklees –'

'Do you think he's noticed yet?' asked Margot.

'That doesn't matter, Margot!' said Wesley, exasperated. 'That wasn't the point.' He turned to me. 'You'd better go home, Jo.'

I shook my head. 'I will in a minute. Look, we've camped, OK, yes, briefly – but we did it, didn't we? Second badge earned! Tick! Tick! We found out that the lights aren't a collective ghostly hallucination, or teens – something weird is happening at Chicane. I saw a man, I swear. Someone is *definitely* out there.'

'Or *something*,' said Wesley. 'Something I don't want to mess with. Whatever that was, it wasn't Grandad, I tell you that.' He shuddered. 'He would *never* freak us out like that.'

'You are right though, Josie,' said Margot. 'It wasn't a failed mission – it was awesome! It had everything: drama, suspense, horror –'

'*Please* stop agreeing with her, Margot!' Wesley shouted. 'Stop scriptwriting and sucking up for just a second – you've lost all your fancy camping gear, and my blanket is gone, along with Josie's mind.'

My mind was firmly where it needed to be, but he had a point about the equipment. A great point. We had to go back – there was no other choice. At the very least, the camping gear was adding to the litter in The Outback, and that was unacceptable.

'OK, Wes, I hear you.' I stroked my chin to suggest I'd just thought of the following idea. 'We have to go and get the stuff. You're right.'

'What, now?' he shouted. 'No way!'

'Of course not now!' I looked up at my bedroom window. 'I have to face the music at home first, instead of the music at Chicane. Tomorrow. Saturday morning.'

Wesley thought for a moment. 'I really *do* want my blanket . . . but I don't need danger and drama, Josephine.'

'I do,' said Margot. 'Sign me back up. I'm still in. I'm not that fussed about the equipment – call it "collateral damage". I have to know more. I need to see how this story ends!'

'Badly. It will end badly!' said Wesley. 'But I'll go back tomorrow. I have to. In the day, Josephine! No night quests.'

'Fine with me. This is a recovery mission after all – we'll need natural light.'

'Excellent,' said Margot. 'So, what now? What are our immediate next steps?'

'Josie needs to step into her house and chat to her mum, that's for sure,' said Wesley.

He was right. That now-familiar feeling of fear and guilt had returned. I swallowed hard and nodded. Margot noticed my nerves.

'Want me to come with you?' she said gently. 'I have a way with Nia and Patrick. I'll help you get them onside.'

Wesley snorted. 'Why do you call them by their names like that? They're parents – not your friends – and you've only known them for five minutes!' He stepped in front of Margot. 'You know that's a terrible idea, don't you?'

I didn't say anything to challenge him out loud, but inwardly I agreed – it was. I had to repair our relationship alone.

'No, don't worry, Margot. I'll be fine,' I replied, really hoping I would be.

CONFRONTING

Face your fears!

Wesley only lives two doors down, but the walk through his house and back to mine felt like an epic odyssey. With each footstep I ran through a variety of parental-crisis-management scenarios, and considered the different ways this situation could play out. All of them ended with me being in multiple degrees of trouble, and I hated that. Margot said goodbye in Wesley's front yard, but I was so deep in thought I barely heard her go. I certainly didn't acknowledge her leaving, which was rude. Staring at the light-blue mattress still stranded in the doughnut, I realized I'd have to apologize to her tomorrow.

By the time I reached my front door, I knew tears definitely wouldn't work.

I'd just have to apologize to them, too. It was the right and only thing to do.

I put my key in the door. It had to be almost eleven o'clock, as the sound of Friday-night TV boomed in the hallway. An eager talk show host joked with their overly excited audience, who whooped with delight in return. It felt like they were laughing at me. I was their entertainment now.

I sat on the bottom step and slowly took off my trainers. I put them in the row of shoes, next to Dad's. I considered getting a glass of water first, but dragging this out would only make Mum angrier. So I took a deep breath, stood up and peered into the living room from the doorway.

The lights were off. The living room was lit only by the vibrant colours coming from the television. Mum was in her favourite position and place – stretched out on the sofa, lips pursed and eyes shut tight. Dad sat at the end, with Mum's feet in his lap. He rubbed at her ankles. Whatever he was doing was working, because they were much smaller than this morning. Well done, Dad.

'Hi,' I said quietly.

Mum opened one eye, shut it quickly and kissed her teeth. Dad looked up and offered me a weak smile.

'Come sit down,' he said. 'The three of us need to talk.' He turned the TV down.

I darted into the room, flopped into the armchair and wrapped my arms across my body. I stared at the TV. Some actor was chatting to the talk show host about some film I didn't know or care about. I sighed, sat up and folded my arms in my lap. I could do this. I could get through this. I was a Copsey now. I had the Copsey Code to guide me.

'Mum,' I started. 'I'm sorry, I –'

'You know what I hate most in the world, Jo?' she said quietly.

'Right now – me?' I said. I fake laughed, matching the energy of the conversation on-screen, hoping it might lighten the mood in the room. Dad shook his head, putting an immediate end to that strategy.

'Lying,' Mum said. 'Lying is one of the *worst* things a person can do.'

She was right. Copsey Code, point one: be truthful and trustful.

'Technically, Mum,' I said. 'I didn't lie – I wasn't walking on the streets.'

'Josephine,' said Dad. His tone was cautionary, but slightly threatening. He shook his head. 'That's not helping.'

'I'm sorry, Mum. I promise I wasn't doing anything bad or wrong.'

'But what about *dangerous*, huh?' said Mum. 'Do you know the kinds of things – what kinds of *people* – might be lurking in those bushes at night? What's the matter with you?'

She had a good point and she was right, but I couldn't concede. Not yet.

'I was doing a good thing.'

That was true. I was. Copsey Code, point two: be proactive – and never procrastinate.

'I don't care what you *think* you were doing!' Mum shouted. She craned her neck, looking like a turtle that had rolled on to its back and couldn't right itself.

Dad winced at the volume of her voice. 'Nia, calm down – think of the baby.' See? It's always about the baby. He tried to touch her arm, but Mum swatted his hand away.

'I'm dealing with this one first,' she said to him, before turning to me. 'I thought you were sensible?'

'I am.'

'I thought I could trust you.'

'You can!'

'Then *why* were you there? I thought we didn't have to worry about you!'

'You don't!' I snapped. 'Worry about your other, more important, precious kid instead!'

Dad and Mum looked at each other and shared a knowing look. I gulped down deep breaths and sat back in the chair. I dug my nails into its arms. I was breaking Copsey Code, point six: be caring. I stared at the TV. Someone from the audience fell backwards from a red chair and disappeared, much to everyone else's delight. I wished that was me.

'Josie, why would you say that?' said Dad softly. 'Of course we worry and care about you. We love you – more than you'll ever know.'

'Aren't you too busy with your new baby?' I snapped. 'Buying things for it, choosing names –'

'He needs things, Jo!' shouted Mum. 'And I *knew* you threw away my list of names, I just knew it!' Dad gently tapped Mum's legs to calm her down. It worked, but only a little bit. 'Be reasonable!' she said. 'If I didn't care, why would I shout, cuss and get vexed?'

'Your mum's right,' said Dad. 'We don't love or care about your brother more than you. He's not your replacement – don't be silly. We're just becoming a bigger team, that's all. Strength in numbers, right?' He smiled.

'Well, no one asked me! I have my own plans – and they don't involve your baby.'

'It's *our* baby!' said Mum, pointing to the three of us. 'Josie, you know we always wanted another child. We planned this. There is no need to be jealous – no reason at all. Enjoy this and get involved.'

'*Involved?* I'm not going to be your babysitter,' I said, fighting back angry tears. 'I've got plans – and you can't stop me.'

I had bigger plans – that was true – but my plan to stick to the Copsey Code evaporated along with my parents' patience and respect for me. The talk show on the television ended. Before either of them could shout – I knew they wanted to and I couldn't blame them – I stomped out of the room. Me, my tired legs and my hot tears ran up the stairs. I threw open my bedroom door and flicked on the big light.

I wanted to throw myself on my bed and sulk, then edit the Copsey Code for real-life situations and go to sleep, but I couldn't – not immediately. There was something in the way. A beautifully wrapped box on my bed – the reason Mum was in my room in the first place. I sighed and slumped down next to it. I considered throwing it down the stairs at them, but I loved presents, and, besides, that wouldn't help matters.

I pulled at its red ribbon, guiltily unfurling it. I removed the shiny, reflective paper, and felt regretful. I lifted the lid from the box and wondered how I would face my parents tomorrow. Inside was a book: a copy of *Becoming*, Michelle Obama's memoir. She was the best First Lady ever and a real hero, just like Josephine Holloway.

I sighed, wondering what Michelle and Josephine would do if they were in my shoes right now – especially Josephine, since she started all of this. It was her fault, really, if I was going to blame someone else. But I couldn't. This was on me. I set the book down, walked to the window and stared out. The lights at Chicane Cars were back on.

Copsey Code, point three: be resilient.

REPAIRING

Make do and mend!

I felt better about the situation with Mum and Dad by morning. I thought about and assessed my performance throughout the argument overnight, and when I woke up I researched ways to improve my skills in dealing with difficult situations. In a nutshell, I just needed to say sorry to Mum and Dad, thank them for the book and mean it. Whether they would accept my apology was a different matter, but that was up to them.

Before I went downstairs to face them, I had to get my priorities in the right order, so I decided to make plans for the day with Margot and Wesley first. I stood by my window and looked down into Wesley's yard. He was wrestling with a washing basket, hanging odd socks and small pairs of pants out on the line to dry. Since his dad had gone and his mum was ill, Wesley really did do a lot around his house – much more than I did in my home. I knocked on the glass to get his attention. He looked up and gestured at me to open the window.

'Still alive, I see,' he said. 'It went better than I thought, then.'

'Yep, it was mostly fine,' I lied. 'I used our code to get me through.'

'Hmmm,' said Wesley. 'Is that so?' He peered up at me through the pegs. 'So, what's the plan for today? When are we going back?'

'Well, it's ten o'clock now, so I need to make nice for a couple of hours and be helpful, and then we can go.'

'They're gonna let you out?'

'Yeah, I reckon. Let's say one o'clock – are you free then? If so, I'll check with Margot.'

'Yeah, one's good,' said Wesley. 'It'll give the washing a chance to dry.'

'Will it?' I said. I put my hand out of the window. 'I don't know. It's November. Drying clothes outside is more of a summer thing, isn't it?'

Wesley sighed. 'Yeah, you're right. I know. The dryer's on the blink and I can't ask Mum – she's with Auntie Molly this morning. Something's definitely going on. They were on the phone last night when everyone was supposed to be in bed. Talking all quietly, whispering, and then she turned up here first thing this morning.'

I drew a sharp breath through my teeth. 'Oh no, really? What do you think is going on?'

Wesley shrugged. 'No idea.'

'Could the Copseys help?'

He smiled. 'Pipe down, Jo. Let's get the stuff back first, then see.'

'OK,' I said. 'If you're sure – I can multitask, you know.'

'Yes, Jo.' Wesley sighed. 'I know.'

I saluted a goodbye to Wesley, who shook his head, and shut the window.

I messaged Margot as I walked down the stairs. She immediately said yes to meeting at one, so my phone went back into my pocket. I sat at the bottom of the steps and fiddled with my fingers for a moment, preparing myself. I knew I wasn't the centre of my parents' world at the moment, but I hoped they didn't hate me or want to throw me out. Surely they wouldn't. No, they wouldn't. I was thinking the worst. I just had to face them and be sorry – or at least act accordingly. I took a deep breath, exhaled, lifted my shoulders and walked into the room. For the first time in forever, Mum wasn't lying on the sofa. She was sitting up, leaning forward, staring at her phone. Dad was standing between her and the television, waving his arms.

'What does that even *mean*?' Dad said, panicked. 'Do you have to go to the hospital now, or not? I told you I should've packed a bag!'

'No, it means you need to relax,' said Mum. 'I've been here before, remember? It's not actual labour – just a warm-up for the main event.'

'You all right, Mum?' I said. I sat down next to her and put my arm on her shoulder. 'Is he coming now?'

Mum pursed her lips. 'No, he's not. Your dad's panicking for no reason.' She winced and lay down. 'Oooh! That feels tight!' she said.

'No reason, eh?' said Dad.

'Just get some water, Patrick, yeah? Please?'

While he ran to the kitchen, I pulled out my phone.

'Are you in pain?'

'Not really.'

'Does this tightness have a pattern?'

'Nah, it comes and goes when it feels like it. Like you do.'

Dad returned with an overflowing glass of water, which he handed to Mum with dripping wet hands. He shook them on to the laminated wooden floor, then wiped them on his jogging bottoms when he thought Mum wasn't looking. 'Drink up,' he said.

Mum took big gulps. 'Ahhh!' She sighed. 'See – I feel better already.'

'I just searched your symptoms, and it seems like you have a case of the Braxton Hicks, Mum,' I said. 'It's basically fake labour.' I shone my screen at her face. She lifted her phone to show me hers in return. We were looking at the same website. She smiled.

'Great minds –'

'Think alike,' she added. 'Well, mostly. I wouldn't put myself in intentional danger.' She kissed her teeth.

I sighed. 'I *am* sorry, Mum. I understand why you're upset with me. I won't be going back there at night.'

'Or in the day,' said Mum. 'I want two children, please – not one at a time.'

I stayed silent by biting my bottom lip.

'Thank you so much for the book, by the way!' I said, changing the subject with enthusiasm. 'You know how I feel about Michelle Obama.'

'See – we *do* buy things for you too,' said Dad. 'Not just stuff for your brother.' His legs started to buzz, and he patted his joggers to find his phone. 'Ahh,' he said, looking at the screen. 'It's Sunny.'

'Don't answer it,' said Mum. 'It's your day off. Let him figure it out – whatever it is.'

'If only,' said Dad. 'Imagine if I actually did that.' He raised an eyebrow and lifted the handset to his ear. 'All right, Sunny?' he said, and stepped into the hallway.

'That's him gone for the day then,' said Mum. 'Good job I've got nothing on but Netflix. Pass me the remote, please?' She lay back on the sofa.

I reached for it and placed it in her hand.

'I'm thinking of grounding you,' she said, looking at the TV while she flicked through films. 'Should I?'

I sat back. 'No, Mum,' I said quietly.

'You see how you've put me in a sticky situation?'

'How?' I replied.

'You're already not feeling your family at the moment –'

'That's not true –'

'– so if I force you to stay in, and sit next to me all day, make you stare at my stomach, it would only make it worse. You'll get all resentful and ratty.'

I had no reply to that, because it was true.

'Your grandad used to make me sit with him when I got into trouble. It was awful. Truly terrible. The worst of times.'

'Sounds it,' I said.

Mum raised an eyebrow, but reached for my hand. 'I *can* trust you, can't I, Josephine?'

'You can trust me to do the right thing, Mum,' I said. 'That's for sure.'

REINVIGORATING

Refresh, renew, return!

'What *exactly* did she say?' Margot said as we stood by the sink in Wesley's kitchen later that afternoon. She popped a handful of raisins into her mouth. 'Where were you standing? How was she lying? Where was your dad? Let me see the scene, so I can write it later.'

'It wasn't all that exciting, Margot,' I said. 'And this is not for any novel of yours! But, yes, they were a bit upset – more worried, really. I understood their point and I said sorry. That's about it.'

'Yeah, right,' said Wesley. 'I know your mum, so I know it didn't go anything like that.'

I shrugged. 'What can I tell you? It's how it went.' Margot and Wesley looked at each other. I put my hands in my coat pockets. 'Shall we go? I did have to promise I wouldn't go anywhere near The Outback in the dark, so let's go now, get your blanket, come back and work on that uniform –'

'I already told you, I'm not wearing no uniform,' Wesley muttered.

'I'd still love to see some drawings, though.'

'The badges weren't enough?'

'Yeah, come on, Wesley,' said Margot. 'Do your bit!'

'So, wait. I'm the *official* Copsey designer now?' asked Wesley.

I nodded. 'Of course. It's good experience for you.'

'In your mind, maybe,' he said. 'I should be paid for this level of work and commitment.'

'You should be paid for what now?' said a voice on the staircase. I turned in its direction. It was Ella. Or, a kind of alternative version of her. The Ella I knew was tall, fit and strong. This Ella seemed shorter, frail and weak. Her glossy Black skin was duller, greyer and lacked shine. She wearily walked into the kitchen, supporting herself by holding her left hand against the wall, a large, tiger-print scrunchie around her wrist. She held a huge mug in her right hand, which trembled slightly. It said 'World's Best Mum' in rainbow-coloured letters.

I tried not to stare, so I instead looked at Margot, who bit her bottom lip. We both turned to Wesley, who briefly glanced down at his black-and-white checked lino floor, and then quickly up at his mother with a smile.

'What you doing down here, Mum? I told you I was going to make you some tea to settle your stomach and bring it up.'

'Eh, I fancied a trip downstairs, Wessy,' she said slowly. 'Can't lie down all day. And I heard talk about money. Conversations about coin are my least favourite, so here I am to put a stop to it.'

Margot and I laughed nervously.

'You look . . . well,' Margot lied.

Ella smiled. 'You reckon? Talking about coins – I've lost a few pounds, don't you think?' She put her hand and her massive mug to her hips. 'Always wanted to be a model,' she said, jutting her chin forward. 'These angles are working for me, no?'

Margot nodded. 'Definitely.'

Ella picked up the kettle and took it over to the sink, standing between Margot and me. As she filled it with water, she looked across at me and smiled.

'What you up to then?' she whispered. Her eyes shone brightly at me. A smile danced across her lips. This Ella I knew and recognized.

'Nothing too exciting,' I said, sneaking a look at Wesley. He tensely shook his head. 'Just a walk. Us kids spend too much time on screens.' I laughed. 'It's important we stretch our legs as much as we strain our eyes. I read the research.'

Ella chuckled and snapped the kettle's lid shut. 'Yeah, right. I know you, young Josephine. You're up to something.'

'I promise we're not.'

She walked to the worktop and plugged the kettle in. She tightened her dressing-gown cord round her waist. 'Well, that's a shame – you should be,' she said. 'Get out there, discover it all. Take my kids with you, too. I keep telling them, don't stay behind them screens – they're boring and too easy. Where's the fun?'

Margot nodded vigorously. 'Right? There are so many stories out there, waiting to be discovered and told.'

'I knew I liked you,' said Ella. She smiled at Margot. Margot grinned at Wesley. He scowled back at her.

Ella plopped a teabag in her mug. 'When I was your age, I was never home, ever. I had this neon bike, right? It was pink and green, and called Tropicana. She had two little palm trees on each side of her name. That bike was my best friend. Me, Tropicana and my other mates ran this town – we rode around all over it all day, until it was dark.'

'It was a different time then, though,' I said. 'People say it's more dangerous now, don't they?'

Ella reached into the fridge for milk. 'Who says that? *That* sounds like Nia.' She laughed. 'Your mum can be dry – but don't snitch and tell her I said that!'

The kettle boiled and clicked itself off. Ella made her tea. She picked up her mug and kissed Wesley on his cheek.

'What's life for, if it's not for living, eh?' she said as she walked through the hallway. 'See you later!' she shouted down the stairs.

Wesley sighed. 'I told her to relax, but she doesn't listen, ever. That's her problem – that's why she gets sick.'

'It was great to see her, though. I loved what she said. Your mum is a real Copsey. When she's better, we should bring her on board, like an adviser. What do you reckon, Margot?'

Margot looked at Wesley and then at me. 'Yes, maybe,' she said slowly and quietly. 'But I'm not sure how Nia would feel about that.'

'Why we still talking about mums?' Wesley sighed. 'Let's get the stuff and my quilt, then figure this – whatever *this* is – out later.'

Margot and I glanced at each other.

'What you looking at each other for?' he snapped. 'Let's go!' He threw his kitchen door open and stepped into his yard, with me and Margot following. Wesley stood by Wesley's Gap for a moment, touching the wire. He crouched down and disappeared. I went to follow him – I didn't want to be at the back this time – but Margot stopped me.

'Did you see what I saw?' she said in a low voice. 'Ella's sick.'

'Yes, she does look ill. Hopefully a few days in bed will fix it.'

Margot shook her head. 'No, Josie. I think she's *really* sick. Like, seriously.'

'What are you saying?' I gulped. My mouth was suddenly dry.

Margot sighed. 'I'm saying I've seen that look on a person before – on my grandma – and . . . and it didn't end well.'

RESTARTING

Sometimes it's smart to go back to the start!

'You two coming or not?' Wesley shouted back through the weeds. I looked at Margot.

'We can't speculate about someone's health, Margot,' I whispered. 'It's not ethical or right – in fact, it's very wrong. She could be fine.'

'Yes, you're right,' she said. 'But there must be *something* we can do?'

'Like what? We're not doctors – not yet anyway – so we can't . . . diagnose her.'

'Maybe we should ask Wesley about it?' she said. 'Then figure out a way to support him?'

I rubbed my head. 'I don't think – no, wait, I *know* he would hate that. He would get so angry with us for even *thinking* this. And you don't want that, Margot, not if you want to be friends with him.'

'OK,' said Margot. 'I do want to be friends with him.' She bit at her nails. 'I'm just worried. Really worried.'

'Me too,' I whispered. 'But, until we know what's wrong, we should wait.'

'All right,' she said. 'That makes sense.'

'So, for now, act normal and don't mention it?'

Margot nodded. 'OK. Let's catch up with him.' Margot looked at me with a concerned frown and pushed her way through Wesley's Gap. I followed behind her. I was at the back and I didn't want to be.

The Outback was just as dark in the day. We walked heavily through the damp undergrowth, one behind the other. We knew the route now, so I didn't need to look at my phone. Instead, I thought about Ella, and just how ill she might be. Margot can be quite dramatic at times and is prone to pulling stories out of thin air, but something didn't feel right or good.

'I reckon we're almost there,' said Wesley from way out in front. 'I can see your tent, Margot. That's a good sign, innit? If anyone's gonna come across the camp and take anything, it wouldn't be my old quilt – it would be that.'

'Yeah, I agree,' said Margot. 'It's got to be there.'

'Let's hope,' I said.

When we reached our campsite, it was mostly how we left it, apart from the absent quilt and a few new items: two beer cans, two apple cores and a splattered pile of dog poop.

'Gross – I definitely don't want the tent back now,' said Margot, eyeing the excrement and kicking the cores away with her foot. 'Someone must have slept on our stuff!'

'Don't worry about that,' said Wesley, rummaging inside the tent. 'Concern yourself with my quilt instead. It's gotta be here!' He lifted the sleeping bags up and threw them into a pile. 'It has to be!'

It wasn't. Wesley's quilt *was* missing.

I crouched close to the ground. 'Those cores aren't brown yet, so these apples must have been eaten recently,' I said, putting my hand to my chin. 'And whoever ate them may also have your blanket.'

Wesley poked his head through the tent. 'What, you're a detective now? You think someone took it?'

I shrugged my shoulders. 'Just a theory.'

'They might have thought it was a rag?' offered Margot.

Wesley crawled out of the tent. 'Watch it, you,' he said to Margot. 'That's no rag. It might look messy, but it means a lot. Who would take it? Why?'

Wesley's eyes widened. 'Wait – you think the man you saw took it?'

'Maybe,' said Margot. 'Ooh – how's this – perhaps taking it is a way of getting us to keep coming back here to find it? Then he can recruit us for . . . for something.'

'It's not the time for tales.' I sighed.

'Are you working with them, Margot? Tell the truth!' Wesley demanded.

Margot shook her head. 'I'm not. I'm not a spy, I told you.'

'Well, it's a trap then,' said Wesley. He stepped away from the tent. 'We've been lured into a trap. Jo – is this your doing? That would be *well* up your street, something you would totally do to keep the Copseys going.'

'Plot twist!' said Margot. 'I love it.'

I was flattered they thought I was that inventive, honestly. 'This really has nothing to do with me –'

Wesley narrowed his eyes.

'– and I *don't* think it's a trap, exciting as that would be.' I stuck my head in and glanced around the tent. 'Look – if we pack everything away properly, we'll know if your quilt is *really* missing. If everything is tidy and cleared, we can survey the site and assess the situation.'

'Yeah, all right. That's a good idea,' said Wesley.

'I don't want to touch any of it,' said Margot. 'What if it *is* a booby trap? What if we were meant to, like, slip in the dog mess, then swallow one of those apple cores, then fall over and get caught up in the tent before being captured?'

Wesley stepped away from the tent towards the stream.

'Margot, stop, that's unrealistic.' I turned to Wesley. 'Do you want to find your quilt or not?'

'Yeah. Yeah, I do.'

'Then help, please,' I said. 'That means you too, Margot. We can earn another cleaning badge, right?' I laughed. They didn't.

We sat with our wrapped-up, rolled-up equipment behind us by the bank and dangled our legs above the stream. We swung our legs into the earth, and small rocks and sediment fell into the water and floated away.

'I'm really gonna miss that quilt,' said Wesley glumly. 'I loved it.' He reached behind him, pulled up a patch of grass and threw it into the stream.

'We know,' said Margot. 'You could make a new one?'

'It wouldn't be the same, would it?' he said.

'Nope, but it could still be good,' she replied. 'You could get your brothers, sister and your mum to make bits of it, too.'

'Hmmm,' he said. 'That's actually not a bad idea.'

'We could help you make it,' I said.

'Sewing badge?' said Margot and Wesley in unison. They laughed.

'You know me so well,' I said. I looked across the stream and up to Chicane Cars. Its broken windows shimmered and shone in the setting sun. Mum would want me home soon. I shook away the image of her folding her arms and pursing her lips, and looked at my friends instead.

'How do you think he – whoever he was – got across the water?' I said.

'Easy,' said Wesley, pointing. 'Look at those big stones there. You can just step on them and go across. The river here is only, like, four metres wide. It's not a big deal.'

I looked over at Wesley. A slow smile crept across my face, and I raised my eyebrows at him.

'Don't even think about it,' he said.

'But what if your quilt is over there,' I said. 'It might be *just* outside the factory and we're so close – only four metres away, according to you.'

Wesley put his face into his hands. 'What have I done now?' he shouted into his palms. 'Why can I never just say nothing?'

I laughed and got to my feet. I picked up Wesley's bag. 'Come on, Copseys – we're crossing!'

MUDLARKING

Get stuck in . . . the mud!

Margot's foot slid against the wet rock in the stream. The bag containing her tent slipped off her shoulder and on to the crook of her arm. 'Oh my gosh, oh my gosh, oh my gosh!' she chanted, looking at her feet and slightly losing her balance as a result.

Wesley's hands slapped his sides in frustration. 'What did we *just* say? Don't look down, silly! We've told you twice now – eyes up! At us!' He turned to me. 'I can't believe this is so difficult for her. It's literally the shortest jump over – stone, bank, done.'

'I heard that, Wesley!' she said.

I turned to Wesley. 'It's not the distance she's struggling with – it's the terrain.'

'What you on about, Josie? What the heck is *terrain*?'

'She means the ground,' Margot shouted.

'So why not just say that in the first place?' He sighed. 'Look, Margot, all you need to do is step forward. If you can't step, stay there. Once we're done looking around, we'll come back for you. Then we can go home, and it will be over.'

'No, no – I want to be there! I don't want to live on this rock forever. Please don't leave me!' she wailed. 'Don't leave me in limbo between life and death!' She glanced at Wesley and then looked at me. 'Sorry, sorry, I didn't mean to say that.'

'What's she on about now?' said Wesley.

'Nothing,' I said, brushing him off. 'You're not going to *die*, Margot,' I said slowly. 'No one is. All you need to do is move forward.'

'But it's so slippery!' she wailed.

'Well, why don't you just step forward for the story?' said Wesley. 'Whatever happens you'll have a tale to tell, won't you?' He laughed.

'Funny,' said Margot flatly.

I crouched down by the bank and leaned over the water. 'You'll be fine. Just walk forward, one foot in front of the other. Then you'll be on this side. Safe with your friends.'

'*Friends?*' said Wesley. He raised an eyebrow. 'I wouldn't go that far.'

'Not now, Wesley,' I pleaded. 'Help me here.'

Wesley threw his neck back and sighed. His shoulders slumped. 'Gah, *fine!*' He crouched next to me and extended his hand. 'Come on, Margot! You can do it!' he said, sarcasm dripping off every word.

'I kind of hate you, Wesley,' said Margot, reaching for his hand. He laughed as their fingers made contact. Wesley wrapped his palm round Margot's digits and pulled her gently forward.

'OK, you're safe now,' he said. 'Just look up and walk. That's all you need to do.'

'All right, all right,' she said. 'I *can* do this, can't I? It's only a few more steps.'

Wesley shrugged, but I shouted, 'Of course you can! This is *easy* for a Copsey.' Wesley stifled a laugh. Margot closed her eyes and stepped forward. The tip of her white trainers grazed the baby boulder in front of her. Her final frontier.

'Good work, Margot. One more step!' I said. Margot squeezed her eyes shut and investigated the air with her foot.

'Hopeless,' muttered Wesley to me. 'And a liability. How the hell are we supposed to get back at this rate?'

He had a point. Margot clearly wasn't cut out for the practical part of the Copsey experience.

'I'm over this,' said Wesley. He tugged Margot's arm and she slid across the final rock, her body slapping the side of the bank. The bag containing her tent flapped around her wrist. I leaned down and reached for it. Once I had a firm grip, I threw it on the bank, and helped Wesley pull Margot up. She slid snake-like up the bank and kneeled when she reached firm ground. The front of her pink jacket was covered in a thick stripe of mud.

Margot stood up and tried to wipe herself off. 'Let's never speak of this again,' she whispered, walking briskly towards the factory.

Behind her, I looked over at Wesley, who snorted out a laugh. 'Absolute bants,' he said, running to catch up with her.

Chicane Cars was just as oppressive and impressive up close, especially in the day. It was so large that we had to crane our necks to look up at its roof, and even then we still couldn't see all of it. It was the definition of dilapidated, and it looked like it was leaning over towards us – it was so old and so neglected that it could be possible. I shuddered in the shadow of its smashed windows.

'I can see why your grandad didn't like this place,' said Margot. 'There's . . . something about it.'

'I thought you didn't believe in ghosts and spirits?' said Wesley.

Margot shook her head. 'I don't, but this place *definitely* has bad vibes.' A bird above us cawed, seemingly in response. 'See?' she said. 'That crow was right on cue.'

'Don't freak me out!' said Wesley. 'You know I don't like it!'

'He's right – don't,' I said. 'Let's search the perimeter –'

'*Perimeter?* You hearing this, Margot?'

'– and locate –'

Wesley snorted. 'Just say find, girl.'

'– the quilt and go. Shall we split up? It will take less time that way.'

'Absolutely no chance,' said Wesley. He pulled at my arm. 'We go together.'

We walked round the edge of the factory twice – through the weeds that grew around it – avoiding the slimy drainpipes that hung loosely from its battered bricks and which bowed towards us. There was no sign of Wesley's quilt. He kicked his feet in the gravel.

'Don't do that!' I hissed. 'Someone might hear us!'

'Who?' he said. 'There's no security here.'

'Which is weird, right?' said Margot. 'This place must be a bit valuable, surely? If I owned it, I'd definitely guard it.'

'No quilt, either. Where's the person Josephine *said* she saw last night?' Wesley said.

'I did see someone!' I insisted. 'Are you saying you want to meet them now? You're not scared?'

'I am, and I don't want to see them – but where are they? And where's my quilt?' Wesley said, crossing his arms.

I looked up and around the building. There was no quilt to be seen. The official entrance was on the other side of the buiding but just round the corner – if I craned my neck back, slightly to the left – was a busted-out window. The other windows in Chicane were gridded and had glass missing, but this one was a void. A void big enough for us to climb through.

I looked back at my friends. 'I have an idea, but you're going to have to trust me.'

Margot nodded. 'I do,' she said.

Wesley sighed. 'I don't, but what choice do I really ever have?'

EXPLORING

You must explore to find out more.

Wesley and I decided Margot would go first – we didn't have all day to wait for her to build courage. The hole that was once a window was roughly two metres from the ground and situated above a small pile of random rubble and ruin. As I was currently the tallest, a full inch taller than Wesley and two taller than Margot, I climbed up and stood with my back against the factory wall. I opened my arms. 'Here, Margot,' I said. 'I'll hold you up while you go in.'

She looked nervously at Wesley and me.

'I know you think I can't do this, but I totally can,' she said.

'Of course you can,' I said. 'This is easy for you!'

'If it's so easy then hurry up,' said Wesley. 'What you waiting for?'

Margot smoothed the front of her pink jacket – the mud stripe was beginning to dry. Small brown flecks fell to the ground. 'I'm just building a *little* more confidence,' she said. She took a deep breath, stepped back and suddenly scrambled into my arms.

'Gah, Margot!' I said, from somewhere underneath her armpit, I think. 'You need to warn me!'

I wasn't ready to receive her, so I just pushed her body in the general direction of up. Margot gripped on to the windowsill and pulled herself into Chicane Cars. She turned round and looked down at us. 'Voila!' she said with a smile and outstretched arms.

'Hmmm. That went better than I thought,' said Wesley. 'Ready for me, Jo?'

I nodded. 'Just give me a leg up, that will do it.' I laced my fingers together and crouched down. He ran up, put his foot into my palms, and I pushed him skywards. Margot grabbed his hands and he was in the factory.

'It's well spooky!' he shouted. He gripped the edge of the window and leaned out to me. 'I'm scared already.'

'Don't be!' I said. 'At least let me get in before you decide you want out!' I thrust my hands in the air. 'Come on then!'

Wesley and Margot reached down and pulled me inside.

'This is *incredible*!' said Margot, turning in circles. 'Don't you think it's amazing, Josie?' She put her hands on her hips and threw her head back to look at the high ceiling.

'It's not amazing,' said Wesley. He stood close beside me. 'It's not right. It's like the town – the whole world – forgot about this place.'

Wesley wasn't wrong, but neither was Margot. Chicane Cars was a vast, impressive place frozen in time.

Light streamed in from its broken windows, and the sound of water echoed around us. It dripped from the floors above, forming lake-like puddles on the otherwise dusty ground. They reflected the rusty, vent-covered ceiling above. The air smelled of oil, dust and damp. Any surface that had been painted years ago was either covered in graffiti or now peeling away. Paint flakes flapped lightly in the gusts of wind that breezed through the building.

This level of the factory must have held part of the assembly line. There were tracks on raised parts of the floor. A rusted car without wheels – waiting forever for its windows – stood on it. Weeds grew where its windscreen would have been. Its bonnet stood, crumpled and dented, to attention. Glass and debris crunched underneath our feet with every unsteady step we took forward. Ribbons of rubber and thick woven straps of fabric lay on the floor.

'Hello?' Margot shouted into the cavernous space. Her voice echoed around the factory. A bird, somewhere above us, flapped its wings and flew away.

'Let's follow that pigeon,' I said.

'Even if I wanted to – which I don't – how would we?' said Wesley, rubbing his nose. He sneezed, then pointed to the twisted metal staircases around this floor of the factory. 'Those steps have rungs missing, and the handrails have rusted away,' he said. 'And, even if we could climb them, I bet they'd come off the wall immediately.'

'They can't have been the only way of getting round this place,' said Margot. 'It's huge – there's no way secretaries and managers were walking up and down those stairs.'

'Yep, there definitely has to be something more stable for us to climb.' I looked around the space. 'Wait, is that some kind of lift over there?' I squinted as I got closer to a pair of huge orange doors that were slightly ajar.

'Be careful!' shouted Wesley. He looked down at his feet. 'I don't trust any part of this building – not at all.'

Margot skipped confidently ahead. She put her head through the gap in the lift, but quickly pulled away.

'I wasn't expecting that,' she said. 'That's made me feel queasy.'

I peered in to see what she'd recoiled from.

The lift was empty – empty because its insides didn't exist any more. It was a vertical tunnel. Its once-creamy-white tiles were now streaked with orange-brown stripes, and the wind raced and rattled through it. Above us, old lights and wires dangled and swayed. One floor below, in what looked like a dark basement, a skinny stray dog barked up at us and trotted away.

'Well,' I said, stepping backwards. 'That explains the dog mess by the tent, I suppose. I bet it was that dog. We'll find some stairs – then think about what to do with that pup later.' I pulled on a heavy, water-warped wooden door. 'Let's try this?'

Behind the door was a concrete staircase. Its bannister or any climbing support – if it ever existed – were long gone. Yellowed newspapers covered the crumbling steps, and I glanced at the front page of a copy of the *Daily Mirror* dated Monday May 3, 1980. We started our ascent. I led the way, with Wesley and Margot following behind.

'Gotta say, I'm not keen,' said Wesley, coughing as he stepped up. 'Not keen at all. This dust is no good for me.'

'Let's just check it out to see if we find your quilt, and then we can go,' I said. 'Also, I was going to surprise you both with this later, but I'm pleased to announce we've just earned our exploring badges.' I smiled down at them. Margot grinned.

'Wow. Great,' said Wesley sarcastically. 'It's all I've ever wanted.' He breathed heavily and looked up the stairs. 'What's the plan then? Where are we going?'

'To the top floor,' I said, without hesitation, and without looking back.

DISCOVERING

Seek and you shall find!

'So, this *was* a scam all along, Josie?' said Wesley. 'You just wanted to get us in the factory to find out about the lights this whole time, didn't you?'

'Well, I –'

'This was never about my quilt, was it?'

It was, partially, but his quilt was really a great way to get him into the building, and to the top floor.

'This was *always* about your quilt, Wesley. I really think we might find it up here,' I replied. 'That man might have it – I saw him turn in the direction of the factory last night.'

'Wait – you're just telling us this *now*?' shouted Wesley. 'Seriously? You just decided to walk us into stranger danger?' Margot stayed silent.

'It's a great plan, though,' I said. 'We find your quilt and solve the light mystery at the same time – it makes sense.'

'It might make sense to *you*, but that's not my point!' said Wesley. 'If you had a scam running this whole time, you should have told us about it *before* we started! It's not fair – and against your code, too, I bet. All that stuff about being "truthful and trustful"? What happened to that?'

'I didn't lie,' I said.

'You weren't exactly clear with us,' said Margot quietly.

Wesley shook his head. 'This Copsey business is changing you, you know.'

'I agree,' Margot said.

'Thank you, Margot. Even you're with me on this, for once.'

'Josie's even braver now, I suppose.' Margot looked at Wesley with a sly smile.

'That's not what I meant. Not at all,' he said.

We reached the top of the stairs. Another heavy door, with a round, smashed window, faced us. I poked my head through the hole.

'This looks like the floor that had offices,' I said. I looked back at Wesley and Margot. 'I'm going in.'

Wesley snorted through his nose in response. 'Look, Wes,' I put my hand on his shoulder. 'I'm sorry you feel scammed, but that wasn't my plan. If you both want to stay here, I understand.'

'Nope, I'm coming. I don't want to miss this,' Margot said, stepping past Wesley. He slumped against the wall.

'And once again I can't leave you, can I?' mumbled Wesley. His hands balled into fists. He breathed deeply and closed his eyes.

I pulled open the door and stepped inside.

There was a long corridor in front of us. On the left were huge panes of broken glass that would have let supervisors look down on the production lines below. To our immediate right was a reception area. A warped walnut desk was moulding and caving in on itself. Behind it, painted in faded pink letters, was the Chicane Cars logo with its intertwined Cs. Smashed frames holding faint photographs of the factory in its heyday hung askew on the wall.

We stepped over a spilled box of chipped, handle-less and otherwise broken Chicane-branded mugs. We walked across overturned shelves and faded paint samples. Once-bright Chicane brochures celebrating their latest models were now various shades of grey, their pages tattered and torn.

'It's quite sad, isn't it?' said Margot, looking down to the assembly line. 'I can totally picture how glamorous and cool it must have been to work here. On this floor, anyway.'

'Nah,' Wesley. 'I heard Grandad say it was hell. The bosses were well mean and tight – that's what I was told.'

We continued forward. To our right we saw what was left of a locker room with lunch boxes on the floor we didn't dare open. Then, a sign on a door indicated that the yellow-walled space we could see within had once been a smoking room, which we were shocked to discover once really existed. Smoking? Inside? Unbelievable. It was followed by a broken-down bathroom with deep-brown crusted toilets. All of the sinks had been pulled off the wall and thrown on the floor. They were each spray-painted a different colour.

'Art!' said Margot.

'Hmmm, sort of, but vandalism, mostly,' said Wesley. 'How much further do you want to go, Jo?' He looked behind him and gulped. 'We've walked so far; I can barely see the door we came in through. And I can *feel* something, you guys. I don't think we're alone. Someone – or something – could jump out at us at any moment.'

'Don't say that,' said Margot quietly. 'I was having a good time, enjoying the energy –'

'*The energy?* Be serious.'

'– until you said that. I'd forgotten about the mission for a moment.'

'All right,' I said, looking back at the door. 'Considering where we entered, and the position of the lights we saw, we need to follow this corridor to the end – to that door right there.' I pointed forward. 'You all right to continue, Wes?' I glanced back at him. He shut his eyes and nodded quickly. I reached for his arm. 'You're being really brave,' I said. 'I'm proud of you.'

Wesley opened his eyes and pulled his arm away. 'Don't patronize me!'

I raised my hands in protest. 'Fine, fine,' I said. 'Sorry.'

We moved closer to the end of the corridor, as the unsteady water-warped floor wobbled beneath us. We stopped at a closed heavy wooden door. 'We're here,' I whispered. 'This is where the lights live.' My heart pounded in excitement, not fear. Our mission was close to being accomplished. I turned to my friends. 'Are we doing this, Copseys?' I said, taking quick breaths through my nose. I reached for the dull brass doorknob, which immediately fell from the door into my hands. We jumped.

'Oh my God, oh my God, oh my God!' said Margot.

I held the knob tightly against the door. We looked at each other and nodded. I pushed the door open. I was *not* prepared for what we saw inside.

MEETING

Meet, greet, don't retreat!

'What *is* this place?' said Margot, stepping into the room. 'It's . . . it's –'

'It's well weird,' said Wesley, panic rising in his voice. 'Way too strange. We have to bounce. Now. Let's go. We've opened a door to a time warp – and you can't get out of those. It's a messed-up version of the past.' He put his back flat against the wall. 'Grandad, if you can hear me, help us!' he hissed.

I stared at the space. It was certainly a meeting room when Chicane was open, but it wasn't now. Now, it was set up like a living room, but not a modern one like any of ours, with long leather sofas and flat-screen televisions. No. It looked and felt much older.

There was a floral rug on the floor, with pink and green buds blooming in neat rows across its width. At the back of the room was a clothes rail, with dresses, pairs of trousers and shirts. There were two tatty green tartan armchairs side by side, with stuffing bursting through their seams. An unbroken, tea-stained Chicane Cars mug rested between them on the floor. The cup and the armchairs faced an old brown, square television that was panelled in fake wood and had a twisted wire coat hanger sticking out of its back.

I pointed to a tall brown lamp with a dust-covered dusky-pink fabric shade. Little loops of gold thread hung from its bottom. 'I think that's the light we've been looking at – been looking *for*!'

'But that's just a regular old lamp,' said Wesley. 'How would we see that from your house?'

Margot reached out to touch it. She fumbled for the switch and turned it on. Bright white light instantly engulfed the room. She winced, shut one eye and turned away. 'That would be why,' she said. 'I think you're right, Jo. This is basically a floodlight under a lampshade. It's way too harsh for the relaxed vibes whoever pulled this room together needed – or were going for.'

'*Relaxed vibes?*' spat Wesley. '*Pulled the room together?*'

'Yeah!' said Margot. 'I reckon they were aiming for cosy, but that light has zero chill. It dominates. Otherwise, I'm into it. I like the aesthetic.'

'You're an ass-thetic,' said Wesley.

Margot laughed. 'That's actually a good one. You're funny when you want to be.'

I walked to the window. What I assumed was once the meeting-room table was pushed against it. An uncountable number of lace doilies covered its surface. Sitting on top of them were candles, a stack of stereo equipment with complicated knobs, a pile of records and a cubed brass clock with a handle and white face. My grandparents had one exactly like it. It was next to a small, square silver photo frame.

'Copseys!' I raised my voice. 'You *have* to see this!' Wesley and Margot gathered round the photograph. I picked it up to get a closer look and brought it close to our faces.

In the fuzzy, faded photograph, a young Black couple smiled back at us from between the rounded corners. They stood in front of a baby-blue car. The man had his arm round the woman's shoulders. He was tall and thin. He wore a clean, sharp, incredibly smart navy-blue suit, and the trousers were flared at the bottom. On his feet he wore tall shoes. They weren't like high heels, but the soles were stacked high, like platforms. The buttons on his crisp white shirt were mostly open so you could see his hairy chest and the gold chain round his neck. He had a neat Afro, and resting on top of it was a flat cap, which was brown and worn at an angle.

The woman was shorter and seemed shyer. She nestled her face into the man's neck a little bit. She had an Afro too, but it was blown out big and it hung around her shoulders. I just knew Mum would love to get her hands on that lady's hair. She wore a long green dress with a gold belt round her waist, and white sandals that showed off her red-painted toenails. She was beautiful. They were beautiful.

'That's a *stunning* photograph,' said Margot. 'They look so cool!'

Someone kissed their teeth behind us. As they did, they sucked all the air out of the room with them.

RUNNING

Keep it moving!

I'm certain Wesley's soul left his body because he bent over at the waist and gripped the table. He looked empty – a husk of his former self. His eyes darkened and popped out of his head; he took deep, panicked breaths. Margot's body froze, but her eyes moved rapidly around the room.

'That's cos we *are* cool!' said a male voice behind us. I dropped the photograph; its frame fell to the floor and one corner came off. I turned round. An old Black couple stood in the doorway. A tall, thin man and a shorter, rounder woman. She held the brass doorknob in her hand and trembled as she stepped slowly into the room.

The minute her foot crossed the threshold, Wesley started screaming.

'Run!' I shouted. 'Run! Just run!' I put my head down and dashed for the door, running straight through the middle of the couple. Both sides of my body brushed theirs as I did, so I knew they weren't ghosts and were definitely real. I didn't look back, but I hoped Wesley and Margot had got out too. Judging by the sound of the footsteps behind me, they had.

'No, no, no!' shouted Wesley as he sprinted past me, leaping over crumpled boxes and fallen shelves.

I turned to look at Margot, who was walking quickly behind me. Her eyes were wide and shining, and she was slightly laughing – at what I didn't know. Margot's smile seemed to fade in slow motion, just before she threw her arms forward and hit the ground. The floor shook beneath her.

'Get up, Margot!' I shouted. Wesley, hearing the commotion, turned to face us from his end of the corridor. I looked up at him – his hands were on his head, and he was pulling furiously at his hair.

'Are you joking, Margot? All you had to do was get to the staircase!' he shouted. He turned his head between the door that led to the exit and back at her. He sighed and ran back to us.

'Can you move or not?' he said, standing over her. She struggled to get up, wincing and squeezing her eyes shut.

'My ankle hurts!' she said through her teeth. 'Give me a moment, a little moment.'

Wesley swore under his breath. 'No. No time for moments. Right, Josie – grab an arm,' he said. Together, we tried to pull her along the floor.

'No, stop, stop, stop!' Margot said. 'My arms! I need them for writing!'

'So what now?' said Wesley. 'That's it? You're giving up?'

'No, no. I'll try again – just be gentle.' Margot extended her arms, and Wesley and I helped her to her feet. She winced, but she was stable.

'I'll be fine,' she said through gritted teeth as she hopped on one foot. She dusted herself down.

'You sure you're all right?' I said.

'Not really,' she said, her eyes welling with water.

'Why are you two chatting?' said Wesley. 'Let's go! Save those tears for later.'

As we crunched over the moulded, brittle paper and shattered glass that paved the way towards the staircase, we heard commotion and crying behind us.

Deep, panicked sobs sounded from the meeting room. I looked back and bit my lip.

'Copseys, hold on,' I said.

'Don't even think about it,' said Wesley. 'We're going. Your girl here is in pain.'

'But, Wesley, can you hear that? That woman's crying – really crying,' I said, looking at Margot. 'You only cry like that when something's *badly* wrong, right?'

'Well, something *is* wrong!' Wesley shouted. 'We found their weird little hideout. If I was them, I'd be bawling, too.' He dropped Margot's arm – she wobbled and grabbed me – and stomped towards the door leading to the staircase. I stood still.

'It's not right to leave,' I said quietly. 'Maybe they can help Margot, too?'

'Of course it's right to leave!' he snapped. 'What did I say about stranger danger, eh? Do you not remember that scary assembly we had in Year Four? I ain't about to be abducted for bants.'

'Of course I remember – I'll never forget it – but look,' I said. 'We're together. We're Copseys. We have to help. Copsey Code, point four: be a true ally.'

'Even potential murderers?' he shouted.

'To be fair, they don't look like murderers,' said Margot.

'And what do murderers look like, hmmm? And why are you speaking, anyway? I thought you were hurt?' snapped Wesley. 'I'm trying to save *you*, you idiot!' Margot stared at the floor.

'We could earn our bravery badge, though,' I offered with a smile. 'How about that, Margot?'

'Well . . .' Margot started slowly.

'I don't give a stuff about your badges!' shouted Wesley. 'Stick them where the sun don't shine, no cap.'

'I know you don't mean that,' I said.

'I do.'

The woman's wails behind us grew stronger and louder. Her sobs rang down the hallway towards us.

I looked at Wesley and shrugged, then turned and walked towards the meeting room. This was the right thing to do. That couple weren't scary. I would go to them, see if everything was all right and get help for Margot. If my friends left me and somehow I didn't make it out – which was unlikely – well, I'm sure my bravery would go viral anyway. *That* would be worth it. I'd leave a legacy at least – just like Josephine Holloway.

Behind me, I heard dragging footsteps, a swear word and someone kicking at the debris. Margot and Wesley were with me. For now.

When we reached the doorway, we stood cautiously by it and peered into the room. Inside, the woman sat in one of the armchairs, her head in her hands. The man was pulling the clothes off the rack and throwing them into a large plastic black-red-and-white-checked bag. She turned to him, tears running down her face and taking her mascara with them. 'Why? Why, Felix? You always have to mess it up. Why you have to attract dem pickney here?' she sobbed. She looked towards the doorway. When she saw us, she was startled. She ran her hands down her chest and then her head returned to her lap.

'Don't look at me,' she said quietly. 'Don't look me in my eye.'

COMMUNICATING

Make contact with the unknown!

I tried my best not to look at the woman – like she asked – but I couldn't help it. I stared at her sitting there, and at the man who rushed around the room. He used his forearm to sweep their belongings from the sideboard into his large plastic bag.

'Excuse me,' I said quietly. 'We're not here to cause any trouble, we promise.' I turned to my friends. 'I'm Josephine, and this is Wesley and Margot. I'm sorry I broke your photograph.' I took a deep breath and stood tall. 'We're the Copseys –' Wesley groaned under his breath. 'We try to help, try to make things better around here, but Margot's hurt.' I nodded at her. Margot hesitated, then hobbled into the room. As she did, she drew a loud, painful breath between her teeth. She stumbled backwards and gripped the door frame. This got the couple's attention.

'What happen? You all right?' Felix said. He hurried over. The woman looked up at Margot from her chair. She leaned over to take a closer look.

'My ankle,' Margot mumbled. 'I fell over in the corridor.'

'You were runnin'?' Felix asked gently.

'Yes, really quickly,' Margot added.

'No, you weren't! You're just well clumsy,' Wesley muttered.

'It definitely sounded like someone had some spring in their steps. I have a limp now, but boy, when I was young, I ran fast – I ran everywhere! But you couldn't catch me runnin' down a corridor like that. All them obstacles?'

'You'd run too, if you thought you were gonna die,' said Wesley. He eyed the man suspiciously.

The man leaned backwards and raised his eyebrow. 'You think we was gonna kill you?'

'Maybe,' said Wesley. 'We don't know you, do we?'

The man laughed loudly. 'Audrey! Hear this? They think I'm a murderer.'

Audrey sighed, then chuckled slightly. 'English kids, they're different,' she said. 'But sensible – it's very wise to be wary. Can't say I blame you.' She looked at Margot. 'It hurts?' Margot nodded a reply. 'Come sit down and let me see.' Margot looked nervously back at us. I nodded, but Wesley shook his head vigorously. She sighed, and carried on hopping into the room.

'Take that armchair, there,' Audrey said, pointing. Margot sat next to her and looked down at the Chicane mug between them. I stared at the woman's small, round face, deep-brown eyes and short, grey curly hair. She was the woman in the photograph, just older. She stared down at Margot's leg. 'Roll up them jeans,' she said. 'I don't have my X-ray specs.'

Margot leaned over, and I could tell even that hurt her a bit. When she finally tugged the denim over her ankle, it was slightly swollen. It looked like Mum's, which made me smile, but it was quickly replaced with nerves because I knew she would kill me if she could see where I was, what I was doing and who I was with. Audrey groaned as she pushed herself up from the chair and kneeled on the floor in front of Margot. She poked her ankle.

'Owww!' Margot shouted.

'Sorry,' she said. 'OK – bend ya foot left, then right. Let me see.'

Margot twisted her foot to the sides, staring at Audrey as she did.

'You'll be all right,' she said, sitting back in her creaking chair. 'Felix, go fetch some ice and one of me stockings.'

'Yes, Missus,' said Felix with a smile. He limped across the room, past Wesley and me.

'You have ice?' said Wesley.

'We got everyting,' he replied with a smile.

'How come?' asked Wesley. 'How have you got electricity?'

Felix chuckled. 'I've been a sparky for a long time – I know me way round wires. I just –' Felix stuck his tongue out slightly and mimed the process of rewiring the factory, I assumed. 'Like that,' he said. 'Easy. You want tea?' he said.

Margot and I nodded. Wesley shook his head. 'No way,' he said. 'I ain't trying to get poisoned out here.'

Felix laughed. 'This boy funny.' He looked closely at Wesley. 'Hmmm,' he said. 'You look like someone. Who is it?'

'I *bet* you're going to say Marcus Rashford,' said Margot from her chair. 'They're like twins to me.'

Felix shook his head. 'Who? Don't know him. Anyway, sit. On the rug, if you like. Make yourself at home.'

'What, like you have?' said Wesley. 'No, thanks, I'll stand.'

Felix shared a tight-lipped smile with Audrey before disappearing into the corridor.

I sat on the rug in front of Margot. 'You all right?' I whispered.

'Yeah,' she said. She looked over at Audrey and extended her hand towards her. 'It's lovely to meet you, by the way. Thanks so much for this,' she said.

Audrey eyed her suspiciously, but put out her hand. Her nails were bitten and broken, slightly yellowed and unpainted. 'Audrey,' she said. 'Audrey Braithwaite.'

Margot looked around the room, and then back at Audrey. 'I really like your place.'

Audrey and Wesley snorted in unison. Margot looked up and smiled at him as Felix reappeared in the doorway. He wore large Perspex safety goggles on his face and carried a pair of sheer brown stockings in his hand. One of the pairs was filled with ice. 'Here you go, young lady,' he said, handing it to Margot. 'Put this pon ya leg – you'll be right as rain in no time.'

'Thanks!' she said. When the stocking touched her skin, she sighed gratefully.

'No problem,' he said, as the sound of whistling grew louder in another room. 'Ah, the kettle boil, tea soon come.' He hopped back to the doorway and adjusted his goggles. 'Might take me a minute – the steam makes me glasses foggy – me can't see too good these days. What tea you want? I make a mean ginger-and-mint concoction; you want to try?'

I nodded.

'Ooh, yes please!' said Margot. 'Sounds super cleansing.'

'Coming right up,' he said. 'Sure I can't persuade you, young man?'

Wesley firmly shook his head.

When Felix returned with the tea, he hadn't used teabags. Pieces of ginger and mint leaves floated on the top of the Chicane cups. 'There you go,' he said, handing one to me. I eyed it cautiously and looked over to Wesley, who shrugged. His movements said, 'Good luck with that, idiot.' I put the cup on the ground. Margot wrapped her hands around her cup and took a sip.

'Ooh, it's so *fresh*. I love it,' she said. 'I love your whole thing.'

'Is that so?' said Felix. He went to sit on the rug, but when Margot noticed she stood up to give him his seat back. He smiled up at her.

'My ankle's much better now and, besides, I respect my elders.'

'Very kind of you, young miss,' he said. 'You nah meet many kids with manners these days.' He looked over at Wesley. Wesley folded his arms crossly.

'So, can I ask?' said Margot, eyes bright. 'What's your story? *Why* do you live here?'

Felix and Audrey exchanged glances. 'You want the truth?' he said. 'The whole story?'

Margot nodded eagerly. 'I absolutely do.'

LEARNING

Acknowledge knowledge!

Felix sat back in his chair and sipped his tea. 'The truth is,' he said, sighing, 'we wanted to do someting different in our old age.' He smiled down at Margot. 'We wanted to experience everyting this life can give. Try it all.' He picked at a piece of mint stuck between his teeth.

'So, you decided to move into a rusty, dusty, musty old factory?' said Wesley. 'Yeah, right.'

Felix chuckled. 'Exactly right.' He reached for Audrey's hand. 'We're retired, have no kids, no grandbabies – so we thought, eh, why not travel? Move around, try different tings.' He squeezed Audrey's fingers tightly.

'That's beyond cool!' said Margot. 'That's *exactly* what I want to do. I went on an amazing houseboat once, when I lived in London. I could have totally lived there.'

'Try it! We did.' Felix smiled. 'Me? I liked it. Missus here, not so much.'

'Water was too rocky – it made me sick to me stomach,' said Audrey. 'And it was cramped and damp.' She shook her head. 'Not for me.'

'That is amazing,' said Margot under her breath. 'I want to be you when I get old.'

Felix laughed.

'No, you don't,' said Audrey quietly.

'Why would you go from a decent boat to squatting in here, though?' said Wesley. 'It makes no sense.'

'It's not just squattin', young man – it's squattin' with *style*,' said Felix. 'This place has everyting we need and we know it well. It's all right for now.'

Wesley raised a disbelieving eyebrow.

'It is an interesting life choice,' I said, sharing some of Wesley's doubt. 'And I appreciate what you have done to help us.' I nodded at Margot, who reached down to remove the now very wet stocking from her leg – the ice inside had melted. She attempted to stand.

'Wait, wait!' said Audrey. 'Felix, the glasses?' He removed the goggles from the top of his head and handed them to her. 'Let me have one last look,' she said, putting them on. 'Can't release you back to the wild if you're wounded.' She bent to the floor and touched Margot's ankle. 'Yeah, it look all right. Felix, the other stocking?'

Felix patted the rug around him, found it and handed it to her. 'There you go, Missus,' he said.

She took it from him without looking and tied it round Margot's ankle.

'Should be much better now,' Audrey said. 'Is it?'

Margot stood up. 'Ah, it feels fine,' she said. 'Really, thank you so much!' She moved her foot left and right. 'It's like the fall never happened!'

'You're welcome,' said Audrey. 'Very welcome.'

'Yes, thank you,' I said. I put my hands in my pockets. 'Erm, we don't have any money to give you . . .'

Felix sat up tall in his chair, stern-faced. 'We don't want no money!' He kissed his teeth. 'We don't take money from children.'

'But I need to repay your kindness,' I said. 'All of us do.'

'No, no! What we don't need is all this coming and going. Best thing you could do is stay away,' Audrey said quickly.

'Agree,' said Wesley.

'This place is dangerous if you don't know what you're doing. We don't want broken ankles next time, do we?' Audrey added, looking down at Margot's leg. 'I don't have enough stockings. The rest of them have runs, so they'll make bad bandages.'

'I'll get you some new ones,' said Felix. 'On that – about staying away – how you find us in the first place?'

I looked at my friends and took a deep breath. 'Well, on Wednesday night I saw a bright light from my bedroom window, and I thought it was strange because I've never seen lights in Chicane before – not in my lifetime.'

Audrey pursed her lips and shook her head at Felix. 'What did I tell you? I *told you* not to fix up that floodlight – them candles did plenty for months and months!' She kissed her teeth and turned sharply in her seat.

'But it gets darker as winter approach, Missus! But, all right, I hear you, me nah use dem again.'

'On Thursday, Wesley and Margot saw them too, so last night we camped on the other side of the river to get a closer look –'

'Ah, I *knew* it was you three!' Felix chuckled. 'Your likkle campsite made me laugh.'

'We heard your music, and Wesley thought you were a ghost,' added Margot.

Felix threw his head back and laughed deeply. 'No, me nah dead yet,' he said. 'Not yet, not yet.'

'It's not funny,' said Wesley. 'We came back today to look for . . . something of mine, then we were conned into coming up here.'

'What you lost?' asked Audrey.

Wesley shuffled his feet. 'I have a special . . . quilt that's been part of my family for years.' Wesley narrowed his eyes. 'Have you got it?'

Felix raised his arms. 'It wasn't me. Me nah touch a ting down there.'

Wesley's shoulders slumped. 'It used to belong to my grandad. He used to work here.'

Felix and Audrey glanced at each other. 'Oh yes?' said Audrey, curiosity piqued. 'When?'

'Not sure, really,' said Wesley. 'Years and years ago, in the seventies and early eighties.'

'What's his name?' asked Felix, his fingers by his chin and one eyebrow raised.

'Alan Evans.'

Felix slapped his thighs. 'Alan Evans?' he said. 'Welshman?'

'Yeah!' said Wesley. 'He was from Wales, yeah! Did you know him?'

'Yes! We know Alan Evans!' said Felix. 'Who doesn't? Oh my God. *Alan Evans*. He's your grandad? I *knew* you looked like someone. Welsh Alan!' Felix shook his head. 'Rhatid, as I live and breathe. You're jus' like him, too.'

'I am?' said Wesley.

'Yes,' said Audrey. 'He was fiery, like the dragon 'pon his flag.'

'He was?'

'Why you say "was" – him dead?' asked Felix.

'Yeah, he died six years ago now,' said Wesley.

'Oh, I'm sorry, young man. So sorry,' said Felix. 'He was a good man. He was the head of the union here, caring about all our rights – making sure we were safe, had holidays, got paid fair and everyting. Always fighting with the bossman. He was a real devil, a bad boss.'

'You worked here at Chicane?' I asked.

Audrey nodded. 'It wasn't a good time here – being Black in the seventies – but Alan made us feel at home.'

'He even joined Chicane Cricket Club for a while – I started that in the eighties. He stayed until someone – I think it was Julian Jackson, him or one of his many brothers – nearly lick his head clean off with a fast bowl.' Felix laughed. 'Then the over was truly over.'

I gave Felix a confused look. 'Cricket joke – forget it,' he said. 'Oh Alan Evans!' Felix shook his head. 'You know, people used to say we were "brothers from another mother" because we sounded alike? Them say Vincy and Welsh accents the same.'

'Never heard it myself,' said Audrey.

'Nor me,' said Felix. 'So, wait, your dad is who then? Creg?'

'Craig, yeah,' Wesley said, correcting him.

'Ah, Craig, Greg Creg – same name to me. He marry that girl, Helen . . . Ellen . . . Elsa?'

'Ella! Yeah, that's my mum!' Wesley smiled widely. Our visit had value for him, after all.

'We went to that wedding – *lovely* reception,' said Audrey. 'Great food. Think Miss Aubrey and her family from Limbury Meads way did the catering. It was at the Lewsey Club, wasn't it?' She smiled. 'Alan was *so* proud that day, I tell you.'

Wesley beamed. 'I didn't know that!'

'It reminded me of our wedding,' said Felix. 'We had ours in the same place, didn't we, Missus?' Audrey nodded. 'And the bride was just as beautiful,' added

Felix with a grin. Audrey swatted him away, but smiled.

'And how's your mum, that lovely girl?' asked Audrey. Margot and I eyed each other. Margot gulped and stared at Wesley.

'Eh, she's been better,' he said.

'And Creg is staying out of trouble?' asked Felix.

Wesley snorted. 'Who knows?'

'What him do?'

I held my breath. Wesley never talks about his dad. Ever.

He shrugged. 'Nothing – that's the problem. Haven't seen him in years. One night he went to bed and everything was fine. The next morning, he was just gone. Weeks later, Auntie Molly saw him in town with a woman who definitely wasn't Mum. That was that, then.'

Margot shook her head, and I put my hand on Wesley's shoulder.

'I'm sorry to hear that, young man,' said Felix.

Wesley sighed. 'Me too, but it is what it is. Nothing I can do about it.'

LEAVING

*Choosing your moment to go is a great
thing to know!*

It was getting dark. I looked out of Chicane, across
The Outback and could barely see our houses.
That meant it was time to go – there was no way I
could get caught creeping through the bushes on
two consecutive evenings. My life would be over.
Besides, I needed space to think about the Copseys'
next steps. After today – after meeting Felix and
Audrey – I had to take stock and readjust our plans.

Wesley was deep in conversation with the
Braithwaites, while Margot listened in intently. I
coughed to get their attention.

'Ahem, I'm sorry, but we need to be going
soon.'

'What, already?' said Wesley, singing quite a different song now he'd made a personal connection to the couple.

'I have to be back before it's too dark,' I said. 'My mum . . .'

Felix nodded. 'Mind how you go, now – be careful in here and out there, yuh hear me? No runnin'.' He groaned as he stood up. 'This day turned out nice, real nice,' he said. 'Lovely to meet you all.' He smiled widely at Wesley. 'Likkle Alan Evans in the flesh.' Felix grabbed his shoulder and shook it gently. 'Be good to mum, now.'

'I will,' said Wesley. 'And sorry for being snappy at the start. I was well nervous.'

'Forget it. I don't blame you for one second for being scared,' said Audrey. We approached the doorway. 'Don't walk around the factory floor,' she said. 'Just take the steps to the bottom, and you'll be all right.'

I nodded.

'I would really like to repay you,' I said. 'For everything.' Margot murmured her agreement, and so did Wesley this time.

Audrey shook her head. 'No, there's no need.'

Felix rubbed his chin. 'I have a likkle idea.'

'No, you don't,' said Audrey.

'Missus, shush,' he said. 'Listen, tomorrow's Sunday. Everyone needs a hearty meal to set them up right for the week. You want to eat?'

'Yes, please!' said Margot. 'What's on the menu?'

Felix laughed. 'Well, I was thinking of doing a small roast: a chicken, potatoes, bit of coleslaw, macaroni cheese . . .'

My mouth instantly watered.

'You can make that here?' said Wesley. 'A whole dinner?'

Audrey nodded. 'There's an electric oven in the old cafeteria. I've cleaned it up, made it nice and bright.'

'I have most of the tings,' Felix continued. 'But I need nutmeg and the macaroni to pull it together. Can you collect some?'

'Not a problem. We promise we'll get those ingredients,' I said. 'Do you need anything else? Some vegetables, fruit?'

'Oh lovely!' said Felix. 'Nothing too hard, though.' He pointed to his mouth. 'Me old teeth can't take it.'

'Deal!' I said. Felix extended his hand for me to shake. He looked in my eyes, and I nodded. The Copseys had a real mission – one that wasn't set by me at least.

'You must promise me one more ting,' said Felix.

'Sure!' said Margot. 'We promise.'

'Margot, hear what it is first before saying yes.' Wesley sighed. 'What is it?'

'Promise you won't tell anyone about us or that we're here, OK?' said Felix. He looked at each of us in turn. 'Because everyone will want to live here, then. Too many cooks will spoil the life broth.'

Audrey raised an eyebrow. 'That doesn't make a lick of sense.'

'It kind of does. I know what you mean, Felix. Don't worry,' said Margot. She ran a finger across her lips. 'These are now sealed,' she mumbled.

Audrey laughed, and walked to the back of the room. She fumbled into their hastily packed bag of belongings. 'Here, take this,' she said. She pressed an old torch into my palms. I turned it on and the bulb glowed for a moment before quickly fading away. 'Maybe not,' Audrey said, and laughed to hide her embarrassment. She snatched the torch away and hid it behind her back.

'Don't worry.' I smiled. 'We have torches on our phones – look.' I reached into my pocket and turned mine on.

'Phones have torches now?' said Felix. 'Well, well, well.'

I nodded. 'They do, and we'll be fine, won't we?'

'Absolutely,' said Margot.

'See you tomorrow, then!' said Wesley.

As we picked up our bags and stepped into the corridor, I took a last look at Audrey and Felix. They stood together, his arm round her, her face half buried in his neck – just like their old photograph. I smiled and walked away. The three of us, now familiar with the terrain in the corridor, walked silently until we reached the door at the end that led to the steps.

'Wow,' said Wesley as he opened it. 'I'm well glad I came today.'

'I knew you would be,' I said. 'You have to trust me.'

'Hmmm,' said Margot. 'We *can* trust you, can't we, Jo? For a minute, when I fell, I thought you were going to leave us. You wouldn't have, would you?'

'No,' I said. 'I knew you were behind me and it was going to be fine.'

'You did?' she said quietly. 'All right.' She sighed. 'Well, I'm sorry we didn't find your blanket, Wesley.'

'Ah,' he said, walking down the steps, shining his torch on his feet in front of him. 'I learned a lot, so it might have been worth losing it, actually.'

Margot looked up at me incredulously.

'Today was really something, wasn't it, Wes?' I said.

'Yeah, it was.'

*

There was a fire-exit door at the bottom of the stairs, so we pushed it open to get outside. We were on the opposite side of the building and had to walk round most of its perimeter to get back to the stream, across The Outback and then home.

'Nervous about crossing the stream, Margot?' asked Wesley. 'Can you do it?'

'I'll be fine. I have experience and courage this time,' she said. She was right – she did. Margot hopped over the stones without an issue. We passed last night's camping spot again, and again, there was still no sign of Wesley's blanket.

'Where *is* it?' I said, looking at the ground. 'Where has it gone?'

'Maybe that dog we saw moved it, and is using it for a bed?' offered Margot.

'Ah, well, in that case, that dog can keep it,' said Wesley with a shrug. 'They need it more than me.' He carried on ahead, through The Outback. I glanced back at Felix and Audrey's window and I was sure I could see them up there, dancing together in the dark.

PRAYING

find - and keep - your faith!

My phone beeped loudly close to my face early the next morning.

Margot had sent a message to our group chat, which I had proudly renamed 'The Copseys'. It read, *The key is under the mat!* I replied with a smiley face, and so did Wesley. He was in a good mood today.

'Enjoy church!' I added. Margot replied with a pair of brown hands in prayer.

Before getting up – and I had to soon – I lay in bed for a moment, replaying and reviewing yesterday's events in my head. It was certainly scary at points and dangerous in others, but really it was brilliant. We stuck together, met interesting people and achieved so much. I leaned out of bed to scramble for my laptop. I looked through the awards and considered a special bravery badge for Wesley, who had really turned his attitude round. I was proud of him, but worried about his mum – and Margot's thoughts about her. I hoped I'd have a chance to raise it with him today. I just didn't know what to say yet. But I'd figure that out.

After taking a hot shower, I bounced down the stairs. Dad was in the kitchen frying plantain. The smell made my mouth instantly water. Mum was sitting as close as she could to the table, her swollen belly between it and her chair. She stretched her arms as she waited for her breakfast. I smiled at her, sat down and poured myself a large mug of tea. I gulped it gratefully. It was exactly what I needed.

'All right, Mum?' I said, reaching for the plate of hard dough bread. I buttered it quickly and stuffed it into my mouth.

Mum raised an eyebrow. 'Hungry?'

I nodded. 'Always.'

'Up to something?'

'Never,' I replied.

Mum laughed as Dad rushed into the room, carrying a plate of plantain. 'Don't touch it!' he said, using his oven-gloved hand to swat mine away. 'The plate's hot.'

'I'm not trying to eat the plate,' I said, stuffing my mouth. My eyes crossed. 'This is so good. Thanks, Dad.'

'You're welcome,' he said. He looked me up and down, then glanced at Mum. 'You're in a good mood today. Enjoying your book?'

'My book? Which one?'

'The Obama one!' Mum said. 'Haven't you started it?'

'Oh, yeah. Not yet, but I will tonight. I'm just . . . busy at the moment. Occupied.'

'With what?' asked Dad.

'It better not be anything to do with going in them bushes!' said Mum.

I looked at her. 'I'm trying to understand my purpose in life, Mum. Thinking about who I want to be and what I need to do when I'm older.'

Mum made a face at Dad when she thought I wasn't looking. She was proud but tried to hide it. Dad didn't.

'That's *great*, Jo,' he said. 'Listen – later, me and your mum are going to take a drive and a walk to Dunstable Downs if you want to come. We're going to look at the birds, the kites and the planes . . .'

I shook my head. 'Thanks, but I can't. Margot, Wesley and I have things to do. Plans we can't change.' I popped more plantain in my mouth.

'Is that right?' said Mum. 'Well, at least you're being productive and not moping. Don't let Wesley's mum put any hippy-dippy tips in your heads about living your best lives, though. That woman is always up to something silly.' She returned to her breakfast. 'She needs to calm down.'

Suddenly, I wasn't so hungry. I put my fork down.

'What?' said Mum. 'What is it?'

'I think something's wrong with Ella,' I said, biting my lip. 'She doesn't look well.'

'Too busy being arty and not eating enough.'

I shrugged and stared at the table.

'Josie?' Mum said. 'What do you know? Should I go over there?' She pushed herself away from her plate.

'No, no, don't make a fuss. It's probably nothing – and Wesley won't like it if he thinks I've been talking about her.' I knocked the end of my fork against the table. 'Listen,' I said, getting up. 'I've got to go.'

'I feel bad doing this,' said Wesley as we stood on Margot's driveway an hour later. He peeked out into the close. 'What if someone's watching and they call the police?'

'Wesley, on Friday night we camped. Alone. In the dark. Yesterday, we broke into an abandoned factory and made friends with strangers. Today, we're only going into our friend's house,' I said. 'This is the easiest, least fun bit.' I reached down under Margot's welcome mat and retrieved her key. I put it in the front door and twisted it. It clunked open. 'See? Done.'

'I've never been here before though,' he said. 'I feel like I need a proper invitation – one from a parent – to go into someone's house.'

'You sound like a vampire.'

'You what?'

'You know – you have to say "Yes, you can come in" before a vampire will come into the room.'

'Is that true?'

'Apparently, according to lore.' I shrugged and pushed the door open.

'This is definitely a shoes-off house,' said Wesley over my shoulder. He bent down to unlace his trainers. 'It's funny – it doesn't feel like anyone *really* lives here.'

I knew what he meant. Margot's house was extremely white, clean and sparse. It was somewhere between an empty house my dad would have to fix before he sold it, and an art gallery. The walls and ceilings were white, the floor was made from light-brown wood and there were framed paintings in bold colours lining the wall up the stairs.

'Ah *this* makes sense. I can see why she's the way she is,' said Wesley. 'And by that I mean a bit weird. It's a nice house – best on the close, I reckon – but is it a *home*? Nah.'

There were a few more personal touches in the living room. On the bright white walls were framed photographs of Margot at various stages of her life to date. One showed her playing her clarinet on an empty stage in front of a large audience. Another was taken on what I assumed was her first day of her old school. She wore a straw boater hat with a red ribbon, white knee-high socks and a blazer. There was a fuzzy, glossy photograph of Margot as a baby – she lay naked and smiling on a shaggy white rug. Wesley pointed to it, laughed, then covered his eyes. 'I can't look – it's way too much,' he said.

There were pictures of Margot's dad, too. He looked stern and professional. He was very serious and very legal in his pictures, apart from one more-candid snap. He stood with one arm in the air, surrounded by people making the same gesture in front of the Statue of Liberty in New York.

'Hmmm,' Wesley said, peering at it. 'Maybe she *does* have family in New York after all.'

'Why would she lie?' I said.

'To impress you, innit. Although, I think she's wising up to you a bit, which is good.'

I took a step back. 'What do you mean?'

'Well, she wondered if you were gonna leave us in Chicane. It was a good question. I know the answer – you would have.'

I put my hands up to protest. 'Wesley, I would never –'

'Yeah, right,' he said, laughing, moving towards the kitchen. 'Tell yourself that.'

Margot's kitchen was similarly stark white and bright. Inside the glossy, shiny cupboards, all of her ingredients and food had been removed from their packets and boxes and placed into meticulously labelled glass jars. It was incredibly organized and I loved it.

'Don't you think that's unnecessary and extra – a bit like Margot herself?' Wesley said, his hand to his chin. He wiped a finger across their light-grey marble worktops. 'Does anyone actually cook in this house? Doesn't seem so. Wait. I know what this is.' He inspected his hands. 'This is a simulation of a kitchen. We've moved into the Matrix.'

I laughed. 'No, we haven't. Just grab the nutmeg, the macaroni, any soft fruit you can find and then we can go, OK? I have to pop to the toilet first. I drank a lot of tea this morning.' Wesley nodded and looked for a packet for the pasta.

I ran up Margot's stairs. Her bedroom door immediately faced the landing at the top. It was open, and I poked my head in. Her room – untidy and colourful – was different from the rest of the house. Her walls were completely covered in ideas for stories, articles and any other tales she wanted to tell scrawled on long sticky notes. There were notebooks, printed copies of scripts with copious notes and coloured pens everywhere. A wave of pride washed over me. Margot, like me, was putting in the work. I loved to see it.

I visited the toilet, and afterwards I enjoyed using Margot's luxurious bottled soaps and creams, spending more time than necessary with fragrant foam on my fingers. As I stepped out of the bathroom, shaking and sniffing my soft bergamot-and-blood-orange-scented hands, I was shocked to see Wesley sitting on Margot's bed. He was smiling and reading one of her journals. He was surprised to see me too, because he shut the book immediately.

SKIPPING

Skip, hop and jump to it!

'I wasn't doing anything!' said Wesley, standing up, grabbing the bag of food and stepping out of Margot's room. He ran down the stairs to the front door and started lacing his neon-green trainers. I flew down the steps after him.

'Yes, you were! I can't *believe* you'd do that, Wesley!' I said, bending down beside him and pushing my feet into my shoes. 'Those are her private thoughts! Imagine if she did that to you? You would be *furious* – and rightly so! What you did is *so* against the code, Wesley. I might have to take action.'

'I couldn't help it,' he said. 'She never lets us look when she's writing her spy notes – you know I think she's sus. I just wanted to know. Confirmation.

Don't shout at me, all right? Those little coloured notes stood out in her well-bleak house. They hypnotized me and pulled me in. How could I stop them?' Wesley opened the front door. 'If you're gonna blame anyone, blame Margot.'

'Blame Margot for what?' she said, standing by her porch. Wesley caught his breath and stared at me. His eyes begged me not to tell her what he'd done.

'Ah, erm.' I coughed and thought on my feet. 'Blame Margot for my hands being so slippery and fresh,' I said, putting them up to her face and feeling terrible that I'd woven myself into Wesley's web of lies. 'That hand cream of yours is something special.' I chuckled unconvincingly.

'It's good, right?' she said. 'Super moisturizing. My mum gives me a tube every time I go back to London.' Margot rolled her eyes. 'I've told her she doesn't need to keep giving me *things*. Just some *time*.' She blinked. 'And attention. Anyway, who cares about cream right now, hmmm?' She clapped her hands. 'Are you excited to spend time with Felix and Audrey, and eat? Dad wanted me to stay after church and have lunch with him, but I, of course, said no. Actually, I said "*No, Daddio*".' Margot laughed. 'Everything all right in the house? Did you find the stuff?'

'Yeah, I found . . . the stuff,' said Wesley with a smile. I sighed deeply while he lifted his bag to show Margot what he had collected.

'Great. Shall we go then?' she said.

'We're ready,' I said. 'But are you? You look nice –'

'Sunday best!' said Margot brightly. She unbuttoned her woollen navy coat and showed us her clean white knee-length dress underneath. She wore her shiny black school shoes.

'But it's not really practical for The Outback and the factory, is it? After what happened to you yesterday . . .'

'Yeah, you need overalls and kneepads,' said Wesley.

'No, it's cool. I know what I'm doing now. I'll be fine.'

'You sure . . . Angel?' asked Wesley. He stifled a laugh. 'I mean you *do* look like an angel in that white dress, don't you?'

Margot and I exchanged confused looks, but she smiled. 'Yeah, I'm sure,' she said, shutting her front door and taking her keys from my hand.

We crossed the close to get to Wesley's. My dad was in our drive, vacuuming the boot of our car. With his wireless headphones over his head and his back to us, he danced as he cleaned. I quickly stepped past him and encouraged Wesley and Margot to do the same. Margot wanted to stop and say hello – of course – but I kept us moving by pushing her across the doughnut. Wesley bounced on and off the mattress that still lay there. He looked back at us and grinned. When he ran towards his house, Margot tugged on my elbow.

'He's in a strange mood,' she said in a low voice. 'Is he excited about talking to the Braithwaites about his grandad, or did you speak to him about his mum? Is she better then?'

'We didn't talk about anything, really,' I said. 'We were busy finding the bits in your kitchen. That's it. By the way, I love how your ingredients are arranged in your cupboards – compliments to the chef. But maybe you're right and he's just excited.' I put my head down because I didn't want to look at Margot any more. It didn't feel right. Together we walked through Wesley's door, straight through the hallway and into the kitchen.

'Where is everyone?' asked Margot, standing by his kettle. 'Your house feels too quiet. I miss your family.'

'Since when? I thought they were Victorian urchins?'

'I was joking,' said Margot, 'and also wrong.' She smiled at Wesley.

'They're at Auntie Molly's,' he said, staring at her. 'It's a bit of a shame I'm not staying here to enjoy the silence.' He shrugged. 'But what we're doing is much better – way more fun!'

Wesley's house phone rang. He ran into the hallway to answer it.

'Wait there,' he shouted.

'Who has a house phone these days?' Margot whispered. 'Doesn't everyone just use mobiles?'

'Clearly not,' I said, leaning on the kitchen doorway and looking into the hall.

'All right, Mum?' said Wesley into the handset. 'What you calling for? Is everything OK over there?' He curled the phone's cord round his finger and looked out of the front door.

Margot looked at me.

'You sure, Mum?' Wesley whispered. 'You know you can tell me, right?'

I shook my head.

'Oh, that's it? That's all you want? I'll do that, but I don't think it will be defrosted by tonight . . . Will that be good for your stomach?' Wesley moved the handset away from his ear. 'All right, all right, don't shout – I'm doing it! Bye, Mum. Yeah, yep . . . See you later.'

Wesley put the phone down, and Margot and I jumped away from the doorway and stood as naturally as we could in the kitchen. He walked in, looking at the floor. He stomped over to his fridge and pulled the bottom door open. He reached into the freezer and grabbed a wrapped package of meat. 'She never listens,' he muttered. 'And she doesn't tell me anything, ever!'

Margot stared at me, then walked towards Wesley. I shook my head and approached him instead. I put my hand on his shoulder. He jumped.

'Why you being creepy?' he shouted, dropping the meat on the floor. He bent over to pick it up, then put it on the counter with his back to us.

'Wesley,' I said, 'you know you can talk to us, about anything.'

'Totally,' Margot said quietly.

Wesley stood still, then wiped his eyes.

'I'm fine, OK?' He sniffed but turned round and smiled. 'It's nothing . . . I hope. All she wanted was this lamb out of the freezer, and now it's done.'

'You sure?' I said.

'Definitely.' He pulled open his back door and ushered us into his yard, locking it behind him.

'After you,' he said, gesturing towards the fence and smiling at Margot with his eyebrows raised.

'Very kind of you,' Margot replied with a slight bow. She stepped into The Outback.

I hung behind for a moment. 'Sure you're OK?'

'I said yes, didn't I? I'm fine. I've had a great morning – read some interesting words.' He laughed.

'No not this again. I don't know what you read, Wes,' I whispered, 'and definitely don't tell me the specifics because I don't want to know. But stop this. You're being weird. Too *nice*. It's not normal.'

'Chill, Josie,' he said. 'It was just a tiny poem –'

I put my hands over my ears. 'Lalalala!' I shouted. 'I said I don't want to know!'

'Calm down. I liked it.' Wesley pulled at my wrists. 'Come on.'

'You shouldn't have done that.' I sighed, keeping my hands tightly to my ears. 'Snooping aside, you know how she feels about sharing her work.'

'Eh, well, it doesn't matter now, does it? It's done,' he said, stepping through the fence.

We caught up to Margot, who sniffed deeply. 'I actually love it out here,' she said, gently pushing a branch away from her face. 'Now we've walked along this path a few times, it's so easy to see everything and know where you're going.'

'Yep,' I replied. 'It's good, isn't it?'

Margot looked up at the factory as it came closer into view. 'I can't believe we're going back, and with a good reason this time, too,' she said.

'Innit,' said Wesley. 'It was awesome learning about Grandad and finding out more about his life.' He kicked wet leaves up in front of him. 'I'm glad Felix and Audrey weren't ghosts, and they're cool, kind of normal people. How decent their food is going to be though, I don't know. I get they have electricity, but do they have running water? If they do, I bet it's all rusty.' He stuck out his tongue.

'That's a good point,' I said. 'OK, right – our strategy here, if the food is suspicious, is to eat just enough to seem polite, but not so much that we get sick. Deal?'

They nodded as we came across Friday's campsite. The ground seemed slightly flatter, and there was another half-eaten apple.

'Someone *really* likes this spot,' I said, kicking the core away with my foot. 'I can't blame them. It's a good spot to take in the sights and enjoy the stream.'

'This girl said *sights*, you know.' Wesley laughed. He stepped on to the bank on the other side of the river. 'Don't overdo it, Josie – it ain't that pretty round here.'

Margot followed behind him. 'Sights *is* a bit strong,' she said. Margot and her shiny shoes skipped across the rocks, turning to look at me as she reached the last one. She smiled, turned to Wesley and slipped face-first off the rock and into the stream. Margot's navy coat and white dress were caked in silt. She wiped the mud from her eyes and screamed.

CLEANING

Cleanliness is next to Copseyness!

Saying 'I told you so' is one of the worst things a person can do, and it certainly doesn't improve any situation. It literally makes everything worse. I therefore bit my tongue very hard and tightened my lips to force those words to stay in my mouth.

I won the battle, but the phrase put up a strong fight.

I quickly crossed the stream to help Margot. She sat there, in the river, back against the bank, screaming and refusing help from Wesley. He lay on his stomach on the grass, arms hanging over the water. Wesley was trying to help her, but he was laughing so hard that his hands trembled, and tears ran down his brown cheeks. If 'I told you so' could take a physical form, it would look like Wesley did in that moment.

'Sunday best!' he shouted. He rolled on to his back and wiped the water from his face. 'More like Sunday mess, innit!' Wesley took deep breaths and exhaled hard. 'Oh my God, I hope the food is as delicious as that was. Phew, my chest! Must. Stop. Creasing. Up!'

'It's *not* funny!' Margot shouted, slapping the stream around her, which only made Wesley laugh more.

'Margot, you have to get up,' I said, offering her a hand. 'And stop screaming – it's not helping, is it?'

She buried her face in her muddy, wet hands.

'Why didn't you make me change my shoes?' she whimpered. 'My trainers were right there.' She pointed down as if she was still in her hallway at home.

'I told –' No. I stopped myself. I wasn't going to say it now. I'd come this far. I started again. 'Listen, you wanted to look nice, special – that's fine. It's important to feel your best and give yourself confidence. We can wash these clothes –'

'Or throw them away,' Wesley added unhelpfully. 'That's probably what you need to do, realistically.'

'– but you must get up and give Felix and Audrey what they asked for first. Then we can go home and get cleaned up. Forget dinner if you have to. But we can't break our code over a bit of dirt, can we?'

Margot sighed and got up. It seemed that most of the stream had seeped into her coat, as it dripped and hung heavily from her shoulders. She finally accepted Wesley's hand and clambered up the bank.

'It ain't that bad, Margot. I'm sure Audrey has granny pants you can put on.' Wesley snorted.

'Shut up,' she said, slapping him with her wet sleeve.

When we got to the safest entrance of the factory, Audrey was waiting at the bottom of the staircase. Her face was stern, and her arms were folded across her chest. 'I could hear you from a mile away, heeheeing, shrieking and carrying on! I had to come all the way down here to tell you off. If you can't behave, you can't come in!'

Margot stepped up. 'I'm sorry, Audrey,' she said. 'I had an accident.' She flicked her hand down her body to show Audrey the extent of the damage.

Audrey's hand flew to her mouth. 'Again? W'happen? You slipped in the river? You hurt?' Margot shook her head, and Audrey put her hand on Margot's shoulder. 'Sorry I shouted. Come, let's clean you up.'

*

Upstairs, we gathered in a small, spotlessly cleaned-up corner of what was once the Chicane Cars cafeteria. Both Felix and Audrey were busy in the kitchen, which was on the other side of a metal shutter that they had pushed up into the ceiling. The wafting smell of chicken roasting mostly covered the funk of the factory. Felix stirred the macaroni as it boiled on the stove.

Margot perched on a water-warped wooden stool, warming herself up by holding a cup of what was now her favourite drink: fresh ginger-and-mint tea. Beside her lay a crumpled, muddy pile of baby wipes, and her dirty clothes were a distant memory – she now wore a long green dress that belonged to Audrey. I was certain it was the one in their photograph and, if it was, it fit Margot well. It really suited her. Wesley didn't think so, however. He kept looking over at Margot and would then hunch over, laughing. I just knew he was replaying Margot's fall in his mind. Every now and again, he would rest his head on the table and shake his shoulders.

'Thanks for the tea, helping me with my clothes *and* lending me this vintage dress,' said Margot loudly so Felix and Audrey could hear her. Her tone told me she wanted to keep it.

'Vintage?' Wesley whispered. 'You mean old.'

Margot closed her eyes and shook her head. 'No, I mean *classic*,' she hissed back at him. She rubbed the fabric of the dress around her neck and face. 'It's really kind of you both.'

'It's the least we could do for the nutmeg and macaroni,' said Felix. 'And the clementines.' He limped over to the hatch to smile at us. 'Dinner will be delicious – just wait!'

'Yes, thanks,' said Audrey, scrubbing away at Margot's dress in the sink. 'Don't you worry about this. It's funny, almost the *exact* thing happened to me back home when I was your age,' she said. Audrey reached for a bottle of bleach, slightly recoiled at its smell and poured some into the sink. She rubbed the folds of the fabric together.

'What happened?' asked Margot. 'Was it as embarrassing as this?'

'Well, when I was growing up, all the houses were connected by these muddy lanes. When it was raining, they'd swamp up and be a real mess. Hard to traverse. My auntie Cheryl, she was getting married. She was wonderful – so young, so funny. She made me laugh until tears come out me eyes.' Audrey smiled at the memory. 'When she told everyone she was engaged, I *knew* she would ask me to be bridesmaid – I would have been very upset if she didn't.' Audrey laughed to herself. 'But she did. So, this one day, I went to her house to try on me dress. Silky peach satin it was, with white lace edges. Little white pop socks, matching gloves and leather shoes that have the buckle across. I was so excited, I had to pop style and show Alfrieda, my friend who lived right across the street.'

'So what did you do?' said Wesley, shuffling to the edge of his seat.

'When Auntie Cheryl and Mommy weren't looking, I snuck out the house and just dash across the lane. But, just outside, right outside, Alfrieda's, I slipped.'

'Oh my gosh, then what happened?' said Margot. 'Did you get into trouble? My grandma says her mum back home in Barbados was *super* strict.'

'Trouble?' said Audrey. 'More than trouble. I got beaten by Alfrieda's mum for showing off, then by Mommy for ruining the dress and wasting money. Wasn't allowed to go to the wedding, either.'

'Really?' I said. 'But it was an accident!'

'Yes, really,' said Audrey. 'Different time, different place.' She returned to her washing. 'England's not like that – children are raised differently here. You have it easy.'

'Compared to that, we do,' I said. 'I'm sorry that happened, Audrey.'

'Ah.' Audrey waved her hands. 'It was years ago and I'm more than grown now. I'd forgotten it until I saw your friend, there. Then it all came flooding back.' Audrey shut her eyes and blinked. Felix put his hand on her shoulder. 'Phew, this bleach strong!' she said.

Felix smiled down at her. 'If you say so, Missus.' He looked up at us. 'Dinner will be served shortly.'

DINING

Bite off more than you can chew . . . sometimes!

I don't know exactly how they did it – especially because Felix and Audrey wouldn't allow us behind the hatch and into the kitchen to check – but cooking the dinner seemed successful. It looked and smelled delicious. Felix carefully carried full paper plates to the table and placed them proudly in front of us. They were piled high with roast chicken and potatoes, macaroni cheese, coleslaw and gravy.

Felix sat down and picked up his plastic cutlery. 'Eat up!' he said with a smile, rubbing his knife and fork together. Then he suddenly slapped the table, making us jump. 'Wait, wait!'

'What?' said Wesley. 'Have we done something?'

'Let me set the scene – light a candle and make this dinner *really* special.' Felix stood up and dug into his trouser pocket. He pulled out a small silver tea light and placed it in the middle of the table. He patted down his jacket and found a small, thin row of matches.

'This looks incredible! Thank you, Felix,' said Margot, leaning over her plate and flicking her hands in front of her face to waft the smell up her nose. Audrey coughed gently under her breath, and smiled at her. 'And you, Audrey, of course.' Margot laughed. She snatched up her knife and fork and dug into her dinner. Wesley and I were more cautious. We held back a bit, questioning the origin and preparation of the meal. Using eye contact between us, we decided to let Margot be the lead tester and taster – the canary in the Chicane Cars coal mine.

Margot's eyes crossed, then closed. 'This is delicious.' She sighed, slumping in her seat. She poked at her plate and piled chicken on the end of her fork. 'So tender and juicy,' she said between mouthfuls. She squealed and wriggled her shoulders. Wesley and I looked at each other and nodded. The food had passed the test, and we started eating. Margot was right – it was so good.

As Wesley ate, he looked intently around the cafeteria, but avoided its darkest corners. 'I can't believe I'm eating in here, just like Grandad. It's well weird.'

Felix laughed and wiped some macaroni from his mouth. 'Oh yes, Alan.' He swallowed his mouthful. 'He was here a lot. Always hungry, but he wasn't just eating. He did his union meetings here, too.' Felix looked around the room. 'Not far from where you're sitting.' He waved his fork at Wesley. 'Yes, he used to stand right there, in front of that window, demands scrawled on the paper in his hand –'

'Shouting over everyone eating,' added Audrey. 'And the people telling him to shut up and sit down.'

Wesley looked in the direction Felix had pointed. I knew he was picturing the past. He smiled, whispered, 'Wow,' and then stared down at his dinner. 'He was a good guy, yeah?' he said to Audrey.

She nodded. 'He really was.'

'A lot like you and your friends,' said Felix. 'Coming up here, helping us. Doing good in your neighbourhood.' He laughed at that line. 'Heh, that's catchy.'

'Very,' said Margot, biting into a potato. 'Good one, Felix.'

'What you say your group's called again?' asked Audrey. 'Crawleys?'

'We're the Copseys,' I said, sitting up straight. 'A youth group for good.'

'How many of you in your group?' she asked.

I pointed to Wesley, Margot and myself. 'Just three for now,' I said. 'We only became official last Thursday.'

Audrey raised her eyebrows. 'So quick? Impressive. Very accomplished.'

I smiled and my chest warmed. I felt incredibly proud, because 'impressive' and 'accomplished' was *exactly* what I wanted to be – how I wished to be – described. 'Thank you,' I said, feeling seen and appreciated.

'It's like Scouts?' said Felix. 'Don't they have Scouts in this town any more? They have this whole ting set up already for you . . .'

'Innit.' Wesley laughed.

'Where's the initiative in that?' asked Audrey, shaking her head. 'Too easy.'

'That's what we said!' said Margot, laughing and nudging me.

'What you got so far?' said Audrey, leaning forward on her elbows. 'You have ideas for badges, tasks and missions?'

'We have a document full of ideas for badges.' I nodded. 'And we've already earned two: camping and litter-picking. I'm trying to make all of the names of the badges end in "ing". It makes them more dynamic, I think.'

Margot nodded. 'Way more action and drama.'

'Also, I think *I've* definitely earned persuading,' I said, slightly laughing.

'You been earning that badge your whole life,' said Wesley. 'Since the moment you came out of your mum.'

Felix chuckled and patted him on his shoulder. 'You really make me laugh.'

'You have uniforms?' asked Audrey, rubbing her hands together. 'I *love* a good uniform. I can stitch and sew – I can give you a hand with patterns.'

'That would be amazing! We're working on the uniforms,' I said, smiling at Wesley in particular. 'Aren't we?'

He snorted. 'Still not wearing one, but yeah.'

'We also have a code, and a pledge – I wrote those!' Margot said proudly.

'Oh yes?' said Audrey. 'Let me hear it.'

Margot opened her mouth to speak.

'No, no! Not like that,' said Audrey, interrupting her. 'Do it properly, with pride. Stand up and say it with your hearts.'

I had no problem doing this; I had secretly been hoping and waiting for an opportunity to present itself so we could. It was also fine with Margot, who was already on her feet. I didn't need to look at Wesley to know he'd be reluctant. He was staring down at his plate, pretending he hadn't heard what Audrey had said.

Felix nudged him lightly in the ribs. 'Go on, Likkle Alan, you can do it,' he said quietly. Wesley looked up at him. I was waiting, just waiting for him to roll his eyes and say something sarcastic, but he didn't. He smiled instead.

Wesley put down his fork. 'Yeah, all right,' he said, pushing himself away from the table.

I was surprised and a bit shocked, but I tried to hide it. If Wesley caught me staring, he'd accuse me of being smug or think I'd 'won'. I glanced over at Felix. He smiled and nodded. Wesley stood next to Margot and I joined them.

'Ready?' I said, looking at my friends. They nodded, so I began. 'I swear I will do my best –'

'To love others – and myself, naturally.' Margot waved her hands between the Braithwaites and us, which made Audrey laugh.

'To ask, "What would the Josephines do?" when things get way too much –' Wesley shook his head at this bit.

'To do good things, and to always keep the Copsey Code,' we said, finishing together.

Felix clapped. 'Nice, nice, very good,' said Audrey. 'Very moving.'

'But who are "the Josephines"?' asked Felix. 'You have a twin?'

'If she had a twin, she wouldn't be called Josephine too, would she, Felix?' snapped Audrey, rolling her eyes while laughing.

'A joke, Missus,' he said. 'Calm yourself. Who is it though?'

'Oh, that's my hero, Josephine Holloway. She started the first Girl Scout troop for Black girls in America almost a century ago, and it really inspired us.'

Felix chuckled. 'Very good. Very important to know your history. Keep your noses in your books and out of trouble!'

'That's our plan,' I said. 'We can't live here forever.'

'Yes,' said Audrey quietly. 'Neither can we.'

GIVING

Give good, receive better!

'I obviously brushed my teeth last night, and again this morning – I'm not an animal,' said Margot, standing by the mattress in the doughnut on Monday morning, kicking it gently. 'But I did want to savour the flavour of that dinner a little longer.' She rubbed her stomach. 'That macaroni cheese was something else.' She kissed her fingers like a chef.

'It was so tasty!' I said, looking towards Wesley's front door as we waited for him. 'I'm really inspired and impressed by Felix and Audrey's inventiveness. We can learn so much from them. We should ask them to be honorary Copseys, don't you think?'

Margot nodded. 'Definitely! They were both so into the concept. And like, how do they live so well in a place like that?' She thought for a moment. 'Oh, I have a *great* idea. Something I can give them! Something that could help both them and us.'

I turned to face her. 'You do?'

'OK, so – what if they wrote a book?' she said, her eyes bright. 'It could be about thriftiness – *squatting with style,* I think they called it – mixed with their stories from back home. Like a mash-up of a manual and a memoir.'

'Hmm,' I said. 'Well, they do want to keep their life in the factory a secret, and this is the opposite of that, but it is a good idea. You'd help them with the writing?'

'Exactly! You could do all the business stuff behind it, and Wesley could design the cover!' she squealed, delighted by her plan. 'They'd be famous, travel to far-flung places and make loads of money. Hopefully they'd give us a bit too, which we could give to charity –'

'Or invest in us and the Copseys?' I added.

'Yep . . . I suppose.'

Wesley's door opened. He smiled, waved and ran over.

'It's a great idea, Margot. You should ask them. Even if it doesn't become a real book, you'll always have their stories. Morning, Wes!'

'Morning, morning,' he said, standing beside us. 'Whose stories will you always have?'

'The Braithwaites',' replied Margot. 'We're going to write a book with them.'

'Maybe,' I said. 'You have to ask them first, remember?'

'Yeah, yeah, of course,' said Margot. We walked towards the end of the close, heading towards Copsey Avenue.

'That's not a bad idea.' Wesley sighed. 'But . . . I just don't know, you know?'

'Don't know about what?' I asked.

'Felix and Audrey,' he said.

'Wait, I thought you liked them?' said Margot. 'What changed?'

'Nothing changed. I think they're cool, but I'm not getting why they live in Chicane. Like really. Why?'

'*Squatting with style!*' said Margot. 'They told us.'

'Yeah, that's what they *said*, but I don't know if I *believe* it,' he said. 'It just couldn't be me, I guess.' Wesley shook his head. He looked at Margot. 'Anyhow, this book – you trying to get writing experience? Josie put you up to this?'

'Nope,' I said. 'This one's nothing to do with me.'

'It was all my idea,' said Margot proudly. 'It just came to me. And, yep, it would be fantastic to help – especially if it makes money for Felix and Audrey.'

'I doubt they'll go for it,' he said. 'But you're quite a good writer.'

Margot was immediately flattered. 'Thanks!' she said, touching her chest. 'But you haven't really read any of my work, not yet.'

Wesley chuckled. 'Oh, I have, Angel.' I spun my head to stare at Wesley and balled my hands into fists. Not this again. If Wesley was going to admit that he read Margot's notebook yesterday, I would commend that. He *should* tell her, but definitely keep me out of it. I also hoped he wouldn't tell her now. It was too early for confrontation. It's best to start the day with a clear mind.

Margot narrowed her eyes. 'What? What do you mean? Why are you calling me Angel?'

'I've read your code and your pledge, haven't I?' Wesley smiled. 'And sorry, but I'm still laughing at your clean white dress turning dirty mud brown yesterday. It was heavenly.' He pressed his palms together as if in prayer.

Margot didn't know whether to say 'thank you' or 'shut up', so she said 'Hmmm' instead.

At the end of Copsey Close, instead of looking up at Mr Kirklees's window, I was drawn to his front door. It was open this morning, and he was leaning against his doorway in his blue jumper, white collar and jeans. His dog sniffed the ground by his feet. As we stepped closer, his smile widened.

'Oh no.' Margot gripped the strap of her schoolbag. 'He's not going to talk to us, is he?' she said through her teeth.

He was. 'Morning, children!' Mr Kirklees said brightly, showing his bright white teeth. Margot took a step back and covered her eyes. When Mr Kirklees's dog noticed us, he galloped in our direction and leaped on Wesley, sniffing him deeply while licking his hand.

Wesley bent down to stroke the dog's thick, wiry fur. 'Ahh, I *love* dogs!' he said, stroking its face and tickling it under its chin.

'Brian!' Mr Kirklees shouted. Brian ran back to Mr Kirklees and stood by his feet. 'So sorry about that – Brian gets very excited meeting new friends.'

'It's fine with me,' said Wesley, who was still smiling, kneeling and making kissing noises at Brian.

'Morning, Mr Kirklees,' I said. 'You well?'

'Oh yes, very well, very good,' he said. He put his hands in the pockets of his jeans and bounced on the spot, creasing his blue slippers. 'Bright, beautiful start to the day – especially for November. Can't complain – mustn't complain, ha!'

'Yeah, it is a nice day,' said Wesley craning his neck to look at the sky. 'You just out here, taking it in?'

'Well, actually, I was waiting for you three to pass by,' he said. Margot instantly narrowed her eyes.

'Oh yeah?' said Wesley.

'Yes!' said Mr Kirklees. He leaned forward. 'I have to thank you for tidying the garden. I just *know* it was you three, and I appreciate it – very kind of you. I have a little something to give you.'

'You do?' I said, surprised. He nodded. 'We didn't do it for gifts!'

'I'm sure you didn't! Wait there. I'll just be a moment.' He hobbled back into his hallway and shut the front door slightly. Brian trotted towards Wesley and wrapped himself round his legs.

'What . . . is . . . happening?' said Margot quietly.

'We're getting a present – what's the problem?' said Wesley. 'Stop moaning! It's a good story, innit?' She pursed her lips.

Mr Kirklees opened the door. In his fist were three ten-pound notes.

FUNDRAISING

Pay it forward!

'Mr Kirklees!' I said, protesting by shaking my head and hands. 'No. You don't need to do that – we didn't tidy your garden for money.'

'We really didn't,' said Wesley. 'We're not about that. We just wanted to help and thought it would be nice for you, and for little Brian there.' Brian wagged his tail and panted.

'Oh, well, Brian he loves his new, clean garden, don't you, Bri?' said Mr Kirklees patting Brian's head. 'And so do I. Therefore, it's only right to show our thanks. No arguments, now – just take it. Go on. I won't take no for an answer.' He waved the notes at us.

I looked at Wesley and Margot. Wesley sighed and shook his head. Margot looked up at Mr Kirklees with questions in her eyes.

'I mean it, children,' said Mr Kirklees. He looked at Wesley's school jumper, peeking out of his jacket. He pointed. 'I often give a bit of money to Larch Hill, but now you can have some for yourselves. Go on!' He pushed the money into my hands.

'Thank you,' I said. Wesley was right – the money wasn't the point of the Copseys, but, as I put it into my pocket, I thought about how we could put it to best use and instantly I had just the thing.

'It was our pleasure. You didn't have to do this,' Margot said with faked enthusiasm.

'You really didn't,' added Wesley genuinely.

'Ah, it's just a little token of appreciation. Get yourself some sweets, or something from the corner shop, Wesley.'

Wesley stood back. 'You know my name?' he asked, confused. 'How?'

'Who *doesn't* know your name, young man?' Mr Kirklees shrugged. 'Everyone on this street – and well beyond, I'm sure – has heard your . . . lovely mother and siblings calling out for you.'

Wesley looked mortified. He stared at the barren flower beds and scratched his neck. Mr Kirklees sensed he'd said something wrong.

'That's nothing to be ashamed of, son – you're clearly a young man in demand,' he said softly. 'I was once, too.' He chuckled. 'But no one shouts for me any more, besides Brian, who just barks. Can't understand a word of it – I don't speak dog. You're lucky.'

'Yeah,' said Wesley, brightening slightly. 'It's nice to have family who care about where you are, I guess.'

'Exactly,' said Margot. 'That matters.' She smiled at Wesley.

'This is so great, really,' I said. 'We have to give you something back – it's what we do.' Mr Kirklees, swatted his hand in our direction, as if to say no. 'The three of us were talking about painting your window frames when the weather warms up, if that's something you'd like?'

He leaned back in his doorway. 'People are so very wrong about kids today. Very wrong. You really are a thoughtful, useful bunch,' he said. 'I'm sure I'll think of something.' He glanced at his watch. 'Now, off you pop – don't be late for school! Go on.' He ushered Brian inside and shut his front door with a smile.

'That was nice,' said Wesley. 'Mr Kirklees is awesome, and I love that Brian.'

'Yeah, that dog *really* liked you,' said Margot. 'Weird.'

'Come on, Margot, *everyone* likes me.' Wesley laughed. 'And *I* really like old people now – they rule.'

'Totally agree,' said Margot. 'About the old people bit, Felix and Audrey – anyway,' she quickly added before coughing, looking away and then over at me. 'What shall we do with the money? Ideas? I think we should give it to a charity for the elderly.'

'Yeah, good idea!' said Wesley. 'Love that. I'm definitely not buying sweets and Felix and Audrey won't take it – you saw how Felix reacted when Josie offered to pay them. He hated it. Josie, what do you reckon? What should we do?'

'Charity is a good idea,' I said.

'Then that's that, then,' said Wesley, dusting his hands. 'Sorted.'

'But what if we gave it to a cause closer to home?' I said.

'Meaning?' said Wesley. 'You ain't trying to keep it, are you?'

'No, no, never – but what if we gave it to the school –'

'What?' Wesley shouted. 'School? *Pfft*. Nah. Why?'

'– for our class Christmas party.' I looked at Margot. 'We *did* promise Mr King we'd plan it. It would be great to put this money towards it. He'll be impressed with our efforts *and* we can buy better snacks – which will also help us recruit more Copseys. We can grow.'

Margot and Wesley eyed each other, checking for the other's reaction.

Margot opened her mouth and spoke slowly. 'Erm, it *is* a good idea –'

'Don't lie, it's not,' said Wesley, shaking his head.

'– but *I'd* rather give it to charity. If not that, then to Felix and Audrey. We could just leave it on their table.'

'They'll hate that, but yeah,' said Wesley. 'It's a much better idea than just giving it to Mr King and the rest of Six K. They don't deserve it. I was thinking last night – we have to do something else for the Braithwaites. Gotta pay them back for dinner – and for cleaning Margot's dress.'

'Exactly,' said Margot. 'Something that doesn't cost much, but means something.' She drummed her lip. 'Something priceless.'

'*I'm* priceless,' said Bobby from class, running to catch up with us. 'You lot could never afford me.' He looked at Margot. 'Maybe you could. I know you've got loads of coins.'

'I don't,' said Margot. 'And this is a private conversation. Bye, Bobby.'

Bobby laughed and turned to me. 'What you trying to do now, Josie?'

'It's not me,' I said, folding my arms. '*They're* thinking of ways to show appreciation that don't really cost anything,' I said.

Margot's arms slapped her sides. 'Why are you letting him in?'

Bobby ignored her. 'What, like do-gooder stuff?' he asked.

'Yeah, kind of.' Wesley laughed.

'Of course – that's what you lot are like.' Bobby thought for a moment. 'You know what, my favourite thing – after having a pee when I'm really busting –'

'Gross,' spat Margot. 'Too much information.'

'– *and* cuddling with Nani when we watch TV, is having a bath. Bubbles and a good soak – unbeatable.' He ran through our school gates. 'Hope that helps!' he said with a grin.

Margot stroked her chin. 'You know, Bobby is beyond annoying, but that's a good idea. They cooked and cleaned my dress, but I *did* have to wash myself down with baby wipes, which, fine – it's OK if you don't have anything else.'

'Yeah, a hot bath is a cool idea,' said Wesley. 'But where? I can't afford no spa day – that thirty pounds won't cut it. And we can't do it at my house – too busy. What about at Mr Kirklees's? We could give him his money back, and ask for this instead?'

Margot and I shook our heads. 'No,' said Margot. 'Felix and Audrey would hate that more than the money. They're very private.'

'They are,' I said. 'I can't bring them to mine, either. There's no way I can get around my mum and dad. Mum's always using the toilet, anyway. She says the baby is sitting on her bladder, but that doesn't seem physically possible to me.' I shrugged. 'That just leaves –'

'Me!' said Margot, grinning. 'Exactly. It's perfect. My house, after school. It's free. It's . . . always free. Also, then we can talk to them about the book.'

Wesley shook his head. 'They are not going to be into it. "*They're very private*",' he said, mimicking Margot. 'Remember?'

'But the bath is a solid plan,' I said. 'Let's head to Chicane straight after school.'

ESCAPING

It's good to get away!

'You calling us unwashed?' asked Audrey, throwing her hands into the air. The three of us stood by their table and awkwardly glanced at each other. This idea was a mistake. 'You saying we smell?' She shook her head. 'That we stink to high heaven?' She swallowed deep breaths and stared out of the window. In the reflection of the glass, I saw her wipe her face roughly. Felix gently placed his hands on her shoulders. While their backs were turned, I gently lifted their clock on the table. I slipped the three ten-pound notes Mr Kirklees gave us beneath it. Wesley and Margot nodded.

'They're not saying we smell, Missus,' Felix said quietly, close to her ear. 'They're just trying to be thoughtful.' She wriggled out of the grip of his fingers and looked at him, and then at us. Her eyes were wet, and her tight lips wavered.

I felt terrible. Upsetting Audrey was not our intention. Our offer of kindness had been flipped and twisted; it had been received as a cruelty, as a cuss.

'I'm so sorry, Audrey,' I said, stepping away from the doorway. 'We just wanted to do something nice for you both. We really didn't mean to hurt you. You deserve it.'

'We think you're great,' said Margot. 'Truly. You're so interesting and amazing. We want to write a book with you and everything!'

I shook my head at Margot; it wasn't the time.

'Yeah,' said Wesley. 'You're the coolest old people I know. Top three, and not three.'

That made Audrey laugh. 'You kids are someting else.'

'We thought a bath would be a treat that we could easily do for you,' said Margot.

'It's a *lovely* idea,' said Felix. 'A long soak would be *so* good for me legs.' He rubbed at them. 'Me knees killing me at the moment.' He looked up at Audrey and he raised his eyebrows, his eyes twinkling beneath them.

'How would we get there?' Audrey said with a sigh. 'What if someone sees us? I don't want nobody to see me – to know we're here. What about your parents? What they going to have to say?'

'Don't worry,' said Margot. 'We'll wait until it gets a little darker, and just go the way we do to get here. My dad's never home, so it's no problem. I promise. Bring your washing, too.'

Felix looked at Audrey with pleading eyes. He laced his fingers together and put his thumbs against his chest. Audrey's shoulders slumped, but she looked up at him with a slight smile.

'Yes, Missus!' shouted Felix. 'Let me fetch me washbag and tings – this beats boiling the kettle for a bucket wash by miles.' He grinned and limped to the back of their room.

We waited until it was almost dusk before we left Chicane. Outside, by the exit, the three of us switched on the torches on our phones to light the way for the Braithwaites. They were slowly making their way down the stairs from the top floor. The three of us were still young – not teenagers for two years yet – so the journey from Chicane Cars to Copsey Close took us no time, especially because we were usually running towards it with excitement or away in terror. We knew it would make sense to allow extra time for Felix and Audrey because, well, they're not teenagers any more. What we didn't take into consideration is that we should have left earlier – if we wanted to complete this task today.

We loitered, waiting for them at the bottom of the steps. Wesley shone his torch towards them and shook his head. 'Still no sign of them. I wish they would've let me help them down,' he said. He lowered his voice. 'How we gonna get them across the stream and through The Outback? Will they be able to make it?'

Wesley had a point. 'I'm a bit concerned, too,' I said, shining my light towards the stream. 'We could link arms, or hold hands to make sure no one falls or gets left behind?'

'Not for the stream-crossing part,' said Margot, shaking her head. 'Not after yesterday. I can't let them fall and get hurt. I'd never be able to live with myself if that happened.'

'Don't you worry,' shouted Felix down the staircase. 'It's just these hard concrete steps that take ages. Crossing the river and going through that likkle bush will be no problem.' The Braithwaites appeared, slightly panting, in the doorway. Audrey wiped her forehead. 'Forward!' said Felix, grinning widely.

*

Felix was right. He and Audrey crossed the river in the dark with ease. On the other side, he looked at us triumphantly, his hands on his hips. 'Told you we've still got some springs in these steps! We've done this crossing plenty of times – just shine your likkle lights in the right direction. It's no problem.' He swung a small, thin plastic bag round his wrist gleefully.

Audrey kissed her teeth, lowering his arm. 'You act younger than these children, Felix.'

'Come on now, Missus. Relax yourself – let me enjoy this!' He limped in the direction of our former campsite. 'Ha, look at your likkle tracks there!' He turned to look at Wesley. 'Oh, you find your blanket yet? It turn up?'

'Nah,' said Wesley, shaking his head. 'No sign.'

'Shame,' said Felix, linking arms with Audrey. 'I hope it does.' Together, the Braithwaites disappeared into the dark. We quickly followed behind.

As we walked through The Outback, Felix looked up and around at the bushes and trees, but Audrey's eyes remained on the ground, making sure they didn't trip. When the houses on the close and the avenue came into view, Felix chuckled bitterly to himself. 'Look, Audrey,' he said quietly. 'Hell House.'

'Devil's lair!' they whispered dramatically in unison, which made them laugh. They shook their heads, unlinked their arms and reached for each other's hands.

'Aww, they're like characters from a romance novel,' whispered Margot, behind the Braithwaites.

'Who, devils? Are devils into love, then?' said Wesley.

Margot laughed. 'Maybe.'

'What are they on about anyway?' he said quietly. '*Hell House?* I don't like that.

'Which house do you think they mean? What's the bet it's number three, Copsey Close.'

Margot laughed. 'Yeah, that would explain those strange students who live there.' Felix put his arm round Audrey for a moment, kissed her head and then continued holding her hand. 'That is *so* sweet. They've been married for so long – like, half a century. My parents couldn't even do a decade,' Margot said as she shook her head, then sighed. I put my hand on her shoulder.

'I'm sorry about that but – on the bright side – your mum and dad don't argue now, so that's good. Plus, you would never have met us, or be here right now, if they didn't break up.'

'That's true,' said Margot. 'Yay for divorce!'

Wesley shook his head. 'Margot, you're not right in the head.'

'Who is, though?'

He laughed. 'Good point.'

Felix turned to face us. 'Where to next, gigglers?'

'We'll jump in front now,' said Wesley, stepping quickly forward. 'We need to go through the fence and then my house.'

Audrey squeezed Felix's hand tightly. He quickly squeezed hers twice in return. 'You have to small up yourself to get through that gap, Missus. Suck it all up and in now.'

She nudged him with her elbow. 'Hush.'

Margot, Wesley and I twisted ourselves round Wesley's Gap, then held it wide open for them. Felix pushed Audrey forward, and then he followed. Together they stood in Wesley's backyard, and stared up and around the backyards of the houses on the close.

'Wow, it change around here!' Felix said as he craned his neck to look up.

I grabbed Felix's arm and repeatedly tapped my lips. I felt so rude shushing an older person – and someone I respect, too – but I had to. We couldn't get caught now. If Mum saw me standing in Wesley's yard with two old strangers when I'd said I was studying . . . well, the rest of my life wouldn't be worth living. It would be over before I really got going.

Wesley opened his kitchen door. 'This way,' he whispered, ushering us into his house. Audrey gulped, blinked and looked around the room. Wesley's kitchen was silent, but the living room was noisy. Wesley crept quickly up the hallway, with us behind him. He poked his head into the living room, and closed the door round his body.

'You lot all right?' he said, sounding so friendly and fake that I was certain his brothers and sister would know something was going on. With his hands waving behind his back, he gestured us towards his front door.

'Yeah, fine,' said Kayla. 'Why you asking?' she added suspiciously.

'What? I can't check in with my sister without getting sassed?' I heard him say as I opened the door.

'I don't trust you when you're not grumpy,' she said. *Exactly, Kayla*, I silently agreed with her. 'Go back to your girls. I'm doing my homework. Bye.'

Wesley left the room and softly shut his front door, and together the five of us snuck quickly past my house where the curtains were closed in the front window. Margot turned to us and grinned as she opened her door. Her dad's car, as usual, wasn't in their driveway.

BATHING

Wash your worries away!

'Fancy, fancy,' said Felix, inspecting Margot's hallway. 'Very plush, young miss.'

'It's nothing to do with me,' she said, kicking off her shoes, which prompted the Braithwaites to do the same. 'I stay in my room, mostly – it's set up exactly how I like it.'

'Who lives here with you?' asked Audrey, touching the white walls, then rubbing at them furiously when she left a light mark.

'My dad, but barely.'

'Huh,' she said, 'I like it. It's sparse. Fresh.'

Felix put his hand on Audrey's shoulder. 'It's called modern, Missus. Contemporary.'

'That's what Mum said when she saw the photos,' said Margot, walking into the living room. 'When we all lived together, our old house in London was very different – much bigger because we had more stuff. I need *things* around me, I think. Things tell stories about your life, don't they?' Margot reached for a small remote sitting on the mantelpiece. She stepped back and aimed it at the fireplace. Small blue flames appeared over carefully arranged logs.

'Like I said –' Felix pointed at the fireplace before folding his arms – 'fancy.'

'Is it?' she replied. 'They're pretty common.'

'Well, I ain't got one,' said Wesley. I didn't have one either.

Margot shrugged. 'Well, let me show you upstairs anyway. The spare room is all yours. I'll start the first bath to make sure it's nice and hot for you.'

Felix rubbed his hands together, gripping the bannister as he hopped up the stairs behind Margot, the handles of his plastic bag still wrapped round his wrist. Audrey followed, hanging her head and dabbing at her eyes.

Wesley and I watched them go, then sat in the living room and sank into the sofa.

'What's up with Audrey?' he asked quietly. 'She seems super down today.'

'I'm not sure,' I whispered. 'Maybe she thinks we're annoying?'

'Well, *you* are annoying, that's true,' he said. 'But that's not news. She's just *different* this afternoon. Her mood was much better yesterday.'

'We were eating then,' I replied. 'Maybe she's hungry? Or tired? My mum gets snappy when she's both of those things.'

'Ha – same,' said Wesley, cuddling a cushion in front of him. 'Normally.'

'How's your mum?' I said quietly. 'She didn't look too well when we saw her on Saturday.'

'Ah, much better today, thanks. Well, this morning at least. Auntie Molly's taking her to the doctor's tomorrow. I heard them talking about an appointment.'

'Oh, that's good! She'll be on the mend soon, then,' I said, hoping that was true.

Wesley nodded. 'Innit.' He threw his head in the direction of the doorway. 'When do you think Margot's coming back down?' he whispered. 'You reckon I've got time to do a bit more reading?' He rubbed his hands together and wiggled his eyebrows.

'Not funny, Wes,' I said. 'When are you going to tell her what you did?'

'On the thirty-fifth of Nevuary.' He laughed, slapping the sofa with glee. 'I heard that in a song once, and never forgot it. Too good.'

Wesley quickly stopped laughing when we heard Margot's heavy footsteps on the stairs. She popped her head round the doorway – in her arms she held a bundle of the Braithwaites' dirty clothes.

'This *was* a good idea.' She smiled. 'They needed this.'

Just over an hour later, Audrey and Felix sat next to each other on the sofa wearing matching fluffy white dressing gowns. Felix stretched out with his head back and his feet on the coffee table that we sat on the other side of. He sniffed his hands. 'Oh, that cream is *so* good. I smell like them clementines.' He laughed. 'Tasty.'

Audrey wasn't laughing. She sat nervously on the very edge of the sofa, drinking a large mug of milky tea and slowly nibbling at the edge of a biscuit. She squirmed in her seat and stared intently at the fire, deep in thought. The reflection of little blue flames danced in her eyes. I watched her, wondering what was wrong.

Margot stepped into the living room with a plate of steaming buttered toast, which she placed down in front of the Braithwaites. 'Thought you might like this. Tea and toast is simple but great, right? Like a bath,' she said as she grinned at them.

'Yes, lovely,' said Felix. 'Lovely.' He leaned forward, folded a piece of toast in half and stuffed it into his mouth. He followed it with a swig of tea, then sighed with pleasure. He nudged Audrey, taking her out of her trance and towards the toast instead. She nodded, but didn't reach for any.

'Your clothes are in the dryer,' Margot said, joining Wesley and me on the floor. 'They'll be ready soon, and once they're done I'll fold whatever you don't want to wear home. Oh, and I'll pack you what I'm now calling "The Outback Hamper" – that's what we had when we camped out. When we were scared of you!' She laughed. 'That was silly, wasn't it?'

'Yeah.' Wesley nodded. 'You aren't scary *at all*, just awesome.'

Audrey looked up as heavy tears fell down down her brown face and dripped on to her white robe. 'We're not *awesome*, not at all,' she spat. She reached up to pull at her damp grey curls. Her fists turned into small balls and her chest rose and fell. Audrey's quiet crying turned into louder sobs. I said nothing, I had no words. Not yet. I only looked with panic at my friends. They looked back at me and then at Audrey with nervous eyes and open mouths. Felix reached for her leg, grabbing it with his wrinkled hand.

'Missus,' he said gently, leaning forward. 'It's gonna be all right. Come on now – don't cry. Not in front of the children.' He shook her knee. 'Audrey,' he whispered. 'Look at me.'

'I can't, Felix,' Audrey sobbed. 'I can't carry on like this no more.'

CONFIDING

Telling someone you can trust is an absolute must!

'Yes, you can, Missus,' Felix said encouragingly. He pushed the coffee table towards us and kneeled on the floor in front of Audrey. She stared down into her lap and squeezed her hands together, pulling at her fingertips. 'We carry on. It's what we do – who we are,' he said, rubbing her knees.

'Who's *we*? Tell me. Because I'm not *this*. This nah me.' Audrey shook her head. 'Not any more.'

'Audrey, please. Stop. Don't involve them – they're kids.'

'*You* involved them, Felix! We're living a lie; we are liars and they should know the truth.'

Wesley sat back on his heels and Margot covered her mouth. She inched closer towards me, sheltering beside me for comfort and safety. She nudged me, urging me to say or do something, *anything*. My heart raced; the room seemed to shrink in size around me.

'What do you mean by lies?' I asked slowly, staring at the Braithwaites.

Felix laughed nervously. 'Nothing, nothing, Audrey just tired, is all.' He tried to swat our worries away with his hand.

'Tired of living like this, yes,' she said. Her eyes were roaring red. 'And I'm tired of lying.'

'We didn't lie, Audrey,' Felix said quietly. 'We just protect them, that's all.'

Wesley got to his feet and scrambled towards the door. 'Protect us from what?' he shouted. 'Are you going to kill us now? Was that your plan this whole time?'

'Boy! No one's trying to kill you!' said Felix, kissing his teeth. He looked at Audrey, her tears flowing freely.

'Who do you think we are?' she asked.

'Well,' Margot started nervously. 'I think you're Felix and Audrey Braithwaite –' Felix nodded – 'and we think you're inspirational people who are enjoying adventure and trying new things while you still can.'

Audrey shook her head. 'You're wrong. *That's* the lie. We're not the care-free, anything-is-possible bohemians you think we are.'

'Knew it,' said Wesley, his arms slapping his sides. 'Told you they weren't living at the factory for fun, didn't I?' He shook his head. 'Who are you, then?' He raised his voice. '*What* are you?'

'We're scared, tired and living in fear,' Audrey said, wiping her face.

'Of what?' I asked. 'We can figure this out.'

'Let's hear what they say first!' said Wesley, raising his hands towards Margot and me. 'I keep telling both of you that!'

'You can't help,' said Audrey. 'Unless you can stop us being deported.'

Margot gasped and her eyes immediately welled up.

'Audrey . . .' Felix whispered. 'Audrey, why?'

'Deported!' I said, hands shaking, heart thumping, stomach twisting and turning. 'What do you mean? Why? Why do you have to leave the country?'

'We don't know. We don't understand it,' said Felix quietly. 'Not at all. *That's* why we keep moving. Because we have to.'

'Wait,' said Wesley, rubbing his forehead. 'I don't understand. You're not allowed to live in England? Nah, that's wrong, right? Surely you're allowed – you've been here basically forever, right?'

'That's what we thought.' Audrey sighed. 'But one day we got a letter in the post, from the Home Office. It said we were here in England illegally, and we had to go back to Saint Vincent immediately. Me and Felix both looked at it. We were *sure* it was a mistake –'

Felix nodded. 'I thought it was a scam – a fake.'

'So we pushed the letter aside. Put it in the kitchen drawer and forget about it. That was, until the officers turned up at our house –'

'The house we paid for by working in this country our whole lives!' Felix turned to slap the coffee table in front of him and, in doing so, spilled his tea. 'The officers were bang-banging on the door, shouting, carrying on. That's when we knew it was serious. Very serious.'

'What did you do next?' I asked. 'Where did you go?'

'We snatched a few belongings and ran out the back door,' said Felix. 'We got no kids, no family here, so we moved from friend's house to friend's house, until the friends started runnin' out –'

'That's what they do at our age.' Audrey sighed with a shake of her head. 'They pass on.'

'Plus, you can't outstay your welcome and make everyone feel uncomfortable.'

'Or involve them in your mess.' Audrey added.

'We stayed with my best friend, Frisco, for a long, long while. When he died, that broke me. We couldn't even risk going to his funeral.' Felix's eyes filled with tears. 'That was it. That's when we started trying different ways to live – not because it was fun, but because we had no choice. We can't rent or buy another house, because we don't have any papers. Or much money, any more.'

'And we'd be arrested as soon as we tried,' said Audrey, tears re-forming in her eyes.

The room was silent, except for soft sobs from Audrey.

'I'm . . . I'm shocked,' said Wesley. 'And disgusted. No one should force you to go anywhere you don't have to, never. But *why* don't you go back to Saint Vincent? It's warmer than here at least, right?'

'Oh yes, definitely warmer,' said Felix, nodding. 'But it's difficult, because it's all different. We haven't been back there for fifty-odd years. We were children when we left. Children! Audrey was your age. All the friends and family we had are long gone. It's changed. It's still our *home* – sort of – but so is England. They would call me English and say I speak like the queen if I went back now. Imagine that!'

'Why did you leave in the first place?' asked Margot.

'It's a long story,' said Audrey shuffling in her seat and adjusting the cord of her dressing gown. 'I reach England from Saint Vincent when I was eleven. Mommy sent for me.'

Wesley looked at her, confused. 'What does that mean? Being sent for?'

'It means Mommy moved here first, looking for a better life. Back then – between the late 1940s to about 1970-ish – people on the islands were told to go to England –'

'America too,' added Felix.

'Yes, for a better life. There were more opportunities here in this country, to make and save money, and to send some home for your family there. When Mommy was all set up in England, they booked me a flight and told me it was time. I didn't want come here – not one bit. I was so happy in Saint Vincent – climbing trees, falling in them muddy lanes.' She laughed. 'I was doing *so well* in school and I wanted to stay with Auntie Cheryl forever. I remember the day I left like yesterday. In them days, in Saint Vincent, your family could come on the tarmac at the airport to say goodbye. Auntie Cheryl wore her brightest red dress that day. Before I boarded, she hugged me so tight – so tight I thought my stomach was going to jump up and fall out my mouth.'

Audrey smiled at the memory. 'The pilot had to pull me on to the plane, kicking and screaming.'

'Then what?' asked Margot, riveted, just like me and Wesley.

'I got on the plane, and I just press my face against the likkle round window. Auntie Cheryl was jumping, waving, looking so silly. When the plane took off, I stared at her until her bright-red dress became the smallest scarlet dot. Then she just faded away. It was the last time I saw her,' said Audrey. 'She told me I'd make something of myself here.' She laughed bitterly. 'And here I am now.'

'Oh my God,' said Margot. She wiped her eyes with the sleeve of her school jumper. 'Felix,' she sniffed. 'What about you?'

'Pretty much the same story,' he said. 'I was a bit older than Audrey when I arrived. Fourteen. We met at Larch Hill High, but I knew I recognized her face –'

'Turns out we both from the same village,' said Audrey. 'Richland Park.'

Felix chuckled. 'Fancy trotting across the whole globe to find someone from your likkle village in the new big country,' he said, shaking his head. 'Crazy.'

'It means you were meant to be,' said Margot, clasping her hands together.

'That's what I say, don't I, Missus?'

Audrey nodded and Margot beamed.

'Then, when we come of age, we had our small wedding and started working at Chicane.' Felix looked at Wesley. 'With Alan Evans.'

Wesley smiled. 'So *that* was true, then? The stories about my grandad?'

'Oh yes,' said Audrey. 'All of that is the truth.'

'If he was alive, he'd definitely help you,' said Wesley. 'I just know it.'

Felix nodded. 'No doubt he would. Welsh Al would give you the shirt off his very back.' As soon as he said that, he put his hands up. 'But we're not asking you for that – you all have done plenty already.'

SHOCKING

Don't be shocked - keep an eye on the clock!

'No, we haven't,' I said, my voice wavering as I stood up. 'We haven't done *anything* for you *at all.*'

Audrey shook her head. 'You have! You've been kind, friendly, thoughtful. It's been lovely meeting you – it made us less lonely. But, this is grown people's business. It's mine and Felix's problem to fix.'

'It's why we didn't want to tell you too much,' said Felix. He sighed and slumped forward.

'No, it's our problem, too!' I said, folding my arms. 'We have to solve this.'

I bit at my nails – something I rarely do. Under normal circumstances, nail biting is disgusting and a sure-fire route to illness, but nothing about this situation was normal, and I already felt sick. What was happening here to the Braithwaites was cruel and unfair, and there was no way we could sit still and do nothing. We were *the Copseys* – we fix things. We just do.

But, in this serious and very real situation, how could we help? This was beyond badges, and maybe beyond me. Realizing this, the temperature in my body rose a few degrees and I instantly felt the heat in my face. I was angry, furious – not only about the circumstances, but also because I didn't have an immediate answer.

'How are *we* going to solve this though, Josie?' said Wesley. 'What can the three of us *really* do? Against the Home Office?'

'Something. Anything.' I paced up and down Margot's living room and then settled by the bay window and looked out across the close. 'I have to think, research and plan.' I rubbed my temples. 'What would Josephine Holloway do, if she was here right now? What would she think?'

'We could write a letter to the council?' Margot offered. 'Then research to find out if this has happened to anyone else?'

Felix shook his head. 'Please, don't do nothing, you –'

'But that will bring attention, then they'll definitely have to leave,' said Wesley.

'What about the news?' Margot said, rubbing her lip. 'We could call the BBC –'

'Did you not hear what I just said?' Wesley shouted. 'No. Bringing. Attention.'

'Come on, don't get angry with each other now. You're friends, aren't you?' said Audrey.

Wesley shrugged, which made Felix slap his thighs. 'What a mess,' he muttered under his breath. 'Disaster. Everyting we do makes everyting else worse.'

I tried to focus by continuing to stare out of the window. I watched a car driving so slowly up Copsey Close, I wondered if it had taken a wrong turn and had missed the motorway. Its headlights grew brighter and stronger as it approached Margot's house. It then swung round and reversed, lining up directly with the driveway in front of me. Its tail lights shone into the living room.

'Margot . . .' I started.

She jumped to her feet. 'It's my dad. My dad's home!'

Felix and Audrey immediately stood up. Audrey began to clear their mugs from the coffee table, while Felix swept toast crumbs into his palm.

'No, no, leave them, leave it!' said Margot from her hallway. 'Don't worry about that. Quick, come to the kitchen! I'll get your clothes.'

'Stay in there while I figure out a way to get you back through Wesley's Gap and to Chicane,' I said.

Margot's dad switched off his engine and the light in the living room dimmed.

'*Wesley's Gap?*' said Wesley. 'You named the hole in my fence?'

Felix limped into the kitchen with Audrey close behind. Margot pulled their clothes from the dryer and handed the warm, steaming bundle of fabric to them. I grabbed their shoes from the hallway and slid them across the kitchen floor.

'Keep the dressing gowns by the way – Dad has a few of them. He won't miss them.' Margot shut the door and ran back into the living room, towards the window. Wesley and I joined her. We sat on our knees and peered up and out. I clutched the windowsill, digging my nails into it.

We could hear the Braithwaites shuffling in the kitchen, hastily getting dressed, when Margot's dad opened his car door. He stepped out, wearing the smartest suit I'd ever seen on a real person in real life. He held his phone in one hand and a big bunch of keys in the other. He stared at his screen as he walked slowly to the front door.

'Margot,' I whispered, panic rising in my low voice.

Margot glared at her dad through the window, then glanced back at the hallway. We heard the faint, soft sound of her back door closing. 'I think we might be OK,' she said quietly, with relief, her body relaxing. 'He does this thing where he loiters by the door doing emails before he comes in. When he comes in, we have to act natural. Sit on the sofa!'

Wesley leaped on to it, sitting in the spot Felix had just left. He reached for a biscuit and bit at it anxiously. I sat beside him, where Audrey had perched. Margot grabbed the television remote and switched on the TV. She sat by my feet and leaned back on my legs. *The One Show* was on – it always was. This evening – ironically, tragically – they were talking about the increasing rates of homelessness in London at Christmas. I buried my head in my hands. When Margot's dad put his key in the door, Margot twisted her body to look at Wesley and me, and she grinned widely to tell us to act accordingly. It was impossible to return the smile.

'Margot, you home?' her dad's deep voice vibrated through the house. 'Upstairs as usual?'

'No, Dad, we're in the living room,' she replied.

'Hmmm,' he said. We could hear him taking off his shoes in the hallway. 'Good. You fancy that sushi

I promised tonight? Because I have some –' He put his head round the door frame. 'Oh, you have friends here. Hi.' His bald head shone under the hallway light. He pushed his glasses up the bridge of his nose. 'How you doing? You're Josephine and Wesley, right?'

'Yeah, and fine, thanks,' said Wesley.

I looked up at him with a weak smile and nodded. 'Yes, good to see you again, Mr Anderson.'

'Michael, please, and you too,' he said with a smile. He perched next to me on the arm of the sofa. I could smell his aftershave. Musky. 'Nice to see more young people in the house.' He leaned down to touch Margot's shoulder. 'More friends here than in London, you see? It *is* better here.'

Wesley enjoyed this insight into Margot's past. He snorted and stifled a laugh. Margot looked up at Michael, mortified. 'Oh my God, Dad.'

'Why didn't you text me and tell me you had company, Margy? I would have brought home much more food,' he said.

'*Margy*?' Wesley whispered.

'That's fine, we're not staying,' I said wearily. 'We're off soon.'

'Well, next time let me know,' he said, standing up and walking towards the kitchen. I held my breath and kicked Margot with my foot. She leaped to her feet.

'Erm, Dad, where are you going?' She stood between him and the kitchen door. Margot laughed and gripped the handle.

'To get some water and a glass of red wine, like I always do. Why?'

'Let me get it,' she said. She smiled at him. 'You've had a hard day, I'm sure. Go sit down and talk to my friends – you never get to see them.'

'I *did* have a hard one, so that's kind,' he said. He smiled at us and nodded his head towards Margot. 'You're clearly a good influence on her.'

He sat down in the armchair while Margot opened the kitchen door, closing it softly behind her. I looked at Michael, who drummed his fingers rhythmically on the chair's arms. 'Why was your day difficult? What happened?'

'Ah, a complicated and complex case,' he said, gesturing with his hand. 'I can figure it out and get them off on a technicality, but I'm going to need to do a lot of research to understand what's at stake first.' Michael laughed. 'Sorry, that's boring and unclear.'

I sat forward. 'It's not boring at all. What kind of law do you do? Is it anything to do with immigration?' I weaved my fingers together, hoping it was.

'No, insolvency,' he said.

'What's that?' asked Wesley.

'It's all about money – losing it and finding ways to get it back,' he said. 'You interested in law?'

I sat back on the sofa, feeling defeated. 'I was,' I said.

Margot opened the kitchen door and returned to the living room with a glass of sparkling water in one hand and a glass of wine in the other. As she gave her drinks to her dad, she nodded at us.

'There you go, Dad. You can relax now.' She looked at me knowingly. 'The stress of the day has *gone away*.'

REASONING

Think it through before you do!

Before Wesley and I left Margot and Michael to their salmon maki, I took a last look into their empty kitchen. There was no sign, not a single indication that the Braithwaites had been there today. Part of me hoped they actually hadn't been, and the entire evening had been a hallucination – a bad one. But I knew that wasn't true. Of course it wasn't. It was real. Too real. I peered into Margot's yard, past my reflection. Margot doesn't have a gap in her garden – Michael wouldn't allow that to happen and has the money to fix it in a moment – so I felt sick, wondering how Felix and Audrey had managed to get out and go 'home'. They must have climbed over the wooden fence – at their advanced age – then scrambled and limped across the gardens and yards in the close before reaching The Outback. No doubt they were stressed and messier now. Dirtier than before their baths.

Our mission had not been accomplished. It was a complete failure.

We said our goodbyes, and as soon as we were far enough away from the house Wesley grabbed my arm in the doughnut. 'Josephine,' he whispered. He stood close to me, his eyes wide. 'Jo, this whole thing has gone next level. Beyond the Copseys. It's too much now. We *have* to tell someone. It's too big. What you gonna do? What are you thinking?'

'What do you mean what am *I* going to do? What are *we* going to do, you mean? Right?'

'Yeah, yeah.' He scratched his chin. 'Of course. But, come on – you're the one with the ideas. I'm the one who says no. Where are the ideas, Jo? I thought you'd have a plan by now.'

I sighed. 'How, Wesley? How could I have possibly done that? What time have I had?' My shoulders slumped and my arms slapped my sides. 'I don't have anything,' I said. 'Not yet anyway.'

'But you *will* think of something, won't you? You have to! You do know they could be arrested? Or worse!'

'I know, Wesley!' I shouted, throwing my hands in the air. 'You think I don't realize this?' My eyes filled with tears, and I wiped at my nose.

When Wesley took a surprised step back – nearly tripping over the mattress in the doughnut – I knew I was firing my frustration and agitation in the wrong direction. 'Sorry. I'm sorry,' I said. 'But I do know,' I added, more gently this time. I looked behind me towards my house. 'I have to go. They'll be wondering where I am. I'll see you here tomorrow?' Wesley looked at me, concerned. He patted my shoulder awkwardly, but gently, from about a metre away. He then nodded and ran to his house. Wesley looked back at me, before closing his door.

I took a deep breath, crossed the close and let myself in. Inside, I kicked off my shoes, leaving them in a messy pile by the front door.

'Hey – you're just in time, Jo,' Dad shouted down the hall from our kitchen. He leaned over a large, steaming pot, stirring whatever was inside with a wooden spoon. 'I'm about to serve up any minute now.'

'Great, great,' I said quietly, walking through the living room to the dining table. I slumped down heavily into the dining chair next to Mum.

'All right?' she asked, without looking up. She scrolled through her phone with one hand, and picked cherry-tomato halves out of the salad sitting in the middle of the table with the other. I stared down at my hands. I tried to think and to plan, asking myself what Josephine Holloway would do in this situation.

'Yep, yep, now *this* is the one. What do you think, Josie?' Mum said between seedy-red mouthfuls, shoving her phone under my nose. There was a bright-blue baby's car seat on her screen. I looked up at her. 'It's good, right?' She smiled.

None of this mattered to me, or to anyone else but her really, but I pretended to care. 'Wonderful,' I offered flatly.

'What's wrong?' said Mum, pulling away. She looked out at me from the corner of her eye. How could I tell her what the matter was even if I wanted to? I didn't want to share. I couldn't. This was my problem. It was on me to find a solution. I shook my head and said nothing. I looked up at her and smiled, biting my lip to stop it trembling.

Dad weaved his way round us at the dining table, holding the large pot with his oven-gloved hands. He leaned over, setting it down heavily on a placemat next to the salad, which instantly wilted from the heat. He ladled its contents into our bowls. Mushroom risotto. It looked fine, and I'm sure it smelled great, but I couldn't tell. I wasn't hungry now. Who knew if I would ever get my appetite back?

I nodded my thanks at Dad. He looked back at me closely, nodding in return. He snuck a look at Mum, who bit angrily at her lips, but her eyes filled with concern. She stared down at her dinner, and so did I. That was easier for everyone. It was for the best.

I picked up my fork and poked at the rice. As I put it to my lips to taste and to be polite to my parents, questions about Felix and Audrey raced through my mind. Did they make it to Chicane? How? Are they eating tonight? Do they even have food? Did we eat it all yesterday? The biggest, most important question was, of course: what am I going to do? I had no answers, not for any of those questions. My eyes burned, stung and welled with tears.

The moment I tasted the risotto, I knew my dad had made it with love and care. I was reminded of how lucky I was to be with my family, knowing that I was safe and secure; that I could sleep in a comfortable bed and have a shower in the morning without worry; that however annoyed my mum might be with me – and me with her – she would still be there for me, whatever happened. No matter what, I had people I could rely on. The Braithwaites didn't. This realization burned my chest. Boiling tears rolled down my face. I quickly tried to wipe them away. I didn't want my parents to see me cry.

'Jo, why are you crying?' asked Dad, grabbing my hand. Too late. 'What's going on? You don't like your dinner?'

Mum put her fork down. 'It's not the dinner, is it, Pat? It's the car seat, isn't it? It's her brother.' She looked over at me. 'Josie, I thought we had moved past this.'

I wished either of the Braithwaites had a brother – someone, anyone, they could turn to today without fear. I burst into more tears at that thought. 'I'm sorry,' I sobbed between breaths. 'Can I be excused, please?' I didn't wait for a response. I pushed myself away from the table and ran up the stairs to my room.

I sat at my desk and threw open my laptop. *Think, Josephine, think!* I urged myself, but I didn't know where to start or where to search. The only results I produced were more tears, which fell in fat drops on to the black keys.

There was a knock at my door, and before I could say 'come in' my dad pushed it open. He sighed at my puffy face and red eyes, then sat down on the bed. 'You need to talk?' he asked, smoothing my duvet. 'Because I think we need to. This –' he waved his hands at me, and around the room – 'has got to stop.' I swallowed and looked at my screen. I put my head in my hands.

'Dad,' I said, between my fingers, 'how and why do good things end up turning out so bad?'

I could feel his concern without seeing his face. 'You in trouble?' The volume of his voice rose at least two levels.

I spun round in my chair. 'No, *I'm* not. Not yet, anyway.'

'This about Wesley's mum? Have you spoken to him?'

'No.'

'Your brother, then?'

I paused for a moment. 'No. Not really,' I said, knowing it partly was.

'Well, what is it? You can't carry on like this, Jo.'

I shook my head. 'I know, Dad, but I can't tell you,' I whispered. 'It might make it worse.'

'Why is it so bad, then?' he asked. 'Can you at least tell me that?'

'Because it's not *fair*, Dad! None of it is.'

Dad narrowed his eyes and stood tall. 'This *is* about the baby, isn't it? Life just isn't fair, Jo – I'm sorry to say that, but there it is. It also doesn't always revolve around you and what *you* want –'

'This isn't about *me*, Dad!' I shouted. 'You've got it wrong!'

'– and you have to think of others, talk with others. They can help! *We* can help.'

'I do, and I know!' I said. I raised my hands in frustration.

He stood up. 'Well, if you know that, then you have to do better,' he said. 'Better than this.' He closed the door and I burst into tears.

SHARING

A problem shared is a problem halved?

I'm comfortable admitting I cried a lot last night. So much so that my face was still swollen in the morning. After a hot shower and dressing for school, I splashed cold water over my red, puffy eyes. I stared at myself in the bathroom mirror, studying my reflection. This morning, I didn't like what looked back at me. I saw a girl – one without a firm answer to the question of the Braithwaites' uncertain future. A girl jealous of a *baby* and what his birth would bring – and mean – for her. A girl too proud to ask her friends and family for help and support.

My stomach knotted as I walked down the stairs. I skipped breakfast and saying good morning, goodbye or anything in between to my parents. I chose the doughnut instead, and headed straight

275

there. Overnight someone – or something – had performed magic. It wasn't me, or anything I had done but, of course, I wish it had been. It hadn't even crossed my mind to do it. The mattress – Wesley's budget bouncy castle – had disappeared from the centre of the doughnut. Gone. I was pleased to see it go, but I knew Wesley would be sad.

Wesley's and Margot's front doors opened at about the same time and they ran down their driveways, rushing to meet me in the middle. We nodded our good mornings and began walking towards Copsey Avenue.

Margot grabbed at my arm. 'I couldn't sleep last night, Jo. I'm so scared and nervous for the Braithwaites.'

'Me too.' I nodded. 'It was hard to concentrate last night. I didn't feel great.'

'Yeah, you look a bit rough,' said Wesley, looking me up and down.

'Thanks,' I said. 'But I did do a bit of research. This has happened to other people – Felix and Audrey aren't alone in fighting for their right to stay in the country.'

Margot shook her head. 'This is awful.'

'We need to work out the ways we can prove they are allowed to live here,' I said. 'And speak to a lawyer – one specializing in immigration. But I don't know how yet, or how to pay for it.' I smiled weakly at them. 'We'll earn our investigating and lawyering badges in the process, but for now we should keep it to ourselves until the plan is ready.'

Margot and Wesley quickly glanced at each other. Wesley tutted. 'See what I mean?' he said quietly.

Margot stared at the concrete and shifted on her feet. 'Wes, no.'

'*Wes?*' I said. 'Since when have you called him Wes? What's going on?'

'Nothing, nothing,' said Margot, shaking her head. 'So, I haven't done this yet – I wanted to check with everyone first – but Dad could help. Immigration is not his area, I know, but I could talk to him and he'll know someone.' She smiled at me. 'He loved that you were interested in law, by the way.'

I shook my head. 'No. I think for now the idea I keep coming back to is –' I sighed. 'Is to just keep being helpful and quiet. Keep visiting, and keep taking things that make them comfortable and cheerful.'

'Are you *serious?*' Wesley exploded.

'Wes!' Margot said. 'Don't!'

'*That's* your idea?' he said. 'Doing basically nothing but earning badges? That's all you care about? Your plan for *the Copseys*?' he spat.

I instantly stopped walking and stared at Wesley. The three of us huddled together at the end of the close. 'No, no!' I demanded. 'And it's not doing nothing! It's something. It's the best I've got right now. What do *you* want to do?'

Wesley scratched his forehead and rubbed his eyebrows. 'I dunno, but not *that*. It's not enough, but this is still too much for me, and Margot too.'

I swung my head to look at her. 'What?'

'It does feel beyond our control,' Margot whispered.

'Look,' said Wesley. 'I only got involved in this Copsey business for a little fun break from home stuff – but, now, being there is easier than having *this* weighing on me. The stress is starting to physically hurt!' He rubbed his stomach. 'I can feel the fear crawling about in my guts,' he groaned.

'Wesley,' I said quietly. 'We'll figure it out.' I put my hand on his shoulder.

'See, I don't think we will, though,' he said softly. 'That's the thing.' He looked in my eyes. 'We have to tell someone, Josie. ASAP. Come on – you must know that? You gotta know your limits. We can't keep this a secret, not for much longer. It's bigger than us. Bigger than your badges.'

I bit my lip to stop it trembling. 'We will figure it out, I promise,' I pleaded. 'Just give me one more day to think, then we can tell someone and get help. Please?'

Wesley sighed, and rolled his eyes.

'Look, in the meantime, at school today, let's go to lost property and see if we can find anything worth taking to Chicane – along with anything from home. We'll go after school, and talk to Felix and Audrey about what to do next.' I looked at my friends. 'Deal?'

Wesley closed his eyes and sighed. He turned to kick the mattress, but of course it wasn't there. 'Fine,' he huffed. 'I don't like it, but fine.'

Margot nodded. 'OK, deal.' She looked at Wesley. 'See, that went well.'

I stood still and raised my hands. 'Wait. What do you mean "*That went well*"? Have . . . have you been talking about me behind my back?'

They looked at each other so cautiously that I knew they had. Margot took a deep breath. 'Yes, but not really – it was nothing bad. Last night, after you left mine –'

'I texted Margot because I was stressed about the situation – and you, innit,' said Wesley with a shrug. 'It ain't a big deal.'

'Not at all,' said Margot.

It was to me. 'Right. So, you're friends now, and talking about me?' I asked, feeling hurt, vulnerable and angry. 'Great. That explains why you keep agreeing with each other.'

'But I thought you wanted us to be friends?' Margot asked. 'Sometimes Wes makes good points.'

'*Good points?*' I spat, feeling my anger rising but not entirely sure why. 'Like what?' I demanded.

'Well, for one, I could tell Margot wasn't loving the idea of you leaving us in Chicane after she buckled –'

'I was never leaving you, I –'

'– *or* when you wanted to give our money from Mr Kirklees to Mr King for the Christmas party. To basically make yourself look good – because, let's be real, that's what that was. And you're heated about your baby brother, cos you're selfish and jealous.'

My eyes narrowed and my temperature rose. 'Is that right, Wesley?'

'Yep,' he said. 'It is. You need to move from *me* –'

he poked my chest – 'to *we*.' He opened his arms widely.

I felt sick at his words, and angry because part of me felt he might be right. 'Well,' I said, not knowing exactly where this was going, but feeling it wasn't anywhere good. 'Did *you* have a good point when you read Margot's notebooks on Sunday?' I smiled smugly, but I didn't feel smug. I felt terrible. I felt hurt, stung to the core.

Margot's mouth hung open in shock. 'What? You *did* what?'

Wesley looked at her with big bugged-out eyes. 'Josie, what the *hell*? I'm sorry, Margot. I am sorry. Your coloured room hypnotized me and I –'

'What did you read?' she asked, panicked. 'What did you see?' Margot glared at me. 'I write about a lot of things in those books – things I can't and don't want to talk about.' She raised her eyebrow, so I was sure what she meant. I knew instantly. She'd been writing about Wesley's mum.

'Can't remember, really,' he said. 'Something religious. It was good, though. And now I don't think you're a spy, so that's cool, right?'

'It's not cool at all.' Margot spun on her heels to stare at me. 'Why didn't *you* tell me, Jo?' she shouted.

It was the first time I'd ever heard Margot raise her voice.

'Yeah, why *did* you tell her?' said Wesley also glaring at me. He clenched his fists in anger.

'I . . . I . . .' I said, my eyes filling with tears.

Mr Kirklees, who had just opened his front door, shouted to us from his front yard. Brian trotted towards Wesley.

'Children! Children!' he said, leaning on his gate. 'It's too early for anger! What's wrong?' He gestured towards the close. 'I thought you'd be pleased I got rid of that mattress for you. I don't like mess – things being where they don't belong frustrates me.'

Wesley breathed heavily, his eyes burning through me. 'I'm gonna tell him,' he said through gritted teeth, jerking his head in Mr Kirklees's direction. 'For my health and whatever *that* just was.' He stomped across the street then bent down to pet Brian, who wagged his tail appreciatively.

'No, wait, don't,' shouted Margot, eyeing Mr Kirklees with suspicion. 'It doesn't matter. I'm over it.'

'Tell me what?' asked Mr Kirklees, confused.

Margot and I crossed the road and I stepped in front of my possibly-former friends and laughed lightly. Unconvincingly. 'Ah, Wesley didn't get a good night's sleep,' I said. I put my hand down across his shoulder and tried to turn him away. 'He's a bit tired.'

'I'm not tired! I ain't a baby.' He shrugged out of my hug and stood up. '*You're* the one that's tired – look at you! Me? I'm upset!' He held his chest, and tears formed in his eyes. Mr Kirklees gave me a confused look, and I shook my head to try to stop him from asking further questions.

'Wesley, please don't,' I whispered gently. 'I'm sorry.'

Wesley began to cry. 'Mr Kirklees,' he said, breathlessly. 'Our friends are homeless and in big trouble!'

My shoulders slumped, and I threw my head towards the sky, wishing the plane passing by could just land, collect me and take me anywhere else but here.

'Stop, stop,' said Margot, reaching for his elbow. Wesley twisted his body away from her, too.

'They've been living in Chicane over there.' He pointed. 'Because they're actually going to get deported! They don't deserve that – they need help. That factory is a *disaster*. It's falling apart. It's no place to live.'

I buried my face in my hands. 'Wes, stop,' I pleaded between my fingers.

Mr Kirklees winced. 'Oh no, that's terrible! Terrible indeed,' he said, drawing breath between his teeth. 'How old are your friends? Can they go home to their parents? Do you know their family?'

'No!' said Wesley, shaking his head. 'That's the thing – they don't have family. Their parents are long dead. They're old – like, your age.' He looked at the concrete. 'Sorry, but you know what I mean.' Mr Kirklees smiled gently and nodded. 'They used to work there – in Chicane – years ago. They were even friends with my grandad Alan who worked with them.'

Mr Kirklees stumbled backwards and leaned on his garden wall. His hand covered his mouth. 'My goodness,' he said. 'This is shocking. Appalling!' His eyes darted between the three of us, then he pointed with his finger curled. 'I . . . I can help you.' 'There are definitely some things I can do to help your friends. Come by after school and let's talk then.'

Wesley breathed a deep sigh of relief, which seemed to instantly lift the weight of his worries from his shoulders. He leaned against the wall next to Mr Kirklees and stroked Brian. 'Thank you,' he said. 'Thank you both so much!' Wesley looked at me and nodded his head towards Mr Kirklees, suggesting I also express my gratitude, but I didn't want to. This situation here was the exact opposite of what should have happened – the plan was now completely out of my hands and my friends were mad with me. None of this felt good. I glanced over at Margot, who was looking at me with a raised eyebrow and also waiting for my reaction.

I swallowed hard. 'We appreciate that, Mr Kirklees. That's very kind of you.' I smiled, but I knew it didn't reach my eyes.

SCAVENGING
Dig deeper, dig it out!

The rest of our walk to school was awkward, tense and silent. I replayed Wesley's words over and over in my head. *From me to we.* My friends thought I was selfish, and so did my parents. They thought that everything I did – every choice I made – benefited me and my needs first and foremost. Margot wore a disappointed look on her face, and mostly stared at the pavement. Wesley was brighter; his backpack bounced on his shoulders as we walked. He glanced over at me, but when he caught my eye he looked away, kissing his teeth. The fabric of the Copseys was coming apart at the seams. I had to mend this. It was up to *me* to make us *we* again, ironically.

'Margot, Wesley,' I said. 'I'm sorry.'

'Are you, though?' said Wesley.

'Yes, I am,' I said. 'I just wish you hadn't told Mr Kirklees –'

'See?' he said, raising his hands. 'You're not sorry. You're only sorry for yourself, because you're not in charge of everything and everyone. I wish you hadn't told Margot that I read her book either, but here we are.' He turned to Margot. 'Again, I *am* sorry about that. That wasn't cool.'

'It's . . . whatever,' said Margot, but I knew she was hurt by both of us. I shook my head and turned away. I didn't want them to see my tears.

'Oi, oi!' said Bobby behind us. He ran forward and stood between Margot and me. I could feel him turn his head to look at me, and then he glanced at Wesley and Margot. 'It's well frosty over here and I'm not chatting about the weather. What the matter?' We didn't answer. 'Ooh, it's like that, is it? The upbeat do-gooders are feeling down?'

'No!' Margot snapped. 'We're fine.'

'Doesn't sound or look like it.'

'We're just working things out,' I said.

'Are we?' Wesley snorted.

'I hope so,' I whispered.

'Innit,' said Bobby. 'I want all the goss, but I don't like seeing you lot like this. It's sad. Weird.'

He was right. It was.

'Cheer up! Go back to how you were yesterday – thinking of nice things to do for people, innit. That's more your energy than this.' He shook his head, and ran into the playground. He put his arms round Kelly Marshall and Jenny Lui, and leaned into their conversation. They shrugged him off and walked away.

Margot sighed. 'Bobby has a point,' she said. 'I'd rather be positive than be fighting.'

'Me too,' I said. 'And I *am* sorry. I really mean that. I'm going to think about what you said, and do better. I promise.'

'OK,' said Margot. 'No more secrets?'

I nodded. Wesley kicked at the gravel. 'Fine.' He raised his eyebrows in my direction. 'So what's the plan, then? Because I know you have one.'

I took a deep breath. 'Well, I have a suggestion. It's the same as before – lost property, the Braithwaites, Mr Kirklees. Then, if he doesn't help, we tell someone else.'

Wesley and Margot nodded, and the air instantly felt lighter.

Although we'd made up, we barely spoke to each other all day. We needed time apart. Margot kept her nose in her notebook, and Wesley played tag with Bobby and the others at both breaks. I thought about how I could do better – be a better friend, a better daughter, a better sister. I thought about Josephine Holloway, who, if she knew me, would probably be shaking her head at my selfishness, because that's what it was, partly. When Mr King asked me at lunchtime if everything was all right, I couldn't answer. I just looked at him until he walked away. I thought about what he said to me last week about thinking of consequences, and buried my face in my hands.

When the bell rang after school, I tried my best to cheer up and think positively. We headed towards the Oaken Road exit. The plan was to pay a visit to caretaker Jim's office-cum-broom cupboard. Margot knocked on his door, but there was no answer.

'Perfect,' she said, reaching for the handle and twisting it to open the door.

'It's not locked?' I said, surprised. 'That's not safe. There are chemicals in there.'

'He's probably just bounced for a second, so we'd better be quick with this,' said Wesley, looking back down the corridor towards our classroom.

Jim's cupboard was dark and smelled vaguely of cigarette smoke. We stared up at the floor-to-ceiling shelves, which were stacked with huge school-sized bottles of various cleaning fluids. Margot ran her fingers across a giant bottle of washing-up liquid. She tried to lift it.

'I don't think we need that, Margot,' I said. 'Let's find the bin bags and go.'

'Straight to lost property?' said Margot.

I nodded. 'Yep.'

We looked up, down and along the shelves, until Wesley spotted them. 'There!' He pointed.

I stood on my toes and pulled the black plastic roll off the shelf. I unfurled it, tore off one big bag each for Margot and Wesley, and took one for myself.

'Right, next stop,' I said, stepping out of the office. Margot and Wesley followed, and I closed the door behind us.

'Oh my gosh,' whispered Margot, grabbing my arm and digging her nails into it. 'She's coming.'

I knew the 'she' Margot was refering to.

Mrs Herbert, our head teacher, was striding towards us.

'Excuse me!' she said, walking quickly and pointing her finger towards us. 'What do you think you're doing? You're not supposed to be in that room – it's out of bounds for children!' Her high heels clacked loudly in the corridor.

Wesley opened his mouth to speak, but I jumped in. I thought quickly. 'Hello, Mrs Herbert!' I said.

'Josephine. Explain,' she said, so close to my face I could tell she'd just had coffee.

I slightly turned my face away, and saw Wesley and Margot staring at me, waiting for a solution to this problem. This time, I had one. I looked up at her and smiled. 'Hi, Mrs Herbert. We just wanted to surprise Jim by doing some litter-picking this afternoon. We went to grab some bags,' I said, raising my sack to show her. Margot and Wesley did the same. 'After we saw him cleaning up the fireworks the Larch Hill High students set off last week, we wanted to help. Didn't we?'

Wesley and Margot nodded. 'It's outrageous how hard he has to work,' said Margot. 'He deserves a pay rise.'

Mrs Herbert stepped back, stared at us and then smiled. 'Oh, I see. That's very nice, very kind of you,' she said, nodding. 'Very thoughtful. Jim will appreciate it – but next time you *must* get permission, understand? That cupboard is *not* for you.'

'Of course, Mrs Herbert,' I said. 'Sorry about that.'

'This time – and this time only – it's fine,' she said, waving us away with her hand.

'Thanks, miss,' Wesley shouted as we ran to the exit. He reached for my elbow. 'Nice one, Josie.'

I smiled at him and nodded. My confidence was returning.

'Hang on,' whispered Margot. 'Do we have to actually litter-pick, now?'

I smiled. 'No, we've earned that badge –'

'Don't start.' Wesley laughed.

'– but lost property is a bust. We'll just have to see what we can get from home instead.'

I opened my front door, and without closing it – or taking my shoes off – I ran straight to the kitchen. I threw open the cupboards and the fridge. Any jar, can or packet that was unopened went into the sack.

'Jo, come here!' Mum shouted from the living room – from the sofa, I'm sure. 'We need to talk about last night,' she said.

'Can't right now, Mum!' I shouted back. 'But definitely later – there are some things I need to say.' I filled the bag, but not too much. I needed to be able to carry it. Glass jars clinked against each other inside.

'What you doing in there? Why you taking all our food? I still have cravings – leave some!'

'I'm . . .' I thought on my feet. 'I'm collecting for the harvest festival at school. I forgot about it.'

'Hmmm,' said Mum. 'But wait – that was October, wasn't it? It's coming up to Christmas! That school's always begging for something,' she muttered. 'That place has gone from Larch Hill to downhill.'

'Yeah, I know! They're doing it again,' I said, heading to the front door with the bag clattering. 'I have to get this all back in time!' I shut the door behind me and ran to Wesley's.

I knew I was right to not overfill my bin bag. Watching both Margot and Wesley struggle across The Outback, over the river and up the stairs with theirs was amusing. A break from the seriousness of the situation. I bit my smiles away as best as I could. I didn't want them to think I was smug – not now. We were just repairing our friendship.

'Laugh it up now,' said Wesley, noticing. 'But you'll feel bad later when the Braithwaites think you're stingy.'

'No, they won't!' I said hopefully. 'They'll understand.' I knocked on the meeting room's door, and, looking underneath it, I noticed it was dark inside. 'Audrey? Felix?' I said quietly. 'Are you there?' I reached for the handle and pushed the door open.

Audrey and Felix were in there, sitting on their armchairs. They held hands across the gap between them. The room was lit only by the light from the screen of their fuzzy, snowy old television. Audrey looked up, surprised to see us.

'You're back?' she said.

'You're here!' I said, relieved. 'We were worried.'

Wesley nodded. 'Really worried.'

Margot squinted at Felix and Audrey. 'I can barely see you,' she said. 'What happened to your light?'

Felix laughed. 'Never again. That light was the source and start of all the problems.'

'Tell me about it,' muttered Wesley.

'Best we keep it off,' said Audrey.

Wesley patted his body, searching for something. 'Well, I brought you this,' he said, pulling a light bulb from his jacket pocket. He stepped over to the lamp on the other side of the room and peered at the empty fitting. 'Ah, it is the right one, thank God!' He screwed the bulb into its socket, and flicked the lamp switch on with his foot. The Braithwaites' living room was bathed with warm, cosy light.

Margot's shoulders relaxed. 'See now, that's much better,' she said with a sigh. 'That works.'

Now that the room was bright, we could see something wasn't right with Felix. He sat in his armchair – still wearing his new dressing gown – but breathing deeply and wincing, like he'd just finished a run. I looked down at his left leg. It was swollen, bruised, scratched and bloody.

'What happened?' I said, dropping my sack noisily on the floor and causing the contents inside to crash together. I walked towards him and kneeled by his side.

'I should ask you the same,' he said. 'Bringing them loud bags up here. You brought your rubbish? Chicane not messy enough for you?' Felix tried to laugh, but it hurt him to do so. He breathed through tight teeth and closed his eyes.

'It's just some bits for you,' said Margot softly. 'But we can look at them later. What's wrong, Felix?'

'Ah.' He sighed, dismissing us with his hand. 'No big deal, no big deal. Took a likkle tumble on the way back after my bath – which was *delightful*, young miss. Thanks.'

'We had to take the scenic route, didn't we?' said Audrey quietly. 'And this is the consequence.' I stared at his leg. I swear I could see it pulsating.

'Must have taken you ages to get up the stairs,' said Wesley.

Felix nodded. 'A whole twenty-four hours.'

'Seriously?' asked Wesley.

'Of course not!' Felix laughed, coughing and holding his chest.

The three of us shared awkward, concerned looks. 'How badly does it hurt?' asked Margot. Audrey glanced at Felix, and then stared at the floor.

'Only a bit,' he said. 'I'll be all right – it's just a knock and scratch.'

I stopped looking at Felix's leg, and looked into his eyes instead. 'You need some help,' I said quietly. 'Medical help.'

'No, no!' Felix tried to stand up, but immediately fell backwards into his chair, which slipped on the rug. He coughed and closed his eyes. Audrey stared at him, and sighed.

This was serious. I bit my nails, waiting for an idea. 'What if we bring you some medicine as soon as we can? I didn't pack any – did you?' Wesley and Margot shook their heads. 'OK – tomorrow, then. We're going to fix this, all of this. We promise.'

'We've told you: you don't need to help, you really don't,' said Audrey quietly. 'It's best to stop now and –'

'No, we can't – we can't leave you like this. We'll find some painkillers –'

'And we'll get some advice,' said Wesley. 'Tomorrow will be better, definitely. Things will change.'

TRUSTING

Knowing who - and when - to trust is an absolute must!

My mind was on Felix – and the condition of his leg – as our footsteps crunched on the short gravel path leading to Beechwood, Mr Kirklees's house. I glanced at the concrete around it, and into his flower beds. The rubbish we'd got rid of last week had started to return; the broken bottles and crinkled wrappers were back. I looked up at his racing-green front door. As we stood on the concrete step under a cold white porch light, I wished Wesley wouldn't reach out and bang the brass knocker against the peeling wood. I didn't want to talk to Mr Kirklees. Not yet.

When Wesley stretched for the knocker, I bit my thumbnail, then quickly put my arm out to stop him.

'Wes, wait,' I whispered. 'Are you *sure* about this?' I asked because I wasn't. 'I don't think Felix and Audrey would want this,' I said, knowing they definitely wouldn't.

Wesley slapped my hand away. 'Yeah, I am. Didn't you see the state of Felix's leg? It was . . . moving.'

I nodded. 'Of course I did.'

'It's not gonna help their situation at all, is it?'

'No, but –'

'You know they're never going to ask for help, don't you? They're like you – too proud.' He slammed the knocker hard against the door. Inside the house, Brian barked. 'So I'm doing it for them. For us, too – my stomach, especially.'

I sighed. 'OK, Wesley.' Padded footsteps approached the door from the other side.

'Telling someone is the right thing, Josie,' said Margot. 'But, yeah,' She pointed at the door. 'I don't know about him either.'

'Just when I was starting to think you were decent, Margot,' said Wesley, rolling his eyes.

'It's shallow to say, but something just isn't right about his teeth,' Margot shuddered.

'Not this again,' Wesley muttered.

The door opened slowly. We saw Brian before we saw Mr Kirklees. He jumped on Wesley, wagging his tail.

'Why is that dog so sexist?' Margot moaned under her breath, making Wesley laugh.

Mr Kirklees's face appeared. 'Hello, children,' he said, smiling warmly, showing us his clean, bright teeth. Margot shuddered. 'You all feeling more positive this afternoon?'

I stayed silent.

'Much better, yeah,' said Wesley. 'Thanks!'

'Very glad to hear it, very glad. Come on, come in, then,' he said, ushering us into the dark-red, high-ceilinged hallway. 'I've been looking forward to this afternoon – I made some small cakes to cheer you up.'

Wesley grinned, removing his shoes. 'Oh yeah? What kind of cakes?'

Mr Kirklees chuckled. 'You'll find out. I hope you have space for a snack.'

'Always!' said Margot, looking up and around at the hallway.

Mr Kirklees smiled and looked at me. 'Are you well? You're very quiet,' he said gently.

'Yes,' I lied. 'I'm fine, thank you.'

Mr Kirklees nodded and stepped in front of me to throw open a tall pair of brown wooden doors. 'Come on, let's sit down and talk.' He walked into his living room, with Brian trotting by his feet.

Mr Kirklees's old-fashioned front room was a world away from any of ours – and the Braithwaites'. It was very large and opulent. If you googled old money and then clicked on images, I'm certain you'd see this room on the first page. The walls were split horizontally in half, with rich red flock wallpaper at the top and polished wood panels at the bottom. Portraits of various sizes featuring horses, farmhouses, fancy people in front of country estates and vintage cars in gilded frames were fixed to the walls. There was a floor-to-ceiling bookcase, full of leather-bound books. Between the books and dotted around the room were little lamps with stained-glass shades – all of them switched on – which made the room feel like a library you see on television. There was a pair of armchairs by the window, with a small table between them and a bowl of apples sitting on top. Mr Kirklees sat in a chair with dark-brown wooden legs that looked slightly scuffed, but in a way that made it look expensive, rather than ready for repair. There was a long racing-green leather sofa adjacent to him, with pushed-in buttons along its back. Mr Kirklees gestured us towards it. As we walked into the room, our feet sank into the deep carpet with each step.

Wesley sat down and looked around the room. Brian leaped into his lap, and licked his face. 'Wow, I like your house,' he said, pushing the dog's face away from his. 'Very plush.'

Margot looked around. 'It reminds me of my old house.'

Wesley spun his head to stare at her. 'Does it?'

She nodded. 'A bit, yeah.'

'Hmmm.' Wesley nodded. 'Explains a lot.'

Margot rolled her eyes.

Mr Kirklees smiled. 'Thank you, I rather like it too. So much so, I've never really lived anywhere else.'

'That's incredible.' Margot leaned forward on her elbows. 'You must have seen lots of changes around here . . .'

'Oh yes!' he said. 'It was *very* different here when I was a boy – very different indeed. Clean and tidy, with everything and everyone in its right place. How it's supposed to be.' He looked wistfully out of his front window. He smiled. 'You know, when my father was your age, this house, Beechwood, was the *only* one on Copsey Avenue. One of the only houses for many miles. It was mostly farms and the families who owned them then.'

'Really?' I said, actually interested.

He nodded. 'So I was told. Father used to say there was nothing but trees and the river. I, of course, don't remember that. I wasn't there, ha! I came along much later, but I know I would have *loved* it.'

'Sounds a bit boring to me,' said Wesley. 'I like things, and stuff happening. You know, buildings, people, the sound of traffic –'

Mr Kirklees smiled. 'Traffic *is* comforting, I'll accept that,' he said. 'You know, without your close in the way, I could see Chicane Cars in all its glory from this window right here.'

I leaned back. 'Well, I'm sorry,' I said. 'We ruined your view and didn't even know it.'

Mr Kirklees barked a short laugh. 'Ha! *View?* No, I was just interested in what went on in there. I loved cars and driving,' he said, looking out of the window. 'Found it fascinating.' He coughed to clear his throat. 'Anyway, before we get down to business, let me fetch the refreshments, hmmm?' He put his hands on his knees and stood up. 'Just a moment.' He ambled out of the room.

I turned to my friends. 'You all right?' I asked. 'It's not too late to leave if you want to.'

'Nah, I'm not leaving,' said Wesley, stroking Brian. 'I love it here. Might ask Mr Kirklees if I can move in.'

Margot wrinkled her nose. 'I wouldn't,' she said. 'It's kind of musty.'

'You're musty.' He laughed, snuggling into the sofa. 'You both are.'

I sighed and sat back.

'Ready for cake?' said Mr Kirklees, stepping into the room. He held a silver tray full of tiny cakes in paper cases in his hands.

Wesley leaned over to me. 'Mr Kirklees or Mr Kipling, eh? Those cakes haven't been baked today – these ain't nothing but shop-bought French fancies,' he whispered, which made me snort with laughter. I covered my mouth to stop it escaping. but Mr Kirklees heard. He narrowed his eyes slightly but smiled. He plonked the tray heavily on the table in front of us, which made the small cakes topple over and crash together. He left the room and returned moments later with another tray, this one carrying a pot of tea, small cups, a bowl of cubed sugar and a little jug of milk. He pushed the bowl of apples on the table to one side and gently placed the tea tray down.

'Tea?' he said. We nodded and he poured hot liquid into china cups, adding milk and sugar for us before passing them over. 'So.' He sighed. 'Back to this morning.' He looked at Wesley sympathetically.

'You looked desperately sad, young man. I've felt terrible for you all day.'

'I was, I was,' said Wesley. 'And thank you, it felt much better getting it off my chest.'

'I'm sure,' said Mr Kirklees. 'Better out than in, that's what Mother used to say. So, tell me about your friends.' He settled into his chair. 'Did you see them today? Are they in good spirits?'

Wesley sat back and cupped his tea. 'Well, Felix and Audrey –'

I winced at Wesley sharing their names.

'Felix and Audrey?' said Mr Kirklees, sitting forward slightly.

Wesley nodded. 'Braithwaite, yeah,' he said.

I shook my head.

Mr Kirklees sat back, stroked his chin with concern and covered his mouth. 'All right . . . and how are they?'

Margot sighed. 'Not great. Felix is hurt and definitely needs a doctor.'

'Good Lord, really? This is *tragic*. It just gets worse.' He lifted his hip and dug underneath the cushion of his chair. He pulled out a small notebook with a pen attached to it by a small elastic loop. 'All right, Felix and Audrey Braithwaite. Need medical help desperately.' He drummed his pen to his lip.

'I do know a discreet doctor who may be brave enough to enter the building.' He looked down and made intense notes in his book.

'Are Felix and Audrey married, or are they siblings?'

'Married,' said Margot. 'They're a beautiful couple.'

'Do they have any children who can help them?'

'Only us,' said Wesley.

Mr Kirklees smiled. 'And what helpful children you are. They'll be as proud of you as I am, I bet.' He stared at his notes. 'Do you know exactly where they're from?'

'An island called Saint Vincent,' said Wesley.

'Oh – not Jamaica, then?' he said.

I narrowed my eyes and spoke up. 'No, not Jamaica. There *are* other islands in the Caribbean.'

'Of course there are.' He chuckled. 'I know the Caymans. Lovely place.' He snapped his book shut and slipped it back in the gap between the arm and the cushion of his seat. 'I think I have everything I need, now.' He looked out of the window. 'Oh, but you don't!' He turned to us. 'Not yet.'

I sat forward. 'What? What do you mean?'

'Just wait,' he said. He pointed at Wesley. 'You'll like this, young man.'

GIFTING

Your presence is also a great present!

Mr Kirklees shuffled to the other end of his living room. 'Shut your eyes, now,' he said. 'No peeking.' Wesley and Margot obeyed, but I didn't. I watched Mr Kirklees bend down and gather fabric into his arms. 'Ta da!' he said. Draped over his arm was a clean, pressed, folded blanket. Wesley gasped, standing up from the sofa, walking towards him.

'My . . . my quilt?' Wesley stammered. 'How? Where?' He reached for it and unfurled it into the room. He peered closely at it, running his fingers over his stitched name, and buried his grateful face in its folds. Margot's gentle murmur of appreciation broke Wesley's moment. He remembered where he was, and who was watching. Embarrassed, he quickly wrapped the quilt into a messy bundle and held it in his arms.

'Ha, I *knew* this belonged to you.' Mr Kirklees laughed. 'Go on, take it!'

Margot nudged me. 'Ahh, *that's* why Brian likes Wesley so much.'

'He could smell him.' I nodded. 'Makes sense.'

'Thank you, Mr Kirklees. Thank you!' he said. 'I thought it was long gone.'

'I hope you don't mind me cleaning it. Couldn't possibly give it back to you in the mucky state I found it in.'

'Where did you find it?' I asked. 'We looked everywhere.'

'I was taking my regular morning walk with Brian here, following the Lea – I do like that walk – and there it was, all scrunched up with muddy little footprints all over it. There are *lots* of rats around there, you know? You must be careful. I saw your name, and thought it surely had sentimental value to the boy so I must return it.'

'I'm so happy,' said Wesley. 'Thank you!'

'No, thank *you*,' Mr Kirklees replied. 'Really.'

Wesley beamed. He was the happiest I'd seen him all week. Mr Kirklees returned to his chair and relaxed into it. 'I have a plan,' he said, nodding.

'Mr Kirklees sounds like you, Josie.' Wesley laughed.

'I'll speak to my lawyer friends first thing in the morning.' He looked up at the grandfather clock in the corner of the room. 'Yes, they'll all be at home now, eating supper.'

Margot looked at the clock and snorted gently. 'It's only six. My dad's a lawyer. He never leaves the office before nine unless he can help it.'

Mr Kirklees leaned forward. 'Ah, but I bet your dad is a young man – my lawyers are much more . . . established, let's say.'

Margot shrugged. 'Maybe.' She bit into a cake, but put it quickly back down and wiped her mouth. 'Stale,' she whispered under her breath.

Mr Kirklees stared up and out of his window. 'Yes, that's the plan. If you're up early enough tomorrow, call by before school. I'll provide breakfast. I will recite what I'll say to the lawyers to make sure you're happy and that it represents your friends and their situation accurately.' That did sound fair, so I nodded. 'I also don't think it's a good idea to share this plan with Mr and Mrs Braithwaite yet. I'm under the impression they are resistant to aid.'

'Deffo,' said Wesley. 'They're well stubborn.'

'And we wouldn't want them running – not if Mr Braithwaite's leg is as bad as you all say.'

Mr Kirklees was right, but I didn't like it.

Wesley wrapped his quilt cape-like over his shoulders and ran in the middle of the road up Copsey Close, towards our houses. Margot laughed, watching him run celebratory laps round the doughnut. 'Well, *he's* definitely happier,' she said. 'That's good.'

'Hmm,' I said quietly. 'I guess.'

Margot looked at me sideways. 'You *guess*? What's wrong?'

I sighed. 'Something doesn't feel right.'

Wesley ran back towards us, his eyes shining bright in the developing darkness. 'That was so sick!' he shouted. He removed the blanket from his neck and kissed the fabric. 'Never thought I'd see you again.' He shook his shoulders at me and Margot and grinned, but I couldn't return the smile – not yet. 'What?' he said. 'Why aren't you happy? We've told someone now, so we're getting help from an actual lawyer *and* I got my quilt back. What's not to smile about?'

'I just –' I said, exhaling. 'I just feel a bit unsure.'

'Because you wanted to win this all by yourself without any help, didn't you?' Wesley said, raising his brows. 'This? Again?'

'No, no.' I sighed. 'This is very much not a game. It isn't fun, and I'm not trying to *win* anything.'

'You don't want the glory then?'

'No, Wesley!' I said, raising my hands. 'I heard what you said this morning, and it's stuck with me all day. You made good points, but I –'

'But what?' said Margot. 'Tell us. I still think Mr Kirklees is strange but at least he's going to help, right?'

'Well, hopefully,' I said. 'But things aren't quite adding up. Not for me. Not yet anyway.'

'Like?' asked Margot. 'Share.'

'Like the cakes he *said* he'd baked for us, for a start,' I said, looking at Wesley. 'Right?'

'*Pfft*, so what?' he replied. 'Who cares about cakes?'

'But why lie? Also, that thing he said about Felix and Audrey being from Jamaica was weird – we never said a *thing* about where the Braithwaites were from. Why did he guess there?' I shook my head. 'How? Of all the countries in the world?'

'Yeah, I agree with that,' said Margot. 'That was a bit of a leap.'

I looked at Wesley. 'Your quilt. He must have had it since Saturday, since he likes to walk in the mornings. Why is he only giving it to you now? It's Tuesday. We saw him yesterday . . .'

'Because he was washing it!' Wesley shouted. 'He told you!' He kissed his teeth. 'Be happy! This whole thing – this drama – is nearly over!'

'I hope it is,' I said softly, mostly to myself. I stared at the concrete for a moment, and then looked up at Wesley and Margot. I tried to smile. 'OK,' I said, nodding and grinning – displaying some teeth to show them I was being friendly and accepting the situation. 'He invited us for breakfast, so shall we meet earlier tomorrow – eight o'clock?'

'Eight it is!' Wesley shouted.

'I might struggle,' said Margot. 'That's early for me.'

Wesley tutted and shook his head.

'Fine,' she said, walking to her house before shouting across the close. 'I'll set an alarm then!'

When I let myself into the house, the light on the landing was on. I looked up the stairs to see that the door to the spare room – my brother's room – was open.

'Nia,' I heard Dad say, exasperated. 'You gonna let me do this, or not?'

'I'm not doing anything!' she protested. 'I'm too pregnant to get involved in arts and crafts.'

'Oh, you're plenty involved,' Dad replied. 'With those eyes and sighs, you're very involved.' He laughed.

I put my head round the door frame. Dad was kneeling on the floor with a screwdriver in his mouth, the long white wooden side of a cot under his arm and an instruction manual in his hands. Mum sat in the corner on a rocking chair, sipping a mug of tea. 'Hi,' I said into the room.

'All right, Jo,' said Mum. 'Why you loitering out there? Come in.'

I smiled and stepped into the room. 'Let me help, Dad?'

'Great,' he said, and, as he did, the screwdriver fell to the floor. He laughed and leaned part of the cot in my direction. 'Got it?'

I nodded and he flicked furiously through the manual. 'It's got no words and the diagrams don't make sense!' He groaned.

'Where did the cot come from?' I asked.

'Gift from your grandparents,' Mum said. 'We got rid of yours years ago.'

I nodded and looked around the room. Its yellow walls were the same, but a slim strip of wallpaper had been added round the middle. Little elephants, lions and hippos danced, tossed balls in the air and held balloons. 'That looks nice,' I said, pointing. 'That's new, right?'

'Nope!' Mum snorted. 'We put that up months ago now.'

'Ah, I've just noticed it.'

'Because you weren't looking,' she said.

'Or trying to ignore it,' Dad added softly, staring at the instructions.

I sighed. 'I've been doing a lot of thinking.'

'Oh yeah,' said Mum. 'About universities again? Another one of those prospectuses came for you today, by the way. It's on your bed.'

'No, not about that,' I replied, shaking my head. 'Dad, after you spoke to me last night, I cried. A lot.'

Dad sighed. 'I wasn't trying to hurt you. You get that, right? I'm trying to help.'

'I do.' I nodded. 'I know. But then today, Wesley *really* had a go at me.'

'That boy's got too much mouth,' said Mum.

'He said that, while I try hard, I'm basically selfish and proud.'

'That boy has some sense.' Mum sipped her tea. Dad stifled a laugh.

'I thought about that all day,' I said, looking out of the window. 'Among other things.'

'And?' said Dad.

'And, well, he had a bit of a point,' I said. 'I think. I know it's good to know your weaknesses so that you can turn them to strengths – and I try to do that – but . . . that hurt. Badly.'

Mum glanced at Dad, raising her eyebrows.

'I saw that,' I said.

'Maybe you were meant to,' she said.

Dad pulled up another piece of the cot and held it next to the part in my hand, screwing the two together. 'So how will you turn this into a strength?' he said. 'You love plans and plots – you got something for this?'

'Not yet,' I said. 'But I've figured out where I need to start.'

'And that's where?' asked Mum.

'By saying I'm sorry and meaning it.'

Mum rocked back in the chair, and spluttered in her mug. She held her stomach in shock. 'New daughter, who's dis?' Dad laughed, holding the two ends of the cot together.

'I am sorry,' I said, knowing I meant it this time. 'I was – am – a bit jealous of the baby. I thought it meant that you loved me less, and you were going to make me babysit –'

'Oh, don't worry about that. We are,' said Mum, stretching. 'Once this baby is born, I'm hitting the town.' She laughed, flicking her ponytail. I stared at her. 'But not all the time, obviously.'

'But,' I continued, 'I am happy for you. For us.'

'Well,' said Dad, reaching for the cot's little mattress. 'I'm proud of you – this is all very mature and sensible.'

'Yeah,' Mum replied. 'I was *nothing* like this at your age.'

'Aren't you glad you've talked it over now?' asked Dad, standing back to admire the completed cot.

'About this?' I said, looking across The Outback into Chicane Cars. The lights were off. 'Definitely. But there are some other things I wish we didn't say today.'

BILLING

Don't delay when it's time to pay!

I slept better last night than I had the night before, but I still woke up feeling uneasy and unsettled. Everything at home was fine and calm now, and I was glad I'd spoken to Mum and Dad and been honest. The trouble was, everything else felt chaotic and confused – emotions I hated.

When I'm feeling like this, I don't want to eat. I didn't want breakfast this morning. Not a bowl of cereal, not a slice of toast and certainly nothing from Mr Kirklees. I thought about him a lot last night – his fancy house, his stale corner-shop cakes and his interest in us and the Braithwaites.

After showering and getting dressed, I rummaged through the medicine cabinet above the sink, looking for any tablets I could give to Felix this afternoon to help him with the pain. I knew he was lying when he said it only hurt a bit. I grabbed packets of aspirin and ibuprofen and pushed them into my pockets, leaving paracetamol for Mum. Pregnant ladies can have paracetamol, I read. My parents' bedroom is directly next to the bathroom so I looked in. Dad had already left for work, and Mum was on her side with one leg dangling off the edge of the bed and her face in her pillow, snoring slightly. I didn't wake her to say goodbye. My brother would be here soon so she needed all the rest she could get right now.

Just before I left – with just a few minutes to go until eight o'clock – I returned to my room. I stared out of my window across to Chicane. I wasn't sure what I was looking for. A glimpse of Audrey and Felix – maybe. A sign they were all right – possibly. Forgiveness for sharing their story with someone I wasn't sure about – definitely. I reached for my phone. I had a feeling I'd need it today. At my front door, another prospectus had arrived for me, from the University of Sussex. I looked at the smiling students on the cover, sitting on benches on their concrete campus. I set it down on the step. University had to wait.

Wesley and Margot were already in the doughnut, ready to eat. I strode over, nodding nervously in their direction. 'Did you remember the medicine?'

'Erm, good morning to you, too,' Wesley snapped. 'Course I did. I didn't think of much else.'

'Same,' said Margot, opening her bag to show us a full first-aid kit.

'All right, let's put it all in my bag – I've got room and it's better if it's all in one place, right?'

'Fine with me,' said Wesley. He handed me a few brown bottles that had 'Ella Evans' printed on peeling labels.

'Are . . . are those your mum's?' said Margot, peering at the bottles. 'You sure she doesn't need them?' She stared nervously at me, gently nodding her head in Wesley's direction.

'Yeah, these are old ones,' he said. 'She went to the doctor yesterday –'

'And?' said Margot quickly, loudly. I bit my lip, breathed deeply and looked at Wesley.

Wesley leaned back, away from her voice, and looked her up and down. 'She's got stomach ulcers again. She needs to relax, eat better and take her meds,' he said. 'Like I keep telling her.'

I breathed a sigh of relief, but Margot slumped forward, her knees grazing the pavement. 'Oh, thank God, thank God for that,' she said, touching her chest.

'Margot,' I said, pulling her to her feet.

When she stood up, she stared at Wesley with wet eyes. 'I'm so glad!' she said, lunging towards him and wrapping her arms round his neck, holding on so tight she almost pulled him over.

'Why you so happy that my mum's got ulcers?' he mumbled behind Margot's arms. 'Why you so weird, man?' he said, but he didn't push her away.

Margot broke their hug and wiped her eyes. 'I'm so happy she's all right.' She sighed. 'When I saw her on Saturday, I was so worried for her and for you, Wes.'

'You were?' he said, looking at her cautiously. 'Why?'

She nodded. 'She just . . . didn't look very well, and I – well, we – were nervous.'

'*We?*' he said. 'Were you two chatting about my mum?'

'We were just worried, like Margot said,' I said quietly, getting ready to receive his rage.

He shook his head. 'Don't do that,' he said. He stared at Margot, who sniffed and dabbed her nose with the sleeve of her jacket. 'But this time it's fine. I'm not going to kick off.'

'You're not?' I said. 'That's not like you.'

'Yeah, well, this time I can clearly see,' he said, pointing at Margot, 'that you weren't just running your mouths and gossiping –'

'Definitely not,' said Margot shaking her head. 'We weren't.'

'– and you can't be a spy, Margot, getting all invested and crying like that. So, you know what?' Wesley said. 'Thanks. Thanks for worrying about us. It's good of you.'

Margot beamed at Wesley. 'No worries, none at all,' she said.

Wesley patted her awkwardly on her back. 'All right, then. We going now or what?' He looked down the close towards Beechwood. 'I ain't eaten yet.'

'I ate,' said Margot. 'After those cakes, I don't trust him with a whole breakfast.'

'I'm not eating either,' I said. 'I don't trust him with anything.' We walked towards his house. Mr Kirklees wasn't waving from his window this morning, or leaning on his gate.

'Josie,' said Wesley. 'We're about to get official, legal, proper help now. Focus on that, even if you don't want the food.' He ran up the gravel drive and knocked loudly on Mr Kirklees's door. Brian, Wesley's number-one fan, didn't bark back.

Wesley stepped down from the concrete step, his hands in his pockets. He looked at us expectantly and knocked again.

'They've gotta be upstairs,' he said. 'They have to be.' He crouched down to shout through the letter box. 'Hello?' He stood up and turned to us. 'Can't see anyone in there.'

I ran up the gravel with Margot behind me. I stepped into Mr Kirklees's flower beds to look into his front-room window. He wasn't sitting in his chair, waiting for us. I couldn't see any cornflakes or other breakfast things on his coffee table. 'He's not there,' I said.

'Is he sick, do you think?' said Wesley, panicking. 'Do you think he might be dead in there or something? He *is* ancient.'

'Should we break in?' said Margot. 'To save him?'

'No and no,' I said. 'If something was wrong, surely Brian would have barked when we knocked? Plus, we already, technically, have our trespassing badges, so we're not doing that.'

Wesley shook his head. 'Wait – unless they're both dead?' he said, stumbling into the flower beds.

'Unlikely,' I said. 'There's nothing wrong with the dog, I don't think.'

'Yeah, that is a bit far-fetched, Wes,' said Margot. 'Even for me.'

'They're just not there,' I said quietly, instead of saying I told you so.

Margot rubbed her forehead. 'You had a weird feeling, and me too. We were right.'

Wesley started grabbing at his hair. 'Nah, nah,' he said. 'Wait a minute! Don't jump to conclusions. They might have just popped out . . . to get us bacon, or something.'

'But he said come early,' I said. 'It's not early any more.'

'I have to trust him!' Wesley shouted. 'Or else I have mucked up – majorly.'

I turned to look at Wesley. 'No, don't say that – you haven't! You did what you thought was best, Wes. You followed the code – every point of it. Whatever *this* is, it's not your fault. OK?'

Wesley swallowed hard, and nodded. 'All right.'

'All right, now move over and let me look,' I said. I gently pushed Wesley to the side, crouched down and opened the letter box. 'Mr Kirklees! Brian!' I shouted. There were no barks, no movement, no 'We're coming!' called down the stairs. Nothing. I removed my bag from my shoulder and peered closer through the letter box into the house, looking around for something – anything – that would help us understand where they might be.

I looked down to the mat at the letters delivered to Mr Kirklees this morning. On the top, facing up, was a letter from iPower, an energy supplier – the one my parents use too. I strained my neck to read the details on the envelope. The letter was addressed to Richard Kirklees, CEO, Chicane Cars.

I gasped and fell backwards off his concrete step.

MEDICATING

An apple a day keeps the doctor away?

'Josie! Josie!' Margot shouted, holding on to my arm. 'What is it?' She bit her lip. 'Do we want to know?' She shook her head. 'What am I saying – *of course* we want to know!'

I took deep breaths in through my nose and out through my mouth, my eyes flicking between Wesley and Margot the whole time.

'Josie, talk!' demanded Wesley. 'You'd better tell us – and quickly!'

'Copseys,' I said slowly. 'There's a letter. Mr Kirklees is connected to Chicane Cars.'

Margot slapped her hand against her mouth, then hurried to the letter box herself. After she'd evidently seen what I'd seen, she slid against the front door and slumped to the ground.

'What does it say?' said Wesley nervously. 'Like, word for word?'

Margot stared blank-faced ahead. 'It's from iPower, addressed to Mr Kirklees here, at Beechwood. I guess it's a bill for the electricity or something?'

Wesley furrowed his brow. 'So?'

'So?' I asked. 'So, at the very least it shows Mr Kirklees hasn't been completely open and honest with us, like we have with him. He never said anything about being involved with the factory, did he?'

Margot shook her head. 'At the very worst, we've been taken advantage of somehow.'

I looked over at Margot. 'And I don't like that.' I breathed deeply and bit my nails. 'I think we might have told him too much.'

Wesley hung his head in shame and swore under his breath.

'It's not your fault,' Margot whispered.

'We have to warn Felix and Audrey as soon as possible,' I said, my hands trembling. 'I've got a bad feeling about this.'

'Like now?' said Wesley. He raised his eyebrows. 'Shall we bunk off?'

I shook my head. 'We can't. Mr King will notice if all three of us are missing, and parents will get involved. Let's go straight after school – as soon as that bell rings, we just go.'

'But what if that's too late?' said Margot.

'We have to hope it's not,' I said. I pulled Margot's arm and she stood up. 'We're going to be late.'

'Liar!' Wesley shouted. He kicked Mr Kirklees's front door before we left Beechwood and broke into a run along Copsey Avenue.

'I can't *believe* Mr Kirklees!' Wesley panted as we stood in the playground, in a rough approximation of a line, waiting for Mr King to take us to class. He took deep breaths and slumped over, his body folded at the waist. Margot patted his back gently. I looked at the pair of them. Margot noticed and quickly put her hands by her sides.

'Mr Kirklees?' said Bobby, spinning round to look at Wesley. 'Him again? Why you *also* banging on about him today?' He shook his head, laughing. 'Is it National Mr Kirklees Day or something and I don't know?'

We stared at each other, then at Bobby. 'What do you mean?' I said slowly.

'Sunny – my brother, by the way, Margot – he was *buzzing* about old Kirklees,' said Bobby. 'He met him at Harrowdens at the crack of dawn.'

Bobby looked at Margot. 'Josie's dad works there too, you know? Him and Sunny are like best friends –'

'They're not,' I said.

'They are! Your dad was at the meeting to help Sunny, so . . . ?'

'What?' I exclaimed. Margot stared at me; Wesley narrowed his eyes. 'I didn't know, I promise!' I protested. 'Carry on, Bobby,' I said, turning the attention back to him.

'Cool, so yeah, first thing, Sunny jumped the queue for the shower and got there first.' He touched his head. 'The hot water was running out by the time I got in – so don't look at my hair, yeah? It's greasy. Anyway, Sunny was pumped; he was literally dancing around the kitchen in his towel.' Bobby made a face at the memory. 'Sunny says it's his lucky day – the one he's been waiting for.'

Mr King appeared at the head of the line. 'Ready to go in, Six K?' he said, leading our class to our room.

We weren't ready. Our classroom was the last place we wanted or needed to be. We needed space to talk freely and urgently, to plan and understand. Wesley pulled on my arm in the corridor. 'Did you know anything about this meeting? Did your dad say anything at all?'

'Not a word,' I said. 'He wasn't home when I woke up.'

'This ain't some part of a messed-up plan of yours?' he said, narrowing his eyes. 'You're not going to spring another surprise on us, are you?'

'No way!' I said, wrestling my arm out of his grip. 'If I knew Mr Kirklees was going to Dad's workplace, don't you think I would've told you? Messaged you immediately?'

'Yeah,' said Wesley. 'You're right. Sorry.'

'I wouldn't have us knocking on his door, shouting through his letter box like fools for fun. Copsey Code, point one: be truthful and trustful!'

Wesley thought for a moment. 'I suppose.'

'You'd better suppose,' I said, taking my coat off and throwing it in the general direction of my peg inside the classroom. 'It would be against our own rules.'

'Right,' said Margot, running to our table. 'Let's figure this out.'

We sat down and huddled together while Mr King began taking the register. Margot pulled her notebook from her bag, and flicked past paragraph-penned pages. 'What do we know?'

'OK,' I whispered. 'Starting with this morning – we saw what we're guessing is an electricity bill.'

Margot nodded and wrote that down.

'Margot Anderson?' said Mr King.

'Here!' she said without looking up.

'He was supposed to be making breakfast, but he went to Josie's dad's work for a meeting,' said Wesley, leaning over.

'To meet Bobby's brother,' Margot said and wrote simultaneously. 'Sunny – what does he do there?' She looked up at me.

'He rents and sells business spaces,' I said.

'Like factories!' Wesley shouted. 'Oh my days!'

The class turned to look at Wesley. He shrank down in his seat and began rubbing at his forehead.

'Wesley Evans!' said Mr King.

'Here, sir,' he said, smiling and pretending to be calm.

'We all know you're here, Mr Evans. That's very clear.' The class laughed. 'But, please, no shouting during the register.'

'OK, sir,' he said, rocking nervously on his chair. 'Understood.'

I spoke up. 'Sorry, sir – we're planning the Christmas party.'

'Very good,' Mr King replied. 'But, please, not now.'

Wesley leaned forward. 'I really thought that letter might have been a mistake,' he hissed. 'But this is joining the dots for me!'

I gulped and looked at my friends. 'And the dots aren't creating a good picture, are they? Why do something with the factory *now*? This morning? It's been sitting there derelict forever.'

'Did you know about this, Josie?' Wesley said, spinning on his seat. 'About Mr Kirklees owning the factory? You're *always* on the internet, researching all kinds of rubbish! How could you not know?'

'Of course I didn't know! And yes, I did research Chicane, but Google doesn't just say, "Hello, Josephine Williams! Thanks for searching that – Oh, and your neighbour Mr Kirklees? He owns Chicane", does it?' I whispered.

Margot laughed a little. 'Fine, but what did it actually say, then?'

I thought for a moment and leaned my head back to access those memories. 'It . . . it said –' I began, feeling like my stomach was going to fall out of my bottom and land on the floor. 'It said that Chicane was owned by a company in the

Cayman Islands. Remember what he said last night?'

'He said he knew the Caymans, didn't he?' Wesley said, his voice cracking. 'But Mr Kirklees lives here – in Luton, in Beechwood – not in no Caymans. What's *that* about? I don't get it!'

'I can help you there,' said Margot, putting down her pen and leaning on her elbows. 'The Cayman Islands is a place where rich people hide their money so they don't have to pay much tax. Or, at least, it used to be. Dad told me – he has loads of cases at work about it. That's how he met Mum, after all – she knows it well, too.' She coughed and looked down. 'Anyway, you definitely don't have to live there to set up a business; you just have to be a bit rich. Which Mr Kirklees clearly is – look at his house.'

Wesley buried his face in his hands. 'I still don't get it!' Wesley moaned softly. 'Help me understand, Josie! What does this mean? For us? For Felix and Audrey?'

'I'm thinking,' I said quietly, biting my nails.

Wesley kicked my ankle under the table. 'Get your phone out! Google Mr Kirklees, google Chicane Cars – google something.'

'I can't!' I hissed. 'We can't take our phones out in class, remember? I don't want Mr King to confiscate it.'

Wesley kissed his teeth. '*Who cares?* This is important! Way more important than detention!'

'But I've never had one, ever!'

'Well, you can earn your detention badge then, can't you?' he said. 'Wait, no, I'll just do it.' He disappeared under the table and opened my bag.

'Don't, Wesley!' I said. 'It's turned off anyway.'

'Josephine Williams?' asked Mr King.

'Here!' I said above the table. 'Wesley, no!' I hissed below. 'If I turn my phone on now, it will be noisy. Mr King will take it and I won't get it back until Friday at the earliest!'

'*Please!*' begged Wesley. 'I'll cough over the little chime thing, then you can just do what you need to, innit.'

'No, Wesley!'

'Miss Williams, please be quiet, or else I *will* separate you and your friends,' Mr King warned. Bobby looked over at us, concerned and confused. He tutted and shook his head.

Wesley grabbed my leg. 'Where is it? I can't find your phone?'

'Wesley, just stop!' I shouted, sharply kicking my bag away with my foot. As I did, the contents of our combined medicine cabinets rattled on to the floor in front of us. Margot's mouth fell open, Wesley meerkat-like, looked up guiltily from under the table. I scrambled to the floor to hide the tablets; Mr King could absolutely not know about this. Kelly Marshall, who was giving out our exercise books at the back of the class, ran over to see what I was doing.

'Mr King! Mr King!' she shouted.

I shook my head and looked up at her. 'No, Kelly, shush! It's not what you think!' I pleaded.

'They've got tablets – loads of them, too!' she said to Mr King while staring at me. 'Come quick, sir! Josie, Wesley and Margot have brought drugs to school!'

DEPARTING

Get up, get out!

I gripped the sides of the green chair and stared past Mrs Herbert's desk, through her open window and across the car park. I dug my nails into the chair's arms and began to battle against the hot tears forming in my eyes and threatening to leak down my face. I tried to blink them away, but there they were on my cheeks, winning this fight. I looked around Mrs Herbert's once-familiar office – I had, of course, been here many times before and knew this particular chair very well, but it was different then. That was under happier, friendlier, more positive circumstances – when I was here for praise and rewards. The whole room felt different now, now I was in trouble. Trouble belonged to and followed other kids, but not me.

I glanced at Margot and Wesley. Margot was scribbling furiously in her notebook. Wesley leaned over, looking at her notes and nodding. He glanced up and caught my eye. 'You crying?' he said. '*I'm* the one who should be bawling – I'm the one who messed up with the medicines.'

'Then why aren't you?' I snapped. Wesley leaned back in his chair, and Margot looked up. 'I'm sorry. I'm scared. I've never been in trouble like this before.'

'You *haven't?*' said Margot. 'Hmmm.'

'What, *you* have?' I asked her.

She nodded. 'A few times at my old school. You'll be OK, I promise. You just have to –'

The door to Mrs Herbert's office swung open, and she walked in with her glistening, black bobbed hair swinging from side to side. 'I thought I said no talking!' she snapped. 'And no writing either!' She pulled her chair from behind her desk and sat down. She sipped her coffee and stared at us.

'What is going on with you three?' she said. 'First, that litter-pick lie you told me yesterday – yes, I checked with Jim – and now *this*? Unauthorized medicine in school?'

'They're *not* drugs, miss, I promise!' I said.

Mrs Herbert sat forward. 'I know they're not, Josephine. But surely you – of all the pupils in this school – understand how incredibly dangerous it is to bring items like those on to the premises?'

I nodded. 'I do, miss. I'm sorry, we were –'

'Imagine if somebody took them, had a bad reaction and got very sick – or worse? The school – and you, and your parents – would be in deep trouble here. Legal trouble.'

'But we weren't doing anything wrong!' I pleaded.

'No, Josephine, you *were* doing something very wrong. Absolutely wrong!' she shouted.

I buried my head in my hands. I knew she was right.

'*Why* did you bring them to school at all? What was the point?'

I looked over at my friends. Margot nodded.

'Might as well tell her,' Wesley muttered.

'Well?' Mrs Herbert demanded. 'Speak up!'

I put my hand on my forehead. 'I . . . we . . . we have these friends –' I started.

'Who don't go here,' added Margot, looking at me. 'They're too old for school.'

'– and they are in trouble, and in pain,' I said.

'We were just trying to help them get better,' said Wesley. 'That's all. It's not a big deal, Mrs Herbert.

Give us detention or suspend us – whatever you want.'

'No, Wesley!' I whispered, leaning forward. 'We don't want that! How will we get to Chicane –'

'Excuse me, young man!' Mrs Herbert bellowed, cutting me off. 'This is a *huge* deal! And *I* decide what happens next, not you.' She looked at the three of us for a moment, shaking her head. 'I don't understand this *at all*. You three are brilliant, incredibly bright children – some of my most sensible Year Sixes. Or so I thought.'

Mrs Herbert stood up and stared at me in particular. 'I'm disappointed in you,' she said.

Those are the worst words someone could ever say, even worse than 'I told you so'. It left me breathless. I sat back on the chair and began to cry.

'It's too late for tears, I'm afraid,' she said. 'I'm going to have to call your parents. You leave me no choice. Excuse me for a moment, while I go to reception. Stay here.' She left her office.

I turned to Wesley. 'Why?' I asked, throwing up my hands. 'If we get detention – or suspended – how will we warn Felix and Audrey?'

Wesley sighed. 'I'm sorry. I just wanted to get out.'

'But now we're even more stuck! *Eurgh!*' I shouted, stamping my feet on the floor. This was so unfair and wrong. Frustrated, I kicked my open, medicine-free bag in front of me and my phone fell out.

'There it is!' Wesley pointed, which made Margot laugh. I wiped my eyes. 'Might as well turn it on now since we're in big trouble anyway.'

I switched it on, and, as it powered up, Wesley coughed over the chime, which made us smile. But my phone continued to chime . . . and chime . . . and chime again. I scrambled to put it on silent. When I looked closely at the screen, I had a stack of messages, all from Dad.

I stared at them and gasped. 'Mum's in labour,' I said. 'They've gone to the hospital.'

'What?' said Wesley. 'For real? Today is too much!' He stood up. 'It's not even, what, eleven o'clock, yet? And we've already had a weekful of drama. I am happy for you, Josie. It will be great.'

'It *will* be.' Margot nodded. 'It's exciting *and* it might get you out of this trouble. Your mum and dad won't have time to be mad with you – they'll be too busy. You're so lucky – when I was suspended from my last school, my dad was *livid*.'

'Suspended?' said Wesley. 'What, you? Fancy Margot? Never!'

Margot shrugged and laughed. 'It wasn't my fault.'

I stared at my phone. Margot looked at me from the corner of her eye. 'Are you all right? You're not still mad about your brother, are you?'

I shook my head. 'No. I'm not – not any more,' I said. 'I'm just thinking.'

'About?' asked Wesley. 'You making a plan?'

I leaned back in my chair. 'We've got to get out of here and get to Felix and Audrey. We can't sit here, doing nothing,' I said quietly.

'I'm standing up, though,' said Wesley.

'Look how things change, and change quickly,' I continued. 'I didn't think I'd become a sister today, but I know it will be all right.' I stood up. 'This situation between us, the Braithwaites and Mr Kirklees gets more serious every second we sit here. It's growing beyond our control, sure. But what can *we* do? We can only control the controllable, right? So let's do that by being honest, proactive and resilient. By being thoughtful and caring allies. By acting according to the Copsey Code. Points one through to six.'

Margot grinned. 'That was great, Josie! Let's recite our pledge.'

'Nope, I'm good,' said Wesley, eyeing me suspiciously. 'You rehearse that?'

'No, just thought of it,' I said.

'Yeah, right,' said Wesley.

'Just thought of what?' whispered Bobby, poking his head round Mrs Herbert's door. 'Oi, are you lot all right? I've snuck out to check on you – I'm well worried. Are you on drugs? Please say no – you're supposed to be the smart ones. You *know* how bad that stuff is!'

'Of course we're not, Bobby!' I said. 'Where's Mrs Herbert?'

'In reception, on the phone.' Bobby's eyes widened. 'She's not calling the cops on you, is she?'

Earning a criminal record was not part of any of my plans. 'I really hope not,' I said. I looked between the door and the window. 'We have to get out.'

'Why don't you just leave?' said Bobby, with a shrug. 'What's Mrs Herbert *really* going to do?'

I looked at Margot and Wesley, who both nodded. 'No, we can't do that.' I shook my head. 'That's bad.'

'Is it, though?' said Bobby with a smirk. 'You're already in trouble – might as well make it worth it. Just tell Mrs Herbert the whole truth later. I'm sure you'll get out of it; you're do-gooders, remember?'

Now I'd experienced walking on the wild side of life, Bobby's twisted logic made sense. It reminded me of something I'd read on the internet that said jails are bad because they create better criminals. I understood that now.

'Oh, I know!' Bobby's eyes glistened. 'I could set off the fire alarm, and then you can escape during the chaos?' He smiled. 'I love a little fire alarm, especially one so close to break time.' He rubbed his hands together.

Wesley turned to look at Bobby. 'You serious, Bobs? You'd do that? *You* could get suspended!'

Bobby shrugged. 'Yeah, why not?' He looked at me. 'As long as you lot let me in – let me be part of your charity thing.'

'That's it?' said Margot. 'That's all you want?'

I put my hand on her shoulder to stop her from speaking. 'Yes, Bobby, you can apply –'

'Apply?!' he said. He thought for a moment, then shrugged. 'Yeah, all right.' Margot sat back in surprise. She looked at Bobby and me, then shook her head.

'When you hear the beeps, just bounce, yeah?' He left the room.

'Bobby's not really going to do that, is he?' said Margot. 'He wouldn't –'

Before she could finish her sentence, the fire alarm blared throughout the entire school and into Mrs Herbert's office.

'He would!' said Wesley. He grabbed his coat and bag. 'Bobs, you are a legend!' he shouted. 'Come on then – what you waiting for?'

Margot and I grabbed our things and ran out of Mrs Herbert's office. We were immediately sucked into the crowd of excited children pushing against each other in the corridor and hurrying towards the exits. 'I want to go the Oaken Road way!' I shouted and pointed to Wesley and Margot over the noise.

'Why?' Wesley shouted. 'It will take longer!'

'I need to do something first,' I said. 'On Mire Road.'

'Really?' said Margot.

'Really!' I said.

Instead of joining the rest of Six K in the line on the playground, we put our heads down and walked quickly to the exit. Nobody stopped or shouted after us and, thankfully, the police weren't waiting for us either. We'd made it. Once we were through the gates, we ran down Oaken Road so fast I could barely breathe. We slowed down slightly on Mire Road.

Margot looked around at the people and the parade of shops. 'I love being out of school when

you're not supposed to be,' she said. 'You know –
like when you go to the doctors, but then you walk
around a bit before you go back, watching what
people do in the day? It's so interesting.'

Wesley looked at Margot from the corner of his
eye, but simply said, 'Yeah, I suppose. Something
for your books, right?'

'Exactly,' Margot said. 'You get it.' She smiled at
Wesley. He smiled back.

We walked past Hair Design by Nia and I put my
head down. I didn't want any of Mum's colleagues
to see me and stop us. When we got to the bakery
next to Harrowdens, I paused and reached for my
phone. I pulled up the Harrowdens website.

'Listen,' I said quietly, staring at my screen.
'We're about to do a bad thing – something so
against the code, it will make you lose your breath.'

'Go on . . .' said Wesley.

'It's for a very good reason, of course. If we do
this, I hope you'll both forgive me.'

ACCOMMODATING

Move over - make some room for others!

I pushed Harrowdens's door open. It caused a little bell to ring, which made Sundeep look up from his desk. Sundeep looks *just* like Bobby, except older, taller and muscular, which I find very weird and unsettling.

We cautiously went in. I'm sure Margot would describe the office as bleak, but it's not too bad. It's functional. It had thin grey carpet and white walls with photographs of available properties in plastic frames attached to them in messy, misaligned rows. There were rows of keys on pegs by the small dark corridor that led to the back of the office. At the end was a small kitchen, a toilet and the fire escape. I know, because I've been here many times before.

'Josephine?' Sundeep said, squinting up at me. I nodded. He put an orange-juice-filled champagne flute down on his desk. 'Josephine!' he said, recognizing me after he put his glasses on. 'Sorry, can't see all that well close up. You all right? Oh! Congratulations on your forthcoming brother. I'm excited for you!' He looked at Wesley and Margot, then back up at me with questioning eyes. 'What you all doing here? If you're not at school, why aren't you at the hospital?'

'We're on our way now. Wesley and Margot got permission to come too.'

Wesley leaned over and waved.

'But,' I said, maintaining eye contact with Sundeep, 'I just got a message from Dad. He said he left his wallet here and –' I laughed – '*of course* he can't leave Mum to get it.'

'He needs it urgently, too,' added Margot, keen to be included in the deception. 'Nia needs some labour snacks.'

'Not a problem,' said Sundeep. 'It's the least I can do. Your dad really came through and helped me this morning – what a legend.' He stood up, reached for his juice and enjoyed a quick sip.

I could feel my heart rate increase. 'Oh yeah?'

'Yeah!' said Sunny. 'I finally got the go-ahead on a property I've had, unlisted, for ages – since I've

348

been here. I can sell the land, get some commission and have a proper pay day.' He wriggled his shoulders in delight.

'What kind of go-ahead?' asked Wesley, biting at his nails. 'I'm interested in becoming an estate agent. I need to know how these things roll, innit,' he lied.

'Ah great! Well, welcome to the profession – if you ever want any work experience, just let me know.'

'Yeah right,' said Wesley. Sundeep seemed confused for a moment, but Wesley quickly smiled.

'I needed sign-off on an order to demolish a building to clear the land – it's much more attractive and valuable without the eyesore that's currently on it. *I* don't think it's an iconic building.' He lowered his voice. 'I could never say that to the owner though – he is very attached to it, holds lots of sentimental value for him. It's been in his family for many, many years.'

'Oh no,' said Margot, her hand flying to her mouth. She turned to look at Wesley and me.

'Oh yeah!' Sundeep smiled. 'It's a *real* blessing, just bang! Out of nowhere – a bit like your brother, Josephine!'

'Ha, yes . . . yeah, exactly,' I said. 'A blessing.' My palms felt wet. 'So it was a sudden decision on the owner's part?'

'Yep,' said Sundeep. 'I got a call randomly last night, asking for a meeting to sign the paperwork first thing.'

I felt dizzy. I leaned forward and held on to Sundeep's desk. He put his arm on my shoulder. 'You all right?'

'Fine, fine, just *giddy* with excitement for you!' I laughed weakly. 'That's . . . so great.'

'Innit?' said Sundeep. 'It was so weird. When he came in this morning, he was cheerful, which is very unlike him – he's one of the rudest people I've ever met. Anyway, yeah, he said he was ready to sell. Some problem he had with old, lingering rats had been resolved.'

I knew which *rats* he was referring to. I grabbed my stomach; it was very possible I was going to vomit. I leaned back and gulped big breaths instead. Margot's hands trembled when she touched my shoulder.

'Wow,' said Wesley. 'Wow!' He shook his head.

'It's funny, because I never saw any rats in that factory – not on the bottom floor, anyway. I never went upstairs – too dangerous and creepy for me.' Sundeep shuddered. 'I don't like ghosts. Bobby had one in his wardrobe for a bit, did he ever tell you? It wasn't fun. Anyway!' He clapped his hands. 'Let me get what you came for.' He smiled at me.

'What?' I said – my mind was a mile away, with the Braithwaites at Chicane.

'The wallet?' Sundeep said slowly. 'Your dad's wallet?'

'Oh yes, right!' I said. I stood tall and exhaled loudly. 'Yes, Dad said it's at the back of the office, in the kitchen, maybe?'

Sundeep nodded and walked down the corridor to find it.

The three of us stared at each other.

'*Rats?*' whispered Margot. 'Mr Kirklees called Felix and Audrey *rats*?'

'I can't believe I thought he was nice,' said Wesley. 'He played us like an Xbox.'

I nodded. 'He did,' I said. 'But I've got an idea that will buy the Braithwaites some time while we work this out.' I took my phone out of my pocket and showed them the Harrowdens website. 'Look at that one – that seems like a good flat, right?'

'It does, but what's your point?' said Wesley. 'Elm Rise is an all-right road, but you can't afford to move out – and it's not legal for kids to live alone.'

'It's not for me!' I hissed.

'It's for Felix and Audrey,' said Margot, a smile creeping across her face. '*That's* what you meant by breaking the Copsey Code?'

'Exactly.'

'Josephine, what's *happened* to you?' Margot's eyes flashed with delight.

'Injustice happened around me, that's what,' I said. I ran to the row of keys by the corridor.

'I can't find his wallet anywhere!' Sundeep shouted down from the kitchen. He began walking towards us.

My eyes darted between the corridor and the keys. 'Did you try the bathroom?' I shouted back.

'Oh yeah,' he said, returning to his task, allowing me to start mine.

I looked at my phone. 'Elm Rise, Elm Rise.' I stared back at the keys and searched for the right set. 'They're supposed to be in alphabetical order!' I said.

They weren't.

Margot and Wesley joined me in the search, peering closely at the keys. 'There!' hissed Wesley. 'Elm Rise!' He pulled the set of keys from the rack, which made the rest of them crash against the wall and jangle loudly.

'You lot all right in there?' said Sundeep, walking quickly towards us from the back of the office.

'Yeah, yeah,' I said breathlessly. 'Fine. I was just coming to find you, Sundeep, and I slipped against the wall. Sorry! Dad's found his wallet. It was in the car the whole time.'

ENDING

Knowing when to stop really means a lot.

Wesley put the keys to the Elm Rise flat into his pocket and we walked sensibly and slowly to the end of Mire Road. We didn't need Sundeep, Mum's colleagues or anyone else watching us, accosting us or generally thinking we were suspicious. When Mire Road turned into Oaken Road, we broke out into a light jog. By the time we reached Copsey Avenue, we were straight-up sprinting – running as fast as we could to the close, to get to Wesley's house and the wilderness beyond it. Racing to make sure we did the right thing for Audrey and Felix.

As we ran along the avenue, we looked up at Beechwood.

'I hate that house now,' said Margot, her face scrunched tight. 'I hate him too. I've never despised anyone more. Told you I didn't trust him, or his teeth, didn't I?'

'You did,' I panted. 'But Mr Kirklees isn't getting my attention, not now. I plan to deal with him later. Audrey and Felix first.'

Margot nodded. 'Exactly.'

Wesley unlocked his front door and we ran through his hallway, straight to the kitchen. Ella was in there, making a cup of tea. She looked better today, but baffled by our arrival.

'Cheese on bread, Wessy!' she shouted, dropping her mug on the floor and stepping away from the hot liquid and broken shards. 'Why aren't you lot at school? Why is Mrs Herbert calling me, telling me you're missing? What's this about *pills*?'

'Can't stop, Mum!' he said, throwing the back door open. 'We've got to right a wrong.'

'Are you in trouble?'

I shook my head. 'We're not, no.'

Ella's eyes shone. 'You on an adventure?'

Margot nodded.

'Well, I never saw you then,' she said, turning round. She reached for a new mug. 'Good luck!' she whispered gleefully.

'Your mum is the best,' said Margot as she slipped through Wesley's Gap. He looked back at the kitchen – and at her, watching us proudly in return. She gave us a knowing nod.

'I know,' he said softly. 'She is.'

I formulated a plan as we ran through The Outback over our now well-worn path. First, we'll get Felix and Audrey away from Chicane, away from Mr Kirklees immediately. Second, we'll give them the keys to the property on Elm Rise. They'd protest of course – Audrey especially. They were going to be annoyed and very upset that we'd told Mr Kirklees, but they'd also be a little bit impressed we found them a flat. We'd persuade them; they'd have a week in that flat at least, I'm sure. Dad would be on paternity leave and Sunny wouldn't notice – not until someone wanted to rent it, and then I'd just slip the keys back on to their hook. Third, I'd get some advice, real advice, from an adult we trusted. We had to get Felix's and Audrey's papers, urgently. It would have to be Michael, Margot's dad. He'd know someone. The plan would be out of the hands of the Copseys at that point, but that's OK. It wasn't about *me* any more. It was about *we*, to quote Wesley. I silently gave him credit for calling me out as we crossed the stream.

We ran round the side of Chicane Cars, opened the door and ran as fast as we could up the concrete steps to the top floor. In the corridor, we stealthily avoided the obstacles on the wobbly floor, leaped over the fallen shelves and the boxes of broken mugs, and ran past the vandalized toilets for what turned out to be the last time.

I couldn't wait to see the Braithwaites again and give them the news. I reached down to open their door, but the brass knob was missing. I pushed it instead, but it didn't budge. I turned to Wesley and Margot, and smiled. They nodded, and I ran and barged into the door, shoulder first, with all my might.

'Felix? Audrey?' I shouted as I burst into their room. 'We have to go! We –'

When I saw the scene, my hand hit my mouth and I gasped between my fingers.

The Braithwaites' living room was empty – mostly.

Their armchairs were gone, their television and its wire coat hanger too. The photograph of the happy couple from the seventies? Missing, along with present-day Felix and Audrey.

Their tall brown lamp was there, but it no longer stood in the corner of the room. It lay snapped into two splintered pieces, tossed on the floor in the middle of the room, on top of their rug.

Wesley put his hands on his head, while Margot crouched on the floor.

'We're too late!' Wesley shouted. He punched the wall, powered by his despair and desperation.

'Wait! Wait!' I said, between tears. My positive, three-step plan had been shattered into pieces. I reached to snatch parts of it. 'M-maybe they've just moved to another part of the factory?'

'Come on, Josie!' said Wesley. 'They've gone! It's over!' I looked at Margot for support, but she shook her head. I sat on the floor and wept with worry.

Later, we slumped back down the corridor, kicking at the broken mugs. We stomped down the steps, and at the bottom Wesley kicked open the door to the outside. Margot patted my back as he dragged his shoes through the dirt and gravel and weeds when we walked round the side of Chicane.

As we approached the river, a dog barked. Its excitement and volume increased with every one of our steps. Wesley cocked his ear in the direction of the sound. He narrowed, then quickly widened his eyes. 'Nah,' he said, tightening his lips. 'I don't believe this.'

Brian – and Mr Kirklees – stood on the other side of the river, on the very spot where we'd set up camp on Friday night. Mr Kirklees was eating an apple. When he saw us, he threw it on the ground, wiped his mouth and waved. 'Hi, children!' he said with a smile, baring his white teeth. 'What are you doing here?' He wagged his finger at us. 'It's naughty to skip school.'

Margot took a step back. 'You have got to be joking,' she whispered, reaching for my hand.

Wesley walked forward. 'What have you done to our friends?' he shouted across the stream. 'Where are they?'

Mr Kirklees shrugged. 'Whether they left or immigration caught them in time I don't know. I don't care, honestly. I'm just relieved the rats finally found their trap and they're gone. I sent some chaps to clean up their . . . droppings this morning.'

I shuddered at each of his hateful, careless words. 'How can you say *that*?'

'What?' he said, raising his arms.

'Call them rats!' said Wesley. 'Felix and Audrey are *not* rats – they're people!'

'Are they though, really?' asked Mr Kirklees, leaning his head towards his shoulder. 'They *were* acting like rats to me – scuttling around, burrowing between here and the bushes. Making *my factory* their home?' He shook his head. 'Rewiring the electrics in there, and leaving me with the bill? How *dare* they? It's unfathomable, honestly. Brian!' he shouted at his dog, who was attempting to cross the river to reach Wesley on the other side.

'Do you not have feelings?' Margot shouted. 'They needed a home!'

'*Home?* Home? That's amusing,' he said with a chuckle. '*Those people* are always talking about going back home, shouting about how things are better there on their simple, primitive islands. Well, they can enjoy it now. Goodbye! I'm glad I put them back on the banana boat they probably came on – all thanks to the details you so kindly provided.'

I gasped for breath and wobbled on my feet.

'Oh yes,' he said, 'I just needed their names and island for the immigration notice, so thank you.'

'No way,' said Wesley, shaking his head. 'I can't believe this.'

'It's true.' Mr Kirklees shrugged. 'Getting your blanket back was your reward.'

I pulled Wesley back from the bank.

'I knew I'd get what I needed – and from Alan Evans's grandson, too? Even better!'

Wesley stumbled, slipping on the grass. 'You knew my grandad?'

Mr Kirklees roared with laughter. '*Knew him?* Of course I did! I was his boss! Keep up, boy! You really should stay in school. That Welshman and those darkies –'

'Wow,' Margot gasped. 'That's the most racist thing I've heard in my life.'

'Get used to it,' said Mr Kirklees. 'They were nothing but a thorn in my side – always calling me a devil.' He shrugged. 'It's what they deserved.' He leaned down to clip Brian's lead to his collar. 'Come on, Bri, let's go home.' He nodded in our direction, before walking away.

I burst into sobs and, as I did, my phone chimed. Through tears, I looked at the screen. There was a message from my dad.

My brother, Nathaniel – all nine pounds and two ounces of him – had just been born.

PARTYING

Get it together and gather!

Do you know what I dislike most during the winter?

Constant Christmas carols. The same ones over and over again. They ruin the season by being aggressively annoying, but Mum seems to love them, so I lowered the volume of Dad's speaker and tried to continue my story over the noise. 'So, this is what happened,' I said, leaning forward. 'I took my eyes off him for one moment, literally *one* second, to turn back to my laptop and search when babies first smile – a true smile generally appears between six and eight weeks, by the way. I looked back at him to check he wasn't choking or hadn't rolled off my bed, and there he was, smiling up at me. Just giving me a little gummy smile.' I sat back on my sofa. 'Talk about timing!' I said, throwing up my hands.

'Yeah, well, that's what happens.' Wesley bit into a mince pie, fresh from the oven. 'Babies smile. Like we do,' he said between bites.

'You smile?' I said.

Wesley grinned at me with his mouth full, mincemeat and pastry between his teeth.

'Gross,' said Margot, turning away.

Wesley chuckled and looked up at Dad. 'These are lovely by the way, Mr Williams!' he said, using his polite voice and raising the mince pie in his direction. 'Home-made?'

Dad nodded. 'I've told you before, call me Patrick,' he said. Wesley smiled and nodded. 'You want me to drop a batch over to yours? I can do it once you've all gone to this class Christmas party of yours –'

Wesley waved his hands. 'The party's nothing to do with me, really. It's all Jo and Margot's work. I only designed the poster.' He said. He looked down at the boxes and crates of food and drink we were taking with us. 'I don't really want to go to school now, on a Saturday evening, but here we are. But yeah, thanks, Patrick – that would be great. Mum loves mince pies.'

Dad smiled. 'Then consider it done.'

'Baby smiles are the best,' said Margot, missing the mince-pie conversation. 'It's all new to me, too.'

'Aren't they?' I said. I reached down to pick up my brother, who was lying on a mat on the floor, looking up at a mobile attached to it. 'What's that, Nathaniel?' I asked. He answered by opening his mouth and dribbling on me, but I didn't care. I wiped my face with a napkin with holly on it and looked at my brother with love.

The doorbell rang. 'Pat, can you get that?' said Mum, distractedly poking at pigs in blankets. She wiped her hands on her apron. 'I think these are just right,' she said. 'Succulent.'

Dad laughed. 'All right – rest yourself, Rustie Lee,' he said.

She looked at him and scowled. 'Don't call me that.'

Dad smiled and went to answer the door.

'Who's Rustie Lee when she's at home?' asked Wesley, reaching for a breadstick.

I shrugged, because I had no idea. 'I'll google her later.'

I heard the front door open. 'Hey!' Dad said in the hallway. 'Come in, come in.' We turned to look at our guests, and Bobby popped his head round the door.

'Ah cool, Bobs is here!' said Wesley, sitting up. 'Yes, Bobs!'

'Hello, hello!' Sundeep said, each arm heavy with clear blue plastic bags that I knew were filled with snacks and sweets. He pulled his beanie from his head and walked over to our patio doors. 'Hey, Pat?' he shouted. 'Can you turn on your garden lights a minute?'

Our yard was suddenly illuminated. There were patches of ice, and it had just started to snow. The falling flakes sparkled in the light.

'Wow – check out my money close up!' he said, cupping his hands round his eyes and leaning on the glass doors. He stood on his toes and stared at the space beyond our garden. 'It looks so *different* from here,' he said, turning towards my dad. 'It's huge and empty without Chicane.'

I sighed and shook my head. Yes, the factory had been demolished two weeks ago and, yes, all that remained was a huge, empty space – only made bleaker and sadder without Felix and Audrey. As it got colder and darker earlier, we wondered where they were and worried. Every day, Wesley, Margot and I looked for them on the internet and in town. Nothing.

Dad nodded and turned to Sundeep. 'So empty. I'm shocked at how quickly your people cut up all the scrub and bushes and pulled the factory down. Josie gets so much light in her room now – even in winter! I'm tempted to ask you not to sell the land, actually.' Dad laughed, knowing it was a ridiculous request.

Sundeep snorted. He turned to me. 'Sorry, but you know I need the commission, right, Josie?'

I looked up at Sundeep. I understood, but I didn't like it. I smiled at him. 'I'm glad it's gone – The Outback, Chicane Cars.' I shuddered. 'Racist Mr Kirklees. Very bad memories for us, but . . . good for you, I guess.'

'We ran him out of town, good and proper.' Bobby laughed.

While the Copseys couldn't take full credit, I hoped we'd played a part in Mr Kirklees leaving Luton. Firstly, we'd told our parents – who were shocked we'd kept this entire situation to ourselves. We'd then told *everyone* else about him, and what he'd done to the Braithwaites. Wesley, Margot, Bobby and I made posters in the three days of detention we had with Mrs Herbert, and then we made copies of them that we taped to every lamp post on Copsey Avenue and Copsey Close. We even got a little article published in the *Herald and Post* about it last week. People had begun to come forward – people who knew both Felix and Audrey and had fond memories of them. People who wanted to help. I *wish* we'd had done this when they were here, but that would have been impossible. They would have hated the attention.

We hadn't seen Mr Kirklees, or Brian, since either. People had come forward about him too – none of them – not a single one – had anything good to say.

Sundeep sighed. 'Richard Kirklees might not be physically here, but he hasn't *gone* – not from my life. I have to deal with him most days, sending me upper-case emails from the Caymans.'

'I don't get it,' said Margot. 'Why would someone so racist go and live in the Caribbean and spread his misery there?'

I shrugged my shoulders. I couldn't answer Margot's very valid question. As for Sundeep, I lacked sympathy. I understand needing money – I'm not unrealistic – but I just could never imagine taking *any* from Richard Kirklees. Apart from that thirty pounds of course, which we'd given away before we really knew him. 'Choices, Sundeep,' I said. 'Make better ones, maybe? Think about *we*, not *me*.'

'Oh my God,' Wesley said, rolling his eyes. 'I'm sorry I ever said that. You'll never let it go, will you?'

I shook my head. 'No, probably not.'

Bobby swatted at my arm. 'Leave Sunny alone, Josie. I make him feel bad about it every day,' he said.

'And Bobby cusses me for letting you guys scam those keys so easily, right under my nose,' said Sundeep.

'I do,' said Bobby, leaning forward. 'So what's next for us Copseys then?'

'Uniforms!' Margot and I said in unison, looking at Wesley.

Wesley waved his hand. 'Nah, we're resting that for now.'

'Forever, hopefully,' Bobby whispered.

'But seriously,' I said. 'Now we've expanded, we need to regroup and discuss our strategy. It's what Josephine Holloway would do. I want us to focus on human lives and how we can make them better, basically.'

'Simple tasks, then,' said Wesley, smiling. 'Let me go back to posters.'

'Posters!' said Mum from the kitchen. 'That reminds me. Josie, you got a something in the mail today. Pat!' she shouted. 'Josie's holding Nat – can you grab it for her?'

Dad looked at Sundeep, rolled his eyes and handed him mulled wine. 'Yes, Missus,' he said with a laugh.

'Oh, you well love post, don't you?' said Wesley. 'What did you order?'

Margot leaned forward. 'New pens? Can I have one?'

I shook my head. I loved post, but I hadn't ordered anything. I turned in my seat to look at my Dad, who walked back into the living room holding a letter.

'Here you go,' he said, handing it to me, then took Nathaniel from my arms.

I held the letter in my hand and looked closely at the postmark. Birmingham. I didn't know anyone in Birmingham. I opened the envelope. It was a Christmas card with an illustration of three children – two girls and a boy – sitting by a roaring log fire. I opened the card, and as I skimmed the words and realized what I was reading, my hands shook.

'What?' said Wesley, hovering over my shoulder.

'It's . . . it's from Felix and Audrey,' I said, my voice wobbling.

Wesley gasped. 'No, it's not. Don't lie!'

'Are you serious?' said Margot.

I nodded.

'Read it, then!' Bobby demanded, bouncing his legs. 'I never met them, but I just *feel* like I know them.'

I took a deep breath. '"To the Copseys: Josephine, Margot and Wesley – Likkle Alan."'

Wesley's bottom lip trembled, and he looked away.

'"We wanted to give thanks to you, for all the wonderful things you did for us this year."' I looked up at Margot as she stared down at the card. She blinked and sniffed.

'"We're sorry for leaving without saying goodbye,"' I read.

'Oh, thank God,' said Margot, slumping back into her seat. 'They didn't get arrested.' She wiped her wet eyes.

'"We could see the trouble and strife we were causing in your life –"' there was a small note from Audrey pointing to this text: 'Felix wrote that' – '"We couldn't put you little ones in any more trouble. We're OK though! We left Luton and travelled to Birmingham. We're back on a narrowboat, now. There are lots of canals up here, and we can keep moving while staying home. Audrey is getting used to the wobbling. Our new friend Claire from Citizen's Advice is trying to help us with our papers

and prove we belong here. That's because of you." '
My eyes filled with tears.

' "You will grow to be great people. We just know
it. Merry Christmas, Felix and Mrs (Audrey)
Braithwaite. P.S. Hope you like the present.'" I
closed the card and held it to my chest for a moment
before passing it to Margot.

'Present?' said Bobby. 'There was nothing in the
card, was there?'

'No,' I said.

'Check again,' said Wesley, leaning over me.

I picked the envelope up from my lap and shook
it with relieved, delighted fingers. The Braithwaites
were safe, for now.

A small, round blue-yellow-and-green embroidered
badge fell out on to my jeans.

I turned it over and peered at it closely. Stitched
on it, in bright white thread that created clean white
letters, was just one word:

Befriending.

Felix, Audrey and the Windrush Scandal

Felix and Audrey are fictional characters, but, sadly, there are many real people suffering a similar fate in Britain today. The Braithwaites' story was informed by the Windrush Generation – and the Windrush Scandal that came to a terrifying, ugly head in 2018.

The Windrush Generation is the name given to Black people from the Caribbean who arrived in England on a ship called *HMT Windrush* on 22 June 1948, along with those who came after from African countries and the Caribbean until the 1970s. After the Second World War, the country needed to rebuild itself, so the government encouraged people from Commonwealth countries – countries controlled by the United Kingdom – to migrate and make better lives for themselves, and to make Britain great again. Those who had the means to afford a ticket decided to do that. Some planned to stay just a few years, while others wanted to settle permanently – and they could. This was legal, and they were promised British citizenship and the same rights as anyone born in the United Kingdom under laws called the British Nationality Act 1948.

When they arrived, many Black people worked in public services – for the NHS, London Transport and British Rail – but they weren't all made to feel welcome. They were faced with shocking racism, attacks and intolerance. Some found it incredibly difficult to find work at private companies and to be accepted for housing. Still, they persevered and made incredible contributions to British life and society.

Many parents had to make the hard decision to temporarily leave their children behind while they began their new life, but when things got easier were able to 'send for' their children so they could be together again. In those days, children didn't need their own passports and could travel under the ones owned by their parents. Because they rightly believed they had British Citizenship, and it was legal to migrate in this way, new arrivals weren't given any official paperwork to prove that they lived and belonged in England.

From the early 1960s, 'alarmed' by the growing numbers of Black people in the UK, the government created new laws to begin to slow down migration from the Caribbean and limit the rights of anyone arriving from there. However, anyone who had arrived in the UK was automatically allowed to remain – if they had not left for two or more years.

All seemed well for forty years. But, in the mid-2010s, the laws changed, and people began receiving letters and messages telling them they no longer had the right to remain in the UK, and they had to leave immediately. If they wanted to stay, they had to prove their legal status by providing documentation – the very same paperwork that hadn't been provided when they arrived as it wasn't required at the time. Documentation that was, therefore, nearly impossible to obtain.

People who had worked hard and paid taxes for many years were suddenly told they didn't have a right to remain in the country they had contributed so much to. It made it difficult for them to continue to live the lives they had built for themselves, with many having their health and housing benefits stopped, or being denied the right to look for work. This forced some Black people into homelessness.

It was a terrifying time. Members of the Windrush Generation and their children were coaxed to come forwards in order get help making their status clear and legal, but some were arrested and detained despite never having knowingly committed a crime.

People were threatened with deportation and told they would be sent back to the Caribbean against their will, and at least 83 people were deported by mistake. Passports were taken away, and anyone whose status was in doubt but who had left the country legally was not allowed back in.

There was a public outcry to the new laws. Minsters resigned and there was an independent review of the scandal, which found that the government showed thoughtlessness; that what had happened was avoidable; and the demands for documentation were irrational. A scheme was set up to give people affected by the scandal compensation and to support them as they rebuilt their lives, but many victims were unable to access this fund, and at least 23 people died before receiving any money.

While the Windrush Scandal seemed to have been 'resolved', the rights of citizens in Britain continue to be eroded. Even as *The Good Turn* is about to go to print, many people are protesting a new set of laws known as the Nationality and Borders Bill, which was proposed in July 2021. One part of it – Clause 9 – would allow the British Government to take away the citizenship of any British person without warning. This could have a catastrophic effect on millions of people – not just British citizens who were born in other countries, but their children and grandchildren, too. Children and grandchildren who may have never visited their relatives' 'home country'. Children and grandchildren just like me.

Sharna Jackson, January 2022

Acknowledgments

On behalf of Sharna Jackson, the Copseys would like to award the following badges:

Badge	People	For . . .
Managing	Hellie Ogden, Ma'suma Amiri, Kirsty Gordon	always being there and looking out for her.
Editing	Kelly Hurst, Pippa Shaw	caring so much about *The Good Turn*.
Designing	Arabella Jones	making it all look brilliant.

Illustrating	Paul Kellam	an amazing cover and chapter head artwork.
Mapping	Luke Ashforth	marking the territory.
Sewing	Jacob de Graaf	making three real badges.
Proofreading	Claire Davis, Leena Lane	keeping an eye out for the mistakes!
Marketing	Clare Blanchfield, Ellen Grady, Chloe Parkinson	spreading the word.
Revealing	AJ at A New Chapter	sharing the cover with the world and being a lovely person.
Reading	Elle McNicol, Sophie Anderson, Katherine Rundell, Alex Wheatle, Anna James	being so generous with their time and giving their thoughts.

Supporting	Alex Wheatle, Dapo Adeola, Patrice Lawrence, Malorie Blackman, Femi Fadugba, Onyinye Iwu, Joanna Brown	lending an ear when things aren't so fun. Being so positive when things are!
Developing	Dean Jackson, Peter Martin	really getting into it with me. And being patient.
Caring	Daniel Anthony, Joseph Jackson Anthony, Margot Jackson Anthony, Lynda and Benn Hunter, Samantha Duffy, Leigh Jackson, Kristina Kuznetsova, Melinda Tuza	everything.